*A long time ago in a galaxy
far, far away. . . .*

STAR WARS

MEDSTAR 1:
BATTLE SURGEONS
A Clone Wars Novel

Michael Reaves and Steve Perry

BALLANTINE BOOKS • NEW YORK

A Del Rey® Book
Published by The Random House Publishing Group

www.starwars.com
www.delreydigital.com

ISBN 0-345-46310-2

Manufactured in the United States of America

First Edition: July 2004

OPM 10 9 8 7 6 5 4 3 2 1

For my son Dashiell
"Never tell me the odds."—M. R.

For Dianne, and for Cyrus, the new kid in town.—S. P.

CLONE WARS
TIMELINE

With the Battle of Geonosis (EP II), the Republic is plunged into an emerging, galaxy-wide conflict. On one side is the Confederacy of Independent Systems (the Separatists), led by the charismatic Count Dooku who is backed by a number of powerful trade organizations and their droid armies.

On the other side is the Republic loyalists and their newly created clone army, led by the Jedi. It is a war fought on a thousand fronts, with heroism and sacrifices on both sides. Below is a partial list of some of the important events of the Clone Wars and a guide to where these events are chronicled.

MONTHS
(after *Attack of the Clones*)

0	**THE BATTLE OF GEONOSIS** Star Wars: Episode II *Attack of the Clones* (LFL, May '02)
0	**THE SEARCH FOR COUNT DOOKU** Boba Fett #1: *The Fight to Survive* (SB, April '02)
+1	**THE BATTLE OF RAXUS PRIME** Boba Fett #2: *Crossfire* (SB, November '02)
+1	**THE DARK REAPER PROJECT** The Clone Wars (LEC, May '02)
+1.5	**CONSPIRACY ON AARGAU** Boba Fett #3: *Maze of Deception* (SB, April '03)
+2	**THE BATTLE OF KAMINO** Clone Wars I: *The Defense of Kamino* (DH, June '03)
+2	**DURGE VS. BOBA FETT** Boba Fett #4: *Hunted* (SB, October '03)

CLONE WARS
TIMELINE

MONTHS
(after *Attack of the Clones*)

+2.5   **THE DEFENSE OF NABOO**
Clone Wars II: *Victories and Sacrifices* (DH, September '03)

+6   **THE DEVARON RUSE**
Clone Wars IV: *Target Jedi* (DH, May '04)

+6   **THE HARUUN KAL CRISIS**
Shatterpoint (DR, June '03)

+6   **ASSASSINATION ON NULL**
Legacy of the Jedi #1 (SB, August '03)

+12   **THE BIO-DROID THREAT**
The Cestus Deception (DR, June '04)

+15   **THE BATTLE OF JABIIM**
Clone Wars III: *Last Stand on Jabiim* (DH, February '04)

+24   **THE CASUALTIES OF DRONGAR**
MedStar Duology: *Battle Surgeons* (DR, July '04)
Jedi Healer (DR, October '04)

+30   **THE PRAESITLYN CONQUEST**
Jedi Trial (DR, November '04)

+31   **THE XAGOBAH CITADEL**
Boba Fett #5: *A New Threat* (SB, April '04)

KEY:

DH = *Dark Horse Comics, graphic novels*
www.darkhorse.com
DR = *Del Rey, hardcover & paperback books*
www.delreydigital.com
LEC = *LucasArts Games, games for XBox, GameCube,
PS2, & PC platforms* www.lucasarts.com
LFL = *Lucasfilm Ltd., motion pictures* www.starwars.com
SB = *Scholastic Books, juvenile fiction* www.scholastic.com/starwars

1

Blood geysered, looking almost black in the antisepsis field's glow. It splattered hot against Jos's skin-gloved hand. He cursed.

"Hey, here's an idea—would somebody with nothing better to do mind putting a pressor field on that bleeder?"

"Pressor generator is broken again, Doc."

Republic battle surgeon Jos Vondar looked away from the bloody operating field that was the clone trooper's open chest, at Tolk, his scrub nurse. "Of *course* it is," he said. "What, is our mech droid on vacation? How am I supposed to patch up these rankweed suckers without working medical gear?"

Tolk le Trene, a Lorrdian who could read his mood as easily as most sentients could read a chart, said nothing aloud, but her pointed look was plain enough: *Hey, I didn't break it.*

With an effort, Jos throttled back his temper. "All right. Put a clamp on it. We still have hemostats, don't we?"

But she was ahead of him, already locking the steel pincer on the torn blood vessel and using a hemosponge to soak and clear the field. The troopers of this unit had been too close to a grenade when it exploded, and this one's chest had been peppered full of shrapnel. The recent battle in the Poptree Forest had been a bad one—the medlifters would surely be hauling in more wounded before nightfall to go with those they already had.

"Is it just me, or is it hot in here?"

One of the circulating nurses wiped Jos's forehead to keep the sweat from running into his eyes. "Air cooler's malfunctioning again," she said. Jos didn't reply. On a civilized world, he would have sprayed sweat-stop on his face before he scrubbed, but that, like everything else—including tempers—was in short supply here on Drongar. The temperature outside, even now, near midnight, was that of human body heat; tomorrow it would be hotter than a H'nemthe in love. The air would be wetter. And smellier. This was a nasty, nasty world at the best of times; it was far worse with a war going on. Jos wondered, not for the first time, what high-ranking Republic official had casually decided to ruin his life by cutting orders shipping him to a planet that seemed to be all mold and mildew and mushroomlike vegetation as far as the eye could see.

"Is *everything* broken around here?" he demanded of the room at large.

"Everything except your mouth, sounds like," Zan said pleasantly, without looking up from the trooper he was working on.

Jos used a healy gripper to dig a piece of metal the size of his thumb from his patient's left lung. He dropped the sharp metal bit into a pan. It clanked. "Put a glue stat on that."

The nurse expertly laid the dissolvable patch onto the

wounded lung. The stat, created of cloned tissue and a type of adhesive made from a Talusian mussel, immediately sealed the laceration. At least they still had plenty of those, Jos told himself; otherwise, he'd have to use staples or sutures, like the medical droids usually did, and wouldn't *that* be fun and time-consuming?

He looked down at the patient, spotted another gleam of shrapnel under the bright OT lights, and grabbed it gently, wiggling it slowly out. It had just missed the aorta. "There's enough scrap metal in this guy to build two battle droids," he muttered, "and still have some left over for spare parts." He dropped the metal into the steel bowl, with another clink. "I don't know why they even bother putting armor on 'em."

"Got that right," Zan said. "Stuff won't stop anything stronger than a kid's pellet gun."

Jos put two more fragments of the grenade into the pan, then straightened, feeling his lower back muscles protest the position he'd been locked into all day. "Scope 'im," he said.

Tolk ran a handheld bioscanner over the clone. "He's clean," she said. "I think you got it all."

"We'll know if he starts clanking when he walks." An orderly began wheeling the gurney over to the two FX-7 medical droids that were doing the patching up. "Next!" Jos said wearily. He yawned behind his face mask, and before he'd finished there was another trooper supine in front of him.

"Sucking chest wound," Tolk said. "Might need a new lung."

"He's lucky; we're having a special on them." Jos made the initial incision with the laser scalpel. Operating on clone troopers—or, as the staff of Rimsoo Seven tended to call it, working the "assembly line"—was easier in a lot of ways than doing slice and stitch on individuals. And, since they were all the same genome, their organs were literally interchangeable, with no worry about rejection syndrome.

He glanced over at one of the four other organic doctors working in the cramped operating chamber. Zan Yant, a Zabrak surgeon, was two tables away, humming a classical tune as he sliced. Jos knew Zan would much rather be back in the cubicle the two of them shared, playing his quetarra, tuning it just right so that it would produce the plangent notes of some Zabrak native skirl. The music Zan was into lately sounded like two krayt dragons mating, as far as Jos was concerned, but to a Zabrak—and to many other sentient species in the galaxy—it was uplifting and enriching. Zan had the soul and the hands of a musician, but he was also a decent surgeon, because the Republic needed medics more than entertainers these days. Certainly on this world.

The remaining six surgeons in the theater were droids, and there should have been ten of them. Two of the other four were out for repairs, and two had been requisitioned but never received. Every so often Jos went through the useless ritual of filing another 22K97(MD) requisition form, which would then promptly disappear forever into a vortex of computerized filing systems and bureaucracy.

He quickly determined that the sergeant—the remnants of his armor had the green markings that denoted his rank—indeed needed a new lung. Tolk brought a freshly cloned organ from the nutrient tanks while Jos began the pneumonectomy. In less than an hour he had finished resecting, and the lung, grown from cultured stem cells along with dozens of other identical organs and kept in cryogenic stasis for emergencies such as this, was nestled in the sergeant's pleural cavity. The patient was wheeled over for suturing as Jos stretched, feeling vertebrae unkink and joints pop.

"That's the last of them," he said, "for now."

"Don't get too comfortable," said Leemoth, a Duros surgeon who specialized in amphibious and semiaquatic species. He looked up from his current patient—an Otolla Gungan observer from Naboo, who had had his buccal cavity severely varicosed by a sonic pistol blast the day before. "Word from the front is, another couple of medlifters will be here in the next three hours, if not sooner."

"Time enough to have a drink and file another pathetic plea for a transfer," Jos said as he moved toward the disinfect chamber, pulling off the skin-gloves as he went. He had learned long ago to cope with whatever was wrong now and not worry about future problems until he had to. It was the mental equivalent of triage, he had told Klo Merit, the Equani physician who was also Rimsoo Seven's resident empath. Merit had blinked his large, brown eyes, their depths so strangely calming, and said that Jos's attitude was healthy—up to a degree.

"There is a point at which defense becomes denial," Merit had said. "For each of us, that point is positioned differently. A large part of mental hygiene lies simply in knowing when you are no longer being truthful with yourself."

Jos came out of his momentary reverie when he realized that Zan had spoken to him. "What?"

"I said this one has a lacerated liver; I'll be done in a few more minutes."

"Need any help?"

Zan grinned. "What am I, a first-year intern at Coruscant Med? No problem. Sewn one, sewn 'em all."

He started humming again as he worked on the trooper's innards.

Jos nodded. True enough; the Fett clones were all identical, which meant that, in addition to no rejection syndrome concerns, the surgeons didn't have to worry about where or how the plumbing went. Even in individuals of the same species there was often considerable diversity of physiological structure and functionality; human hearts all worked the same way, for example, but the valves could vary in size, the aortal connection might be higher in one than in another . . . there were a million and one ways for individual anatomies to differ. It was the biggest reason why surgery, even under the best of conditions, was never 100 percent safe.

But with the clones, it was different—or, rather, it *wasn't*. They had all been culled from the same genetic source: a human male bounty hunter named Jango Fett. All of them were even more identical than monozygotic twins. *See one, do one, teach one,* had been the mantra back on Coruscant, during Jos's training. The instructors used to joke that you could cut a clone blindfolded once you knew the layout, and that was almost true. Ordinarily Jos wouldn't be working on line troops, but with two of the surgical droids down for repairs, the only option was to let the injured triage up out in the mobile unit's hall and die. And, clones or not, he couldn't let that happen. He'd become a doctor to save lives, not to judge who lived and who didn't.

The lights abruptly blinked off, then back on. Everyone in the chamber froze momentarily.

"Sweet Sookie," Jos said. "Now what?"

In the distance, explosions echoed. *It could have been thunder,* Jos thought nervously. He hoped it had been thunder. It rained here pretty much every day, and most nights, for that matter; big, tropical storms that tore through with howling winds and lightning strikes that lanced at trees, buildings, and people. Sometimes the shield generators went down, and then the only things protecting the camp were the arrestors. More than a few troopers had been cooked where they stood, burned black in a heartbeat by the powerful voltages. Once, after a bad storm, Jos had seen a pair of boots standing with smoke rising from the hard plastoid, five body-lengths away from the blackened form of the trooper who had been wearing them. Everything in the camp worth saving had arrestors grounded deep in the swampy soil, but sometimes those weren't enough.

Even as these thoughts went through his head, he heard the staccato drumming of rain on the OT roof begin.

Jos Vondar had been born and raised in a small farm town on Corellia, in a temperate zone where the weather was pleasant most of the year, and even during the rainy season it was mild. When he was twenty he'd gone from there to Coruscant, the planetary capital of the Republic, a city-world where the weather was carefully calibrated and orchestrated. He always knew when it would rain, how much, and for how long. Nothing in his life up to now had prepared him for the apocalyptic storms and the almost vile fecundity of Drongar's native life-forms. It was said that there were places in the Great Jasserak Swamp where, if you were foolish enough to lie down and sleep, the fungal growth would cover you with a second skin before you could wake up. Jos didn't know if it was true, but it wasn't hard to believe.

"Blast!" Zan said.

"What?"

"Got a chunk of shrapnel intersecting the portal artery. If I pull it loose, it's gonna get ugly in here."

"Thought you said you had this one signed, sealed, and transported." Jos nodded to Zan's circulating nurse, who opened a fresh pack of skins for Jos to slip his hands into. He wiggled his fingers, then stepped in alongside his friend. "Move over, horn head, and let a *real* doctor work."

Zan looked around. "A real doctor? Where? You know one?"

Jos looked down at the patient, whose interior workings were brightly illuminated by the overheads and the sterile field. He lowered his hands into the field, feeling the slight tingling that always accompanied the move. Zan pointed with the healy grippers at the offending chunk of jagged metal. Sure enough, it was angled into the portal vessel, blocking it. Jos shook his head. "How come they never showed us stuff like this in school?"

"When you get to be chief of surgery at Coruscant Med, you can make sure the next batch of dewy-eyed would-be surgeons has a better education. Old Doc Vondar, nattering on about the Great Clone Wars and how easy these kids today have it."

"I'll remember that when they bring you in as a teaching case, Zan."

"Not me. I'll dance at your memorial, Corellian scum. Maybe even play you a nice Selonian étude, perhaps one of the Vissëncant Variations."

"Please," Jos said as he gingerly spread tissue apart to get a better look. "At least play something worth hearing. Some leap-jump or heavy isotope."

Zan shook his head sadly. "A tone-deaf Gungan has better taste."

"I know what I like."

"Yeah, well, *I* like keeping these guys alive, so stop embarrassing yourself in public and help me get this liver working."

"Guess I'd better." Jos reached for a set of healys and a sponge. "Looks like it's the only way he'll have a fighting chance, with you as his surgeon." He grinned behind his mask at his friend.

Working together, they managed to extricate the shrapnel from the artery with minimal damage. When they were done, Jos looked around with a sigh of relief.

"Well, kids, looks like a perfect record. Didn't lose a single trooper. Drinks are on me at the cantina."

The others grinned tiredly—and then froze, listening. Rising over the steady pounding of the rain on the foamcast roof was another sound, one they knew very well: the rising whine of incoming medlifters.

The break was over, as most of them were, before it had begun.

2

The drop from orbit to the planet was faster than normal, the pilot explained to her, because of the multitude of spores.

"Dey gum up *everyt'ing*," he said, in thickly accented Basic. He was a Kubaz, gray-green and pointy-headed, a member of the long-snouted species whose enemies referred to them derisively as "bug-eating spies." As a Jedi Padawan and a healer, Barriss Offee had learned early not to be judgmental of a species because of its looks, but she knew that many in the galaxy were less open-minded.

"'Specially d'ventilators," he went on. "D'rot'll eat t'rough d'best filters we got in a hour, mebbe less; y'got to change 'em every flight—you don't, d'Spore Sickness get into d'ship and get into *you*. Not a good way to go, b'lieve it, coughin' up blood 'n' cooking in y'own juices."

Barriss blinked at the graphic scenario. She looked out of the small shuttle craft's nearest viewport; the spores were visible only as various tints of red, green, and other hues in the air, and an occasional spatter of minute particles against the transparisteel, gone before she could see them clearly. She probed a bit with the Force, getting nothing like a sentient response, of course,

merely a chaotic impression of motion, a furious muta-
bility.

"D'spores are, um, adepto . . . uh . . ."

"Adaptogenic," she said.

"Yeah, dat's it. Every time d'mechanics and d'medics
come up wit' new treatments, d'spores *change,* y'know?
And d'treatments, dey stop workin'. Weird t'ing is, dey
don't cause problems at ground level, only when y'get
up above d'trees, y'know?"

Barriss nodded. It didn't sound pleasant. In fact, very
little about this planet sounded pleasant, even though
her information on it was still sketchy. According to the
hurried briefing at the Temple on Coruscant, the Republic's forces and those of the Separatists were more or
less evenly balanced on Drongar. The war here was limited mostly to ground troops; very little fighting took
place in the air because of the spores. On the ground,
things were even worse in many ways. Among the problems the forces on both sides encountered were monsoons
with devastating electrical storms, soaring temperatures,
and humidity over 90 percent. As if that weren't enough,
the atmospheric oxygen level was higher than that
found on most worlds habitable for humans and humanoids. This often caused dizziness and hyperoxy-
genation for nonindigenous life-forms, and, for the
Separatists' battle droids, rust. Hard to believe, Barriss
thought, but even the incredibly tough durasteel alloy of
which the droids were constructed would oxidize if
conditions were extreme enough. The high oxygen content also limited military engagements, for the most
part, to small-arms fire: sonic pistols, small blasters,
slugthrowers, and the like, because of the high risk of
fire from laser and particle beam armament.

What kept both sides struggling for control of this

pestilential quagmire of a world was bota, a plant somewhere between a mold and a fungus, which, to date, had been found almost nowhere else in the galaxy. It grew thick on this backwater planet, but all attempts to transplant it offworld had failed. The plant was extremely valuable to both sides, because, like the spores and other flora and fauna on Drongar, bota was highly adaptogenic in its effects. Many species could benefit from it—humans used it as a potent broad-based antibiotic, Neimoidians sought it as a narcotic painkiller, Hutts utilized it as a valuable stimulant almost as powerful as glitterstim spice, and many other species found it useful for still other functions. Moreover, the stuff had virtually no side effects, making it a true wonder drug.

Processed by freeze-drying, the resulting product was readily transportable. Its only drawback was that, once harvested, it had to be processed quickly or it degenerated into a useless slime. And, to make things worse, the plant was quite delicate. Explosions going off too close to it could shock it to death, and it apparently burned like rocket fuel when ignited, despite the general dampness of the landscape. Since bota was the reason both sides were here, this was yet another reason for military engagements to be limited—fighting over a field of the stuff would be useless if it burned up, died, or went sour before it could be collected.

Bota was also one of the main reasons Barriss was here. It was true that her primary mandate was to augment the doctors and surgeons who cared for Republic troops, using her skills as a healer, but she was also supposed to keep an eye on the harvesters, to make sure that the bota was being packed and shipped to offworld Republic ports as it was supposed to be. The harvesting

operations had been folded in with the Rimsoo procedures to save money and expedite shipment. Neither
she nor her superiors had any problems with that. Any
advantage the Republic could gain over the Confederacy was valuable and desirable—the Jedi certainly had
no love for the rogue Count Dooku, who had caused
the deaths of so many of them two standard years earlier on Geonosis.

She strongly suspected that she was here for another
reason as well: that this assignment was part, or all, of
her trials. Her Jedi Master, Luminara Unduli, had not
told her that such was the case, but not all Padawans
were warned in advance that they were about to be
tested. The nature of the trial, and whether or not the
Padawan would know about it beforehand, were matters left entirely to the discretion of the Jedi Master.

Once, about six months ago, she had asked Master
Unduli when she could expect to begin her Jedi trials.
Her mentor had smiled at the question, and said, "Any-
time. All the time. No time."

Well. If her sojourn on this world was to be her trial
by fire, the test that would determine whether or not she
had what it took to be a Jedi Knight, she would probably know before too—

The transport slewed in a sudden yawing turn, inertia
shoving Barriss hard into the seat. The ship's internal
gravity field had obviously been turned off.

"Sorry 'bout dat," the pilot said. "Dere's a Sep'ratist
battery in dis sector, an' every now and den dey try
t'track one'a us an' knock us down. Standard procedure
to t'row in a few 'vasive maneuvers on de way down.
Kanushka!"

The exclamation of surprise in the Kubaz's native
tongue drew Barriss's attention. "What?"

"*Big* battle goin' on, off t'starboard. Coupla mech units an' troops goin' at it—dere, y'see? I'll do a fly-over—we're high 'nough, dey can't hit us wit' hand weapons. Hang on."

The pilot made a broad turn to the right. Barriss looked down at the scene. They were, she estimated, about a thousand meters high, and the air was reasonably clear; they were below the main spore strata, with no clouds or mist to block her view.

As a Jedi Padawan, she was knowledgeable in the ways of war. And she had been trained in personal combat with her lightsaber from an early age, so her observation was more critical than most.

The trooper units moved across a field of short, stubby plants, with the sun at their backs—a sound tactical move when facing biological opponents, but of little use against battle droids, whose photoreceptors could easily be adjusted to tune out glare. There were perhaps two hundred troopers; they had a slight numerical advantage over the droids, which, Barriss estimated, had maybe seventy or eighty units on the field. From this height, the crescent attack formation of the Republic force was apparent as it sought to envelop the droids and gain superiority in field of fire.

The battle droids were mostly of the Baktoid B1 series, as nearly as she could tell from high overhead. There were also several B2 super battle droids, which were basically the standard model with an armored casing overlay and more weaponry. They had broken into quads, each unit of four fanning out to deal with the tactic of envelopment, concentrating its fire on the same section of troopers.

Classic formations on an open battlefield, she knew,

just as she knew that the outcome would be decided by which side could instigate the most accurate firepower the fastest. She could almost hear the voice of her Master echoing in her memory:

It does not matter how fast you are if you miss the target. It is the one who hits the most who will have the victory . . .

Blaster beams lanced through the engaging forces, which were now separated by no more than a short sprint's distance. Vapor boiled up from misses that hit vegetation, and small fires quickly flared here and there. Troopers fell, seared black and smoking, and battle droids ground to a halt, scorch marks and flashes of electricity on their white metal chassis marking where blasterfire had struck.

It was all eerily silent, no sound reaching this height as the pilot slowed to give her a longer look.

It appeared that the Republic forces would win this engagement—both sides seemed to be losing combatants at the same rate, and in such a case, the side with the larger force would win—though the victory would be costly. A unit that lost eight out of ten troops won only in the technical sense.

"We can't hang 'round," the pilot said. "D'filters'll be in d'red in 'nother fifteen minutes an' we're five away from Rimsoo Seven. I like t'have a margin 'f error."

The shuttle craft gained speed, and they left the battle behind.

Barriss mused on what she had seen as the transport shot over lowland vegetation and steaming, miasmic swamps. Whatever else this assignment might be, it certainly was not going to be dull.

* * *

Jos was snatching a few precious moments of sleep in the cubicle he shared with Zan when he heard the transport's approach.

At first, only half awake, he thought it was another medlifter bringing in more wounded, but then he realized the repulsor sound was pitched differently.

It has to be the new doc, he thought. *No one else in their right mind would make planetfall on Drongar without being ordered to.*

He pushed through the osmotic field that covered the cubicle's entrance; it had been set to let air circulate freely, but it kept out the eight-legged, bi-winged insects they'd come to call "wingstingers" that constantly buzzed about the unit. He'd heard that the newer-model fields came with an entropic overlay feature that bled energy from the air molecules as they passed through the selective barrier, thus lowering the inside temperature by a good ten degrees. He'd put in a requisition for a batch of them; with any luck, they might arrive a day or so before the war ended.

Blinking in the harsh light of Drongar Prime, he watched the transport spiral down to the pad. He noticed Zan, Tolk, and a few others emerging from the OT as well. It was a time of relative quiet at Rimsoo Seven, which meant that triaged patients weren't queued up, waiting for surgery and treatment, and that the surgeons weren't in a life-and-death race with time to save them. They were enjoying the respite while it lasted.

A couple of Bothan techs ran up to the shuttle and sprayed the exterior with spore disinfectant. This particular batch of chemicals, Jos knew, would probably be good for another standard month; it took about that long for the spores that attacked the craft's seals to develop immunities to the spray. Then various chemical precursors would have to be altered, and molecular configurations shifted just enough to produce a new type of treatment that would once again be effective—for a time. It was a constant dance that went on between the guided mechanisms of science and the blind opportunism of nature. Jos wondered, not for the first time, what the odds were of the spores mutating into a more virulent pathogen that could strip-mine a pair of lungs in seconds instead of hours.

Then the shuttle's hatch opened, and so did Jos's mouth—in surprise.

The new doctor was a woman—and a Jedi.

There was no mistaking the simple dark garb and accoutrements of the Order, and certainly no mistaking the shape beneath them as anything other than feminine. He'd heard that the latest addition to the team was a Mirialan—which meant human, basically—a member of the same species as himself, whose ancestors had spread in several ancient diasporas across the galaxy, colonizing such worlds as Corellia, Alderaan, Kalarba, and hundreds more. Humans were ubiquitous from one spiral arm to the other, so to see another one—male or female—arrive here was no great surprise.

But to see a Jedi, here on Drongar—*that* was surprising.

Jos, like most other beings intelligent enough to access the HoloNet, had seen the recorded images of the Jedi's final stand in the arena on Geonosis. Even before that, the Order had been spread mighty thin across the galaxy. And yet one of them had been assigned here, to Rimsoo Seven, a ragtag military medical unit on a world so far off the known space lanes that most galactic cartographers couldn't come within a parsec of locating it on a bet.

He wondered why she was here.

Colonel D'Arc Vaetes, the human commander of the unit, received the Jedi warmly as the latter disembarked from the transport. "Welcome to Rimsoo Seven, Jedi Barriss Offee," he said. "Speaking for everyone here, I hope you will be——"

But before he could finish his sentence, Vaetes stopped, for a sound was rising in the thick, humid air—a sound every one of them at Rimsoo Seven knew very well.

"Incoming lifters!" shouted Tanisuldees, a Dressellian enlistee. He was the aide-de-camp to Filba, the Hutt supply officer. He pointed to the north.

Jos looked. Yes, they were coming, sure enough—five of them, black dots against the sky, which at this time of day was a faint verdigris in color, like the algae that coated the surface of the Kondrus Sea. Each medlifter could carry up to six wounded men—clones and possibly other combatants. That meant at least thirty injured, possibly one or two more.

After the first moment of realization, everyone began moving purposefully, each doing his, her, or its duty to prepare. Zan and Tolk headed for the OT at a run. Jos was about to follow, but instead he turned and moved quickly to where the Jedi, looking slightly confused, was standing.

Vaetes took her hand and gestured toward Jos. "Jedi Offee, this is Captain Jos Vondar, my chief surgeon. He'll get you briefed and prepped for what's coming." The colonel sighed. "It's something we're all quite used to, sadly. What's even more sad is that you'll get used to it as well, very quickly."

Jos wasn't quite sure what the proper protocol for greeting a Jedi was, but he didn't see much point in worrying about it at the moment. "Let's hope the Force is with you, Jedi Offee," he said, having to raise his voice to be heard over the rising whine of the repulsors. "Because it's going to be a long, hot day." He started toward the open landing area in the camp's center, where the initial triage calls were pronounced on the wounded as they came off the lifters.

Barriss Offee moved quickly to keep up with him. He trusted she was willing to tackle whatever was in store. *She's a Jedi,* Jos told himself—*she's probably got what it takes.*

For her sake—and the troops'—he hoped so.

3

The full-spectrum light in his office was dimmed—as a Sakiyan, Admiral Tarnese Bleyd could see farther into the infrared than most beings, and he preferred to spare himself the harsh glare that many of the galaxy's species needed for illumination. Most sentients considered themselves enlightened to some degree, but to those who could see things as they really were, the rest of the galactic population was stumbling about half blind. Unfortunately, the sighted few were all too often handicapped by the blindness of the masses.

Bleyd frowned. He knew himself to be one of the Republic's most capable admirals: smart, clever, and deft. Given the proper venue, he could have risen easily to the top of the military's chain of command in short order. Become a fleet commander, at the least; perhaps even a Priority Sector High Commander. But instead, his superiors had seen fit to shunt him to this Maker-forsaken, backrocket planet in the hind end of nowhere, to preside over the administration of a lowly MedStar, a medical frigate fielding Rimsoo units charged with patching up clones and collecting an indigenous plant.

He feared for the stability of a commonwealth that could make such ill-advised decisions.

Bleyd stood and moved to the large transparisteel viewport. Drongar filled a quarter of the sky "below" him. Even from orbit the planet looked vile and pestilential. From the surface, he knew the sky would have a sickly copper tint caused by the clouds of spores constantly adrift in the upper atmosphere, and the rampant, almost virulent growth that covered everything.

He shivered, rubbing his upper arms. His skin was the color and texture of dark, burnished bronze, but that didn't mean Tarnese Bleyd didn't feel the cold occasionally. Even when the temperature was set to a comfortable thirty-eight degrees.

The only parts of the planet, with its vast, continent-spanning jungles and marshlands, that remotely reminded him of the veldts of his homeworld were the few isolated patches where the bota grew. He couldn't even see those from orbit. By far the largest fields were on Tanlassa, the bigger of two landmasses in the southern hemisphere. The Jasserak engagement—the only active conflict zone on the planet, at the moment—was taking place on the Tanlassan western shore.

Bleyd turned away from the port and made a gesture. A hologrammic display appeared before him, showing a translucent image of the rotating planet. Alphanumerics cascaded on either side of the globe. The admiral brooded on the stats. He knew most of them by heart, and yet he often felt compelled to review them. Somehow, it was comforting to know everything about the planet that was going to make him rich.

According to the Nikto survey team that had first discovered the system, nearly two centuries ago, Drongar was a relatively young world, with a radius of 6,259 kilometers and a surface gravity of 1.2 Standard. It had two small moons—nothing more than captured asteroids, really. There were three other planets in the system, all gas giants orbiting in the outer reaches, which meant Drongar was well shielded from meteor and cometary impacts. Drongar Prime was approximately the same size as Coruscant Prime, but it burned hotter. That explained Drongar's current near-tropical climatic zonation. But the lack of a large moon to stabilize its obliquity meant that, in a few hundred million years, Drongar would probably become a "snowball" world as cold as, or colder than, Hoth.

Bleyd gestured again, and the holo faded. He thought about Saki, his homeworld. True, it was mostly tropical as well, with large stretches of jungle and marshes—but not like Drongar. Neimoidia and Saki together couldn't match Drongar for sheer fetid, noisome area.

Saki also had forests, and savannas, and lakes . . . and, unlike Drongar, a stable axis, anchored by the gravity of a single, large moon. Thus, seasonal variations on Saki were mild, the air was sweet, and the hunting was good. Saki Prime was an older star, its spectrum shifting more toward the red. From the planet's surface it looked like a swollen crimson jewel hanging in the azure sky.

Bleyd had heard it said on occasion that Sakiyan were too insular, that they tended to stay on their own world rather than venture out into the galaxy and play with the big kids. He never responded to these charges. He knew that, if most of the other sentients voicing the complaint could spend even one day on Saki, they would understand why few of its children ever wanted to leave.

True, he had left—but only because circumstances had forced him to seek his fortune offworld. His pride-father, Tarnese Lyanne, had invested heavily in various black-market and smuggling operations—far too heavily. Shiltu the Hutt, a Black Sun vigo, had double-crossed

Lyanne. Clan Tarnese had been ruined—and Bleyd had left to find employment in the Republic military.

But one day he would return. That was never in doubt. And he would return in style.

The Sakiyans were a proud and predatory race—Bleyd's ancestors had been legendary hunters. It was his *monthræl* to be no less of a legend than they.

Bleyd stopped reminiscing. He could not afford to lose his focus now. A decison had to be made, a decision that could determine the rest of his life's course.

But there really was only one choice. If the Republic was unable or unwilling to recognize his abilities, then it was the Republic's loss, not his. He had known all along, after all, that it was up to him to make certain that he came out of this war wiser—and richer.

Much richer.

With sufficient credits Bleyd could reclaim his clan's holdings. It was too late to wreak any sort of delayed revenge on Shiltu—the old reprobate had died a decade before from sudden massive cellular hemorrhage, a sort of full-body stroke that had ended the Hutt's life far too quickly and painlessly, in Bleyd's opinion.

But it was just as well that he not be tempted. Revenge, he knew, was an expensive and dangerous luxury. Retiring from the war a rich man would be his best vengeance upon a military too foolish to know what they had in him.

If Filba continued to come through . . .

Bleyd was certainly not blind to the irony that required him to trust another Hutt in dealing with Black Sun again. It was risky—very risky. Allying with Black Sun was like gambling with a Wookiee: even when you know he's cheating, sometimes it's best to let him win. But the stakes were too high to walk away from. With the credits they stood to make, he could become a landed person, perhaps even enter politics. He closed his eyes, picturing it: the wealthy Senator from Saki, with his own palatial spire on Coruscant, affecting the lives of trillions with his every command . . . he could certainly get used to such a lifestyle.

Yes, it was risky. Going after the big game always was. But he'd hunted razor-tailed tigers in the Dust Pits of Yurb; he'd fought lyniks that had tasted his blood and therefore knew every move he would make; he had even trapped a nexu, one of the most ferocious beasts in the galaxy.

He was more than capable of outwitting even a many-headed beast such as Black Sun.

His secretary droid appeared in the doorway. "Admiral, you asked to be reminded of the time."

Bleyd glared at the droid, annoyed at being pulled back from his visions of glory. "Yes, yes. All right, you have reminded me. Go on about your business."

The droid, a standard protocol unit, quickly shuffled away. It knew better than to hesitate when Bleyd told it to move.

The admiral glanced down at his desk and the mountain of flimsies and datapads there. Bleyd set to work. It would be best to have a clear mind, unencumbered by trivial business, so that he could concentrate on his plans. He had to keep things running smoothly; there was far too much at stake for any mistakes to be made at this point. Bleyd thought of the billions of credits he would realize from the Hutt's scheme. Those billions would buy him the top floor of a monad in Coruscant's prestigious equatorial belt, and servants to cater to his every whim. The means to accomplish all this was there—all he had to do was be brave enough to seize the opportunity.

Den Dhur swaggered into the cantina.

It wasn't much of a swagger, but after all, he was a Sullustan, waist-high to and only half the weight of most of the patrons within. It was understandable that conversation didn't cease and heads turn to mark his progress. He could live with that.

What was harder to live with were the lights and the noise. There were fluorescent globes on every table, and a quadro unit near the door was pounding out something loud and thumping and syncopated that they called music these days. *Big milking surprise,* he told himself; *a noisy cantina. Who'd have thought?* But the fact that it was unremarkable didn't make it any less unpleasant.

Added to the wail blasting from the speakers were the patrons. Most of them were military and all were chattering loudly, which only added to the cacophony. Like all Sullustans, who had evolved for underground living, Den had relatively large eyes and sensitive ears compared to most sentients. He was wearing polarized droptacs and sonic dampeners, but even so, he knew he was going to have a walloping headache if he stayed in here too long. Still, he was a reporter, and places like this were where the most interesting stories could be heard. Assuming one could hear anything through this din . . .

He ascended the ramp, designed for shorter and legless species, to the bar, gaining enough height to put him on eye level with the tender, whom he signaled with a wave.

The tender, a phlegmatic Ortolan, came over. He looked at Den without speaking—at least, without speaking anything Den could hear. Most Ortolans conversed in ultrahigh or ultralow frequencies. Even the Sullustan's ears, sensitive as they were, weren't as good as the blue-furred flaps the tender sported. Den was sure the chunky, long-nosed alien wore sonic dampeners as good as his own, if not better.

Fortunately the dampeners had selective blocking—either that, or the Ortolan was good at lip-reading, because when Den said, "Bantha Blaster," the tender promptly began pouring liquids into a glass, building a swirly orange-and-blue concoction. He was pretty good, Den noted. In a matter of moments the Ortolan handed the drink to Den. "On the tab," the tender said, his voice low and resonant.

Den nodded. He took a long, slow sip. *Ah* . . .

The first drink of the day was the best. After a few more, you couldn't really taste them.

He had enough swallows to blunt the harsh edges of the lights, then looked around. First thing a good reporter did upon spacing to a new planet was find the local watering holes. More stories came out of cantinas than anywhere else. This one certainly wasn't much: a dilapidated foamcast building in the middle of a swamp—most of the planet seemed to be either jungle or swamp, Den had noticed on the shuttle coming down—set up to serve the clone troops, soldiers, and assorted support staff; the latter mostly medics, given that this was a Rimsoo.

Lightning flickered outside, leaving, in his eyes, a momentary faint blue afterglow to everything. Thunder boomed almost simultaneously, hurting his ears even with the dampeners. If the weather here worked the same way it did on most planets Den was familiar with, the rumbles dopplering through the sky meant imminent rain. He watched as most of the cantina's occupants repositioned themselves. *Uh-huh. Roof leaks.* The regulars undoubtedly knew the spots where the water would drip through. He watched gaps opening in the crowd as they shifted to new areas, their movements almost unconscious. Rain's coming, don't stand there, you'll get drenched. Unless, of course, you were a water species, in which case the leaky spots were prized. *One person's trash, another person's treasure . . .*

Another thunderclap—a sound easily differentiated from that of artillery, if you'd been in and out of war zones for as much time as he had—sounded. In the momentary ringing silence that followed, heralding drops of the storm pattered on the foamcast roof. Within seconds, the sky opened up, and the drumming of the rain became a constant barrage.

And, just as he'd anticipated, the leaks began streaming.

The water puddled on the floor for the most part, without hitting anybody as it cascaded. A newbie here and there was surprised and awarded laughter by his comrades for his soaking. At the end of the bar, an Ishi Tib mechanic stripped out of his lube-spotted coveralls and undulated under a steady stream, moving his eyestalks and clacking his beak in time to the music.

Den shook his head. What a life. Cantina-crawling in yet another dung-hole, all in the service of the Public's Need to Know.

A blast of hot, wet wind swirled over him as the door seal parted. Den knew without even turning around who had entered; he could tell by the smell of damp Hutt that suddenly filled the room.

The Hutt shook himself, ignoring the annoyed looks and exclamations the spray of water brought from nearby patrons, and slithered toward the bar. He came to a stop on the ground level next to Den.

Den drained the last of his drink and took a moment to compose himself before looking at the Hutt. "Filba," he said. "How's it flopping?"

The Hutt didn't seem surprised to see him here—no doubt he'd been notified of the arrival of the press. He hardly spared Den a glance. "Dhur. Why aren't you out somewhere making up more lies about honest working folk?"

Den smiled. "I can make them up just as well in a dry—well, relatively dry—cantina." *Honest working folk, my dewflaps,* he thought. If honest work came anywhere near Filba, the huge gastropod would probably shrivel up and die like his remote ancestors did when covered in salt.

The tender approached. *"Dopa boga noga,"* Filba growled in Huttese, holding up two fingers.

The tender nodded and drew two mugs of something yellow and fizzy, which he set in front of the Hutt. Filba knocked them both back, barely taking a breath between them.

"Not one to savor your drink, I see," Den said.

Filba turned one enormous, bilious eye in his direction. "You have to drink Huttese ale fast," he explained. "Otherwise it eats through the mug."

Den nodded in sage comprehension. The tender filled his glass again, and the reporter raised it. "War and taxes," he said, and drank.

"Koochoo," Filba muttered. Den wasn't familiar enough with Huttese to recognize the word, but from

Filba's tone it sounded like an insult. Of course, most of what Filba said sounded like an insult. The Sullustan shrugged. Either Filba still had a problem with him, or he was just venting. Either way, Den wasn't particularly worried. In his experience there were very few problems in this galaxy that couldn't be cured, or at least put in proper perspective, by liberal doses of alcohol or its many equivalents.

The rain stopped almost as quickly as it began. Den stared at the puddles on the floor, knowing it would take days for them to evaporate in the humid air. And long before they did, it would have rained again. He asked a Bothan who stood at the bar a few steps away, "Why don't you guys throw a field over this place, keep it dry?"

The Bothan looked at him. "Tell you what—if you can rec one from Central or find one around here that's not being used, I'll be happy to put it up. And don't suggest fixing it the old-fashioned way—we do that all the time. As soon as we get one hole patched, the milking spores eat open another one."

Den shrugged again—he had a feeling he would be doing a lot of that on Drongar—and turned back to his drink. Before he could give it the attention it deserved, however, he noticed a group sitting at a table a couple of meters away. There were four: two males and two females. One of the males was a Zabrak; the rest were humans. Den made a wry face. Although he tried to be open-minded and tolerant, he had to admit that he had little use for humans. They tended to be louder than most species, and whenever a ruckus started in a place like this, it was usually a human at the bottom of it. He remembered one time, on Rudrig, when—

He blinked.

One of the human females was wearing the robes and trappings of a Jedi.

There was no disputing it; the plain dark hooded robe, the lightsaber hanging from her belt, and, most of all, something as indefinable as it was unmistakable in the way she comported herself—all these identified her as surely as if a neon holo had been blinking JEDI above her head. The Order had been in the holonews quite a lot lately, Den knew. He felt his pulse quicken a bit as he thought about the possible implications of her being here, on Drongar. Something to do with the bota, perhaps? Or was it something more secretive, more clandestine . . . ?

His reporter's curiosity could not be denied. Den picked up his drink and started toward the table.

After all, the public needed to know.

4

Jos didn't recognize the Sullustan, but that wasn't surprising. Rimsoo Seven wasn't exactly one of the Coruscant spaceports, but a small amount of traffic did cycle through. Most of the newcomers were observers or officers on tour, and, of course, there was an endless parade of clones. Some, however, were civilians: supply and matériel supervisors, bota harvesters, and various hired laborers. He'd even heard rumors that the base might be included in a HoloNet Entertainment tour. Many base functions were performed by droids, but most droids didn't last very long on Drongar. The WED Treadwells were constantly breaking their many delicate armatures, and the medical droids—the MDs, 2-1Bs and FXs—needed constant maintenance due to the humidity and high oxygen quotient. Jos had had parts on back order from Cybot, Medtech, and other factories for months, but no joy was in sight anytime soon.

So when the Sullustan strolled over with a drink in one hand and a friendly expression, the four made room for another chair. He introduced himself, adding that he was a string reporter for the *Galactic Wave,* one of the smaller holonews services. "Been asked to come over to HoloNet several times," he said, grabbing a handful of shroomchips from the bowl in the table's center. "But they're too mainstream, too party line for me. I like working on the edge."

"Do you disagree with the Republic's policies toward Dooku and his Separatists?" Barriss Offee asked.

Dhur's huge eyes appraised her for a few seconds while he swallowed. "Kind of unusual to see a Jedi Knight this far out," he said.

"I'm not a Jedi Knight as of yet. Until I complete my training, my title is still Padawan," Barriss said. "And you haven't answered my question."

"You're right—I haven't." Dhur looked steadily into the Jedi's eyes. "Let's just say I disapprove of some of Dooku's methods."

The silence that followed threatened to become tension. Zan said quickly, "We'd just offered to give our new healer the five-decicred tour. Care to join us?"

Dhur drained his drink. "Wouldn't miss it."

Five decicreds would be robbery for this tour, Jos thought as the four walked through the base. There really wasn't much to see: several foamcast buildings, the biggest of which contained pre- and postmed and the operating theater. Then there were the officers' quarters—smaller cubicles, for the most part—the cantina, mess hall, landing pad, refreshers, and showers. All this in a small valley overshadowed by tall, tree-like growths, mostly draped with something that looked similar to Naboo swamp moss.

The storm had stopped as suddenly as it began. Jos was sweating after a dozen steps; the air lay sodden and heavy, without a breath of movement. He watched Barriss Offee, wondering how she stood the damp heat in that heavy cloak. She didn't even seem to be sweating.

He wondered what she looked like under those robes . . .

"We do triage over there, where the lifters put down," Zan said to her, pointing to the west. "We keep a separate pad for the shuttles; that's where you two landed, near the harvesters' quarters." He pointed south. "The front's about seventy kilometers back. The lifters usually come around from the east, because of the winds."

Jos became aware of Tolk's gaze upon him; she was watching him watch the Jedi. He glanced at her, and she grinned at him. He grinned back, somewhat sheepishly. No use trying to disguise his thoughts to her—she was a Lorrdian, and could read anyone's body language like a holo on max-mag. It was almost like telepathy.

He shrugged. *Just idle curiosity,* he thought, and saw one of the nurse's eyebrows arch: *Oh, really?*

He felt a moment of slight embarrassment as he glanced back at Barriss. Since she was a Jedi—well, one in training, at least—had her connection with the Force already alerted her to his taking notice as well?

He had been most impressed by her work in the OT—her hands were fast and assured, wielding laser scalpels and mini pressor fields as she cauterized spurting arteries and even aided in transplanting a kidney. If she had used any of the healing powers it was rumored that the Force had given her, Jos hadn't seen it—but then, he'd been rather busy himself.

He knew very little about the Force—not even how to test for it, because that knowledge was supposedly reserved for the Jedi. He was aware of the power of the mind–body connection, of course, but he had no talents in that direction. He was a surgeon; he knew how to slice and splice the innards of a dozen species, including his own. That was his talent, his gift, and he was very good at it. So good that at times he felt almost bored with the routine plumbing repairs he had to make, for the most part, on the clones. He very rarely lost one, and when he did, due to sepsis or hidden trauma or some other nasty surprise, it was hard to feel too much grief. Even in wars fought by individuals the doctors often grew numb. It was easier still to do so when the next body to come under his laser looked exactly like the last one.

They really do all blur together sometimes . . .

It had bothered him at first. Now he'd grown used to it. After all, it was common knowledge that clones weren't true individuals, in the strictest sense of the word. Their mind-set had been standardized, just as their somatotype had been, in order to make them more effective fighters. No one ever heard of a trooper freezing under fire, or letting his fellows down on the front lines. It just didn't happen, due to subtle behavioral adjustments mass-programmed into the amygdala and the other emotional centers of their brains. Jos wasn't sure, because he'd never had the opportunity to run tests, but he suspected that their serotonin and dopamine levels had been adjusted as well, making them more fearless and aggressive. The bottom line was that one clone was pretty much just like another, and not only in appearance.

Of course, they weren't interchangeable units of a hive mind. Jos had seen evidence of individuation, but only in areas that didn't interfere with their ability to fight, or their loyalty to the Republic. They were true universal soldiers, genetically hardwired to fight without fear of death or sorrow at the deaths of their comrades. It made them more effective warriors, to be sure, but it also made it hard to think of them as being each a unique organic sentient. He'd often heard them referred to disparagingly as "meat droids" . . . he didn't care for the term, but as a description, it seemed apt.

". . . right, Jos?"

Jos blinked, realizing Zan had asked him something, but he had no idea what it was. He looked up at Zan, Barriss, and Dhur; they were standing on a small rise coated with the pale pink growth that was Drongar's idea of grass. A slight breeze had started, but it provided little relief from the heat. The Jedi's cloak was stirred slightly. It parted momentarily in a gust, and Jos could tell that the body beneath the robes was . . . *Not bad. Not bad at all.*

"Hey, partner," Zan said, amused. "How's about dropping out of hyperspace and rejoining the group?"

"Sorry." He moved quickly up the rise to stand beside him, Dhur, and Barriss. "What was the question?"

"I was wondering if that storm was the start of the monsoon season," Dhur said.

"It doesn't start," Jos said, "because it never stops. Except for the poles, the whole planet is like this."

Jos didn't think Dhur's eyes could get any wider, but his last statement proved him wrong. "You mean it's like this all the time?"

"Pretty much," Zan said.

"Actually," Tolk said as she joined the group, "this is a rather nice day. Only one lightning storm so far."

A far-off rumble of thunder came from the east. They all turned and saw a new storm front massing dark gray on the horizon.

Jos glanced at Tolk. "You really should know better than to say things like that."

* * *

The second storm subsided around midnight, though the skies remained cloudy. Drongar had no large moon, and so Barriss, standing just outside one of the doors to the officers' quarters, was surprised to see the huts and grounds illuminated by a wan light that shifted among green, pearl, and turquoise hues, as if the clouds were somehow noctilucent.

"It's the spores," Zan told her. She was not surprised that he had stepped out alongside her; she'd felt his presence in the Force before she could see him. "Some strains glow in the dark," he continued. "Clouds make a good backdrop for them. Though you'd think all the rain would wash them out of the air."

She nodded. The bands of variegated light, twisting slowly far overhead, were more impressive than many rainbows and auroras she'd seen on far more hospitable worlds.

It was nice to know that even Drongar had some beauty to offer.

"A lot prettier than the night sky, actually," Zan said. "We're so far out on the Rim that you don't see that many stars. And the whorl itself isn't visible from this hemisphere." He grinned at her. "Not even a full moon to walk hand-in-hand under."

Almost by reflex, she felt his aura gently with the Force, and found nothing in him but friendliness. She smiled back at him. "Did you have a moon on . . . ?"

"Talus. No, we had something much more spectacular: Tralus, our sister world."

"Ah. The Double Worlds of the Corellian system. Two planets, orbiting each other as they circle their sun."

Zan nodded and looked impressed. "You know your galactic cartography."

"I would be a poor excuse for a Jedi if I did not."

He looked at her for a moment. Barriss could hear the sounds of the night all about them: the buzzing of the scavenger moths, the dopplering hum of a worker droid as it pursued its tasks, and, far away, the occasional distant crackle of energy weapons and sharper cracks of slugthrowers. She might have thought she was imagining them, but she could feel the reverberations of death and destruction quite clearly through the Force.

"And who were you," Zan asked, "before you became part of the Order?"

She hesitated as well before replying. "No one. I was brought to the Temple as an infant."

"Have you never tried to contact your parents, to find your homeworld's—"

Barriss looked away. "I was born on a liner in deep space. My parents' identities are unknown. I call no world save Coruscant my home."

Zan said softly, "My apologies, Padawan Offee. I didn't mean to pry."

She turned back and smiled at him. "It is I who must apologize. There is no excuse for rudeness. As Master Yoda says, 'If in anger you answer, then in shame you dwell.'"

"He's your instructor?"

"I am not Padawan to him; my Master is Luminara Unduli. Master Yoda is one of the most respected members of the Council." She hesitated, then added, "He has been a mentor to nearly all the Jedi currently in the Order. One student, to his great disappointment, left the Order and turned to the dark side of the Force."

"I don't have children," Zan said, "though I hope to change that once I'm off this damp rock. I would imagine that to lose a pupil like that must be almost as bad as a parent losing his child."

She nodded. "I hope that, someday, after this war is over, he will be able to return to training students. He has much to offer."

"As do you, Padawan Offee." Zan yawned and turned back to the door. "I'm going to grab some sleep while I can. You might want to do the same; if we're lucky, maybe tomorrow won't be too much worse than today."

He disappeared into the building. Barriss lingered a moment longer, thinking.

She had deflected his questions about her path by changing subject of the conversation. *Why?* she wondered. She wasn't sure. It had nothing to do with her assignment, and she was not ashamed of her origins. Perhaps it was just the shock of the new, of being on a different world once more.

She looked up again at the glowing spores overhead. There were species and cultures that believed souls traveled among the stars, flitting endlessly from one celestial object to another. Those strands up there could almost be mistaken for something like that.

She noticed then that another strain of spores was working its way across the clouds; a band of crimson. It interwove with the subtler colors, its borders increasing steadily. By the time dawn broke, she knew, it would be the dominant hue.

Barriss turned away, going back inside the barracks before she could see the other strands overwhelmed by the red one.

5

Sitting in the chow hall and eating a breakfast of grainmush cakes, poptree syrup, and dried kelp strips, Barriss Offee suddenly sensed a disturbance in the Force. The energy of it was that of impending combat—something she had learned to recognize. She stopped and tried to focus on a direction.

"Something?" Jos said. He was sipping a mug of parichka a few seats away.

She turned to look at him. "You said we are well behind our own lines here?"

"Yes. Why?"

"There is some kind of confrontation happening, quite close by."

The surgeon looked at his chrono. "Ah. That would be the teräs käsi match. Want to go take a look?"

Last night's rain had washed away some of the acrid pollen and spore-float, but the afternoon air still had a moldy, sour tang to it as Jos led her from the compound. A hundred meters away, in a small natural amphitheater eroded from rock, perhaps twenty or twenty-five people were gathered; troops, mostly, though Barriss could also see a few humanoids of various types. They sat or stood in the rough semicircle formed by the rocks, watching intently the unfolding spectacle before them.

There were a few shouts of encouragement, but the crowd was, for the most part, silent.

On the floor of the amphitheater was a large, spray-foam mat, and upon this stood two humans. The men were bare to the waist, and wore thinskin briefs and wrestling slippers. Both appeared to be physically fit, though neither was particularly large or bulky. One was short, dark-haired, and swarthy, thick with muscle through the chest and shoulders; the other was tall and slender, almost blond, and had several unrevised scars on his arms. The scars didn't look like ritual ones—if there was a pattern, Barriss couldn't see it. But it was obvious from their shapes that the marks had come from blades.

Barriss felt another roil of the Force, and knew this was where the disturbance had originated.

As they moved closer, Jos said, "Hand-to-hand combat instructors. The short guy is Usu Cley—he's from Rimsoo Five, about ninety kilometers toward the south pole from here. Cley was the Ninth Fleet Middle-Mass Champion two years running. I've seen him fight a couple of times—he's very good.

"The other one is new; he's a replacement for our unit's instructor, who got blown up by a suicide droid last week. I haven't seen him move yet. Are you a betting woman, Jedi Offee? They aren't due to start for a few more minutes. You could make a few credits—line is two-to-one in favor of Cley."

The Force swirled again in her, imparting a definite sense of menace, and it came, no question, from the blond fighter. "What the new man's name?"

Jos frowned, searching his memory. "Pow, Fow . . . something . . ."

"Phow Ji?"

"Yeah. You know him?"

"You have a bet down?"

"Ten credits on Cley."

Barriss smiled. Jos looked puzzled. "What?"

They stopped at one of the higher bluffs overlooking the sparring area. The two fighters moved toward the middle of the mat. The referee, a Gotal, stood between them, giving them instructions. It didn't take long; apparently outside of killing one another, just about anything went.

She said, "A couple of years ago there was a teräs käsi tourney on Bunduki—that's where the art originated, you know. In the final match, a Jedi Knight, Joclad Danva, met the local champion."

"A Jedi? Against a local? That hardly seems fair."

"Danva had the peculiar skill of being able to divorce himself from the Force at times. He never used its power in his matches; only his personal skill, which was considerable. He was a virtuoso with twin lightsabers, one of the few ever to master the Jar'Kai technique. I've seen holos of him, and he was a fantastic fighter. He could hold his own with most of the Jedi in practice."

"And . . . ?"

"And he was defeated in the Bunduki match."

Jos raised his eyebrows, then looked away from her toward the bare-chested men on the mat. The ref backed away, and the men assumed fighting positions.

"No," he said.

"Yes. Master Danva was beaten by the local teräs käsi champion, Phow Ji. Your new combat instructor."

Jos sighed. "I see. Well, it's only credits. And it's not like there's anything to *buy* around here . . ."

As they watched, the two fighters circled, watching each other. Cley kept his left side facing his opponent, his legs wide in a bantha-riding pose, left hand high, right hand low, fingers formed into loose fists.

Ji stood aslant to Cley, his right foot leading, his arms held wide, hands open. He looked vulnerable, but the invitation was false, Barriss knew. They were a step and a half apart, and Barriss recognized this as knife-fighting distance—just outside the range of a short blade.

They kept circling. Cley was too wary to fall for the obvious trap. It looked more like a jetz match than a fight, the delicate balance between them holding as one man shifted, ever so slightly, and the other responded with an equally subtle move.

The onlookers rumbled uncertainly, aware something was going on, but not sure what.

Then Cley made his move. He lunged, driven by powerful legs churning hard, and he was *very* fast. He launched a two-punch combination, a left and a right, low and high, and either would have been enough to end the fight, had they landed.

Ji didn't back away, but instead stepped in to meet the attack. His own punch crossed the centerline and deflected Cley's highline strike a hair, just enough so that his hit missed. Then Ji's punch caught Cley flush on the nose, but that wasn't the end of it. He continued his step in, put his right leg behind Cley's leading foot, caught the man's throat in the V of his thumb and forefinger, and swept him, shoving him down onto the mat hard enough to momentarily imprint Cley's form into the resilient foam. Then he dropped into a deep squat and drove the elbow of that same arm into Cley's solar plexus. Cley's breath burst out in a rush.

Ji stood, turned his back to the fallen man, and walked away. Cley lay on his back, trying to regain his wind, unable to rise.

Just like that, the fight was over. Once the attack had been launched, the entire sequence had taken maybe three seconds, total.

"Sweet soalie!" Jos said. "What did he do?"

"Looks like he just cost you ten credits, Captain Vondar," Barriss said.

Jos watched as the fight medic checked Cley over and decided that the man wasn't hurt badly enough to need more than first aid. He had never seen anything like that before—a fighter as experienced as Cley getting floored so fast and so easily. Phow Ji was *good*.

Jos had taken the basic training required of all military personnel, of course, and had learned a couple of tricks, but those were nothing compared to what he had just witnessed. He still wasn't sure what he had seen. One moment the two men were jockeying for position—the next, Phow Ji was strolling away and Usu Cley was on his back trying to remember how to breathe.

What would it be like to know that you could really take care of yourself like that, when push came to shove?

That you could defeat a *Jedi* in hand-to-hand combat?

It was hard even to imagine. Of course, the fastest moves in the galaxy couldn't block a blaster's particle beam or a projectile from a slugthrower. Although he'd heard that Jedi were actually able—through the Force, he supposed—to anticipate such attacks *before* they were launched, and thus block or avoid them—seeing the immediate future, in effect. He wasn't sure if he believed that. But one thing was for sure: his credits would be on the new guy from now on.

Beside him, Barriss stiffened, and Jos looked up to see the fearsome Phow Ji approaching, wiping his face with a towel.

Seen up close, the man's features were lean and hard; his lips seemed set in an expression not quite a sneer. This was a man who knew just how dangerous he was, and wasn't shy about letting others know as well.

"You're a Jedi," he said to Barriss. It was not a question. His voice was even, quiet, but full of confidence. He ignored Jos as if the latter weren't there. Jos decided that was fine with him.

"Yes," she said.

"But not fully fledged yet."

"I am Barriss Offee, a Padawan."

Ji smiled. "Still believe in the Force?"

Barriss raised an eyebrow. "You don't?"

"The Force is a tale made up by the Jedi to scare away anybody who would stand against them. Jedi are not impressive fighters. I hardly broke a sweat, dropping one a while back."

"Joclad Danva did not use the Force when you fought him."

"So he said." Ji shrugged, wiped his face with the towel again. "Hot day. You look a little sweaty yourself, Jedi. Here—"

He tossed the towel at her.

Barriss raised her hand as if to catch it. The towel stopped in midair. It hung there for maybe two seconds. Jos blinked. What in the—?

The towel dropped and landed at Barriss's feet. She had not taken her eyes off Ji. "The Force is real," she said, mildly.

Ji laughed and shook his head. "I've seen much better illusions from traveling carnival mages, Padawan." He turned and walked away.

Jos looked at the towel, then at Barriss. "What was that about?"

"An error in judgment," Barriss said. "I allowed myself to become annoyed." She shook her head. "I have so far to go . . ." She turned and started back toward the compound. Jos watched her go for a moment, then picked up the towel and looked at it curiously. It was a perfectly normal sheet of absorbent syncloth, the kind that one usually did not see hanging in midair as if from an invisible hook. It was damp from the teräs käsi master's sweat, but otherwise unremarkable.

He had just seen his first demonstration of the Force.

As shows went, it wasn't in the same league as dodging blaster rays, turning invisible, or shooting laser beams from one's eyes—all of which he'd heard that Jedi could do. But it had been pretty impressive, all the same.

He wondered what else she was capable of.

When he'd looked at her, standing on the rise of ground outside the base, the wind blowing her robe behind her, he'd felt a powerful attraction—or thought he had, at least. There was a sense of inner strength and peace about her that appealed strongly to the healer that he, too, was at heart. But that same tranquillity also made her seem remote and unapproachable; more like a simulacrum of a woman than the real thing. Some men were attracted by the appearance of aloofness, but not Jos.

On top of that was this power she had. Though he'd heard about the Force all his life, he realized now that he'd never really believed such a thing could exist. Like so many others in his profession, Chief Surgeon Jos Vondar was a pragmatist—he believed in what was real, what was quantifiable and measurable. What he'd just seen had been—there was no other word for it—spooky.

A sudden crackle nearby caused him to start and spin

around. The perimeter field was not far away, and something had brushed against it and gotten zapped for its trouble. The charge wasn't strong enough to kill, but it was definitely unpleasant to anything smaller than a Tatooine ronto.

Jos started back toward the cluster of huts. Not that there was anything in the jungle anywhere near that big to worry about; it had probably been a wriggler. This was the largest land-based life-form they'd noticed so far: a sluglike thing about five meters long and half a meter thick that undulated in a zigzag pattern across the ground. Its cilia could deliver a powerful electrical charge, enough to knock a grown man off his feet, but it wasn't usually fatal. All the terrestrial fauna they'd seen so far, even large ones like the wriggler, were invertebrate. Supposedly there were aquatic creatures of much greater size and variety in Drongar's oceans, but he'd never seen one, and was just as glad to keep it that way.

His thoughts turned to Barriss again, and he sighed. It was pointless to wonder if he was attracted to her or not. Even if he was, and even if her Order condoned outside relationships—something he had no data on, one way or the other—it was still impossible. The Jedi were not the only ones with traditions.

Any further thinking on this was interrupted by the signature whine of approaching medlifters. Almost glad of the distraction, Jos started to trot back to the base.

6

This run was a bad one. There were four full lifters, which meant sixteen wounded troopers. Three had died en route, and one was too far gone to attempt resuscitation—one of the nurses administered euthanasia while Jos, Zan, Barriss, and three other surgeons scrubbed up.

One of the clones was covered with third-degree burns; they had to cut his armor free. He had literally been cooked by a flame projector. Fortunately, one of the three working bacta tanks they had was empty, and the trooper was quickly immersed in a nutrient bath.

The condition of the remaining eleven ranged from critical to guarded, and were triaged accordingly. Jos pulled on his skin-gloves while Tolk briefed him on his first case.

"Hemorrhagic shock, multiple flechette injuries, head trauma . . ."

Jos glanced at the chrono. They were about ten minutes into the "golden hour"—the time window most critical for a trooper's survival of a battlefield injury. There was no time to waste. "Okay, let's get him stabilized. He's lost a lot of blood, and he's got an asteroid belt's worth of metal in his gut. Pump in some vascolution, stat . . ."

Barriss watched Jos at work for a minute, admiring his skill and quick decisions. Then she opened herself to the Force, letting it tell her where her abilities would be most needed. She felt it guide her feet toward Zan's table, where the Zabrak was working on another trooper, assisted by an FX-7.

"Is there a problem?" she asked.

"Take a look," he replied.

She stepped closer. The naked body lay on the table, intubated and dotted with sensor lines and drips. He did not appear wounded or injured, but the skin was a mottled purplish color—it looked like one gigantic bruise.

"He's been hit with a disruptor field," Zan said. "Bioscan shows his central nervous system's been fried. I thought we could do something, but he's past that. Autonomic functions are stable on life sustain right now, but they won't last. And even if we could reestablish consciousness, he'd be nothing but meat."

"What can be done?"

He shook his head. "Nothing. We can harvest his organs, use 'em to patch up the next one who needs a kidney or a heart." He started to gesture to the droid, but Barriss stopped him.

"Let me try something first," she said. Zan blinked in surprise, but stepped back, indicating the patient was hers.

She stepped closer, hoping that her nervousness would not show. She extended her hands through the field and placed both palms on the clone trooper's chest.

Then she closed her eyes and opened herself to the Force.

It seemed to her that the Force had been with her, always, from her earliest memories of childhood. One of those was particularly vivid, and for some reason it often came to mind when she was about to invoke the power. She could not have been more than three or four, and had been playing with a ball in one of the Temple antechambers. It had rolled beyond her reach, through an open arch she had not yet explored. Barriss had followed the ball, and abruptly found herself in one of the gigantic main chambers. Far overhead, the vaulted ceiling loomed, and huge pillars rose majestically from the tessellated floor. Her ball was still rolling across that floor, but Barriss, awed by the sheer size and magnificence of it all, wasn't about to go after it.

Instead, she made it come back to her.

She had not known she was capable of that. She simply *reached* for it, and the ball stopped, hesitated, and then rolled obediently back to her.

As she bent to pick it up, she sensed someone behind her. She turned and beheld Master Yoda, standing in the far entrance to the antechamber. He smiled and nodded, quite evidently impressed with what he had just seen.

That was all. She remembered nothing after that, whether Master Yoda had gone on his way and she had continued playing, or if he had spoken to her, or if something else entirely had happened. One would think such an encounter with one of the most legendary Jedi of all would be impressed in one's brain far more thoroughly than the part about playing with a ball. But that was how it was. She even remembered the ball's color: blue.

That memory came to her now, as it did, sometimes fleetingly, sometimes in great detail, nearly every time she prepared to call on the Force.

Barriss felt the palms of her hands growing warm against the trooper's belly. She didn't have to visualize the process—she *knew* that healing energy was pouring from her into him. No—not from her; *through* her. She was only the vessel, the conduit through which the Force did its work.

An unknown time later—it could have been a minute or an hour, as far as she knew—she opened her eyes and lifted her hands.

"Wow," Zan murmured behind her. He was looking at the readout panel. She saw that the trooper was stabilizing. Also, the discoloration had vanished; his skin was a healthy color.

"You must've been top in your class. How'd you *do* that?" Zan asked, without taking his gaze from the panel.

"*I* did nothing," Barriss replied. "The Force can heal wounds on many occasions."

"Well, it sure worked on him." Zan gestured at the panel. "His brain wave pattern's within normal limits, and most of the secondary trauma seems gone. Pretty impressive, Padawan."

The FX-7 guided the gurney out. By the time Zan had finished changing gloves there was another body before him. "Stick around," he said to Barriss. "There's plenty more where he came from."

Seated on a bar stool, his left foot propped on a rung higher than the right foot, Zan adjusted the tuning mechanisms on his quetarra, bringing the strings into tune. The instrument had eight of these, bucky-fibers of varying diameters and texture, and eight was three more than Zan had fingers on either hand. The first time he had seen his friend play the thing, Jos had been impressed. The Zabrak's fingers had danced nimbly up and down the instrument's fret board, and he had now and then leaned way over and pressed his chin against the instrument, using it to fret the strings. The quetarra was a hollow, ornate, and beautifully grained pleek-wood box, polished to a dull sheen, with several holes in it, shaped something like a figure eight. A flat board protruded from the box, and eight geared turnkeys on a carved headpiece attached to the ends of the strings.

The cavalcade of war-torn bodies had finally stopped coming nearly five hours after the last lifters had arrived. During the final hour another lightning storm had passed through—a bad one, with bolts stabbing down quite close to the camp. The entire area was electrostatically shielded, of course, but it was hard to remember that when the thunder was loud enough to shake the building, the sudden flares of white light through the windows left purple afterimages in his eyes, and the pungent scent of ozone filled the air, expunging even the stench of battle-charred flesh.

But the storm had passed as quickly as it came, and by unspoken agreement everyone had wound up in the cantina. Jos had come in a few minutes late, and had been surprised at the relative silence within, until he saw Zan.

The anticipation in the air was almost as piquant as the ozone smell had been. People sipped drinks or inhaled vapors or chewed spicetack, and watched Zan adjust the quetarra. No one was even so much as glancing at the silent quadro box that usually provided canned music. The globe lights had been toned down to a soft, effulgent level. Various harmonic sounds rang out as Zan turned the keys, modifying the various tensions until the atonal notes came to blend together just right. At last, satisfied, he sat up a bit straighter on the stool, settled the instrument on his left leg, and nodded at the audience.

"I'm going to try two short works. The first is Borra Chambo's prelude to his masterwork, *Dissolution by Self-Intention*. The second is the fugue from Tikkal Remb Mah's *Insensate*."

Zan began plucking the strings, and the music that came from that rapport between fingers and fibers filled the cantina with a haunting melody and a counterpoint bass line that, despite Jos's gripes about how much he hated classical works, immediately swept the human into its embrace.

Zan was a master musician, there was no question of that. He should have been on a concert stage on some quiet, civilized world, where sentient beings appreciated such artistry, his talented hands occupied creating art with Kloo horn and omni box instead of wielding vibroscalpels and flexclamps.

War, Jos thought. *What is it good for?* Certainly not for the arts. He wondered how many other talents like Zan were being squandered in battles across the galaxy. Then he forced such depressing thoughts from his head and just listened to the music. There was little enough beauty on this world, he reminded himself—might as well enjoy it while it lasted.

Around him, others stood or sat quietly, caught in the musical web Zan was weaving. Nobody spoke. Nobody rattled dishware or clinked glasses. It was silent, save for the distant rumble of thunder and the sounds of Zan's quetarra.

Jos glanced around and saw Klo Merit. The Equani was easy to spot; he towered nearly a head taller than any other biped in the crowd. The pale gray fur and whiskers helped, too. Jos was glad to see the Rimsoo's minder there. The Equani—what few were left, after a solar flare had scorched their homeworld—were intensely empathetic beings, capable of understanding and psychoanalyzing nearly every other known intelligent species. Jos knew that Merit, in many ways, carried the emotional weight of the entire camp on his sleek, broad shoulders. Now, however, he seemed caught up in the spell Zan was weaving, just like everyone else. *Good*, Jos thought. He remembered a quote from Bahm Gilyad, who had formalized the rules and responsibilities of his profession five thousand years before, during the Stark Hyperspace Conflict: "The sick and the injured will always have a healer to salve their wounds, but to whom does the healer go?"

As Zan played on, Jos found it easier not to think about the war, or how tired he was, or how many shards of metal he had removed or perforated organs he had replaced in the last few hours. The music carried him to its depths, raised him to its heights, and refreshed him like a week's worth of rest. He realized that, in a great many ways, his friend was doing for the doctors and nurses of Rimsoo Seven what the Jedi had done for the wounded clone troops—he was healing them.

Time seemed to stand still.

Eventually, Zan reached the end of the last composition. The last clear note shivered away, and the silence was nearly absolute. Then the cantina patrons began whistling and clapping, or pounding their empty drink mugs on tabletops. Zan smiled, stood, and bowed.

Den Dhur was standing next to Jos, who hadn't noticed when the reporter had come in. "Your partner's good," Dhur said. "He could be working the classical circuit, making serious credits at it."

Jos nodded. "Probably would be," he said, "except for this little problem called interstellar war."

"Well, yes, that." Dhur paused. "Let me buy you a drink, Doc."

"Let me let you."

They stepped over to the bar. Dhur waved at the tender, who lumbered toward them. "Two Coruscant Coolers." As they waited for the drinks, Dhur said, "What do you know about Filba?"

Jos shrugged. "He's the supply sergeant. Processes requisitions, changes in orders from upstairs, that kind of thing. Smells like he uses the swamp for cologne. Outside of that—nothing, really. Who knows anything about Hutts? And why do you care?"

"Reporter's instinct. Hutts make news, more often than not. Also, Filba and I go back a ways. I don't want to be speciesist or anything, but you know the old saying: 'How do you know when a Hutt is lying? His—"

"—lips move,' " Jos finished. "Yeah, I heard that one. They say the same thing about Neimoidians."

"And Ryn, and Bothans, and Toydarians. It's a tough galaxy, or so I've heard." The reporter grinned at Jos, who grinned back. Though he came across as sarcastic and irascible, still there was something likable about the scrappy little fellow.

The bartender brought their drinks. Dhur dropped a credit on the bar. "Hate to break it to you, but I've heard it applied to humans, too."

Jos drained his mug. "I'm deeply shocked and offended. On behalf of humans across the galaxy, I'll have another drink." He signaled the tender, then added, "Filba can be a pain in the glutes, but he seems to do his job pretty well. Or maybe I should say 'jobs.' He's got his pudgy little fingers into everything, seems like. He's even in charge of the bota shipments."

Dhur was about to take a sip of his second drink; he

stopped and lifted an eyebrow instead of his mug. "Excuse me?"

"That's what I hear. Bleyd's given him full control over processing, harvesting, and shipments."

"Imagine that." Dhur seemed suddenly nervous. "Hey, did you hear about Epoh Trebor and his HoloNet Entertainment tour? Looks like Drongar's on their list."

"I'll make a note to get excited about that later." Jos had never been overly fond of the popular HoloNet star, although he seemed to be in a minority, judging from Epoh's ratings. He was still curious about Dhur's interest in Filba, but before he could say anything more, the Sullustan drained his cup and said, "Align with you later, Doc. Thanks for the drink."

"You paid for it," Jos reminded him.

"Right, so I did," Dhur said. "Well—you'll get the next round," and then he headed for the door as fast as his stubby legs could carry him.

Jos looked around, wondering if Filba had come in while they were talking. He didn't see him, and the Hutt was pretty easy to pick out in a crowd.

He frowned. Obviously something had gotten Dhur's dewflaps in an uproar, and it seemed to have to do with Filba. The base was expecting a few hours of relative peace and quiet before the next wave of wounded arrived, unless there was an emergency evac from the front lines, which was always a possibility. Jos had intended to spend the time getting some sleep. Sleep was even more precious than bota on this world. Maybe, though, he would stop by the supply hut, see how Filba was doing.

First, however, he would finish his drink.

7

The spy had been on this miserable soggy mudball of a planet for more than two standard months now, and was intensely, seriously sick of it already. Two months since the agents in the higher echelons of the Republic military had arranged for the transfer to this Rimsoo. Two months in the heat and the sun, besieged constantly by all manner of flying pests . . . and the spores! Those irritating spores, constantly clogging up everything. There were days when a filter mask was a necessity, or he would strangle before he could walk the length of the base.

The spy missed home with an unnerving desperation. The mild weather, the ocean breezes, the subtle scents of the fern trees . . . the nostalgic ache was dismissed with a growl and a headshake. No point in dwelling on the past. There was a job to do, and finally, the seeds that had been planted more than a year before were starting to come to fruition.

Although the exact nature of the machinations by which Count Dooku had accomplished this grand scheme were still unclear, ultimately they did not matter. In fact, it was better to be ignorant so that, if caught, not even drugs or hypnoscans could extract the truth.

Not that exposure was very likely. This new identity had been impressively documented, and the position in the chain of command was high enough that almost every piece of important data coming through could be evaluated. The confederacy had laid the groundwork well. The spy glanced at a wall chrono, then sat down behind the large, impressive desk. Built into the desktop was a flatscreen that displayed various views of the Rimsoo buildings, the transport ship hangar, and the bota-processing docks. There really wasn't too much more to the place. Everything combined wouldn't be worth the waste of a single proton torpedo, except for one thing: the bota.

The different flatscreen scenes showed everything looking normal. That would change soon enough—in just a few minutes, in fact.

A push of a button stopped the screen on the "space-dock"—much too grandiose a term for a slab of ferro-crete ten meters square—where the shuttle, bearing a load of processed bota, was about to lift off. The spy watched as the transport rose silently on invisible repulsor waves. It climbed quickly, building up speed for a quick dash through the main spore strata to minimize damage. It reached the height of a thousand meters in mere moments, dwindling to an all-but-impossible-to-see dot. Then the dot abruptly bloomed, blindingly white, becoming for a second brighter than Drongar Prime.

A few seconds later, the rumble of the explosion rolled over the base, like tumbling, crashing breakers of sound.

The spy couldn't feel any joy over this act. People had died in the doing of it, but it was necessary. One had to cling to that. It was part of a distant, but important, goal. One had to keep that in mind.

*   *   *

Den Dhur was thinking hard. It would soon be time for him to go back to his cubicle and dig out the small but powerful comm unit he had bought on the black market for his war assignments. It had cost him a pile of credits, but it was worth it. Disguised as a portable entertainment module, it was actually capable of sending a holocoded message packet through hyperspace on a bandwidth that was all but undetectable by both Republic and Confed monitor stations.

The problem was, there didn't seem to be a whole lot to report. While it wasn't general knowledge that the Drongar engagement was primarily about claiming the bota fields, it wasn't a big surprise, either. Den's problem right now was that he didn't have a good story to follow.

That problem didn't last long.

Den was crossing the compound when he saw his shadow turn pitch black for a fraction of a second. He turned and looked up carefully, squinting so as to maximize the polarization factor in his droptacs. Even with ambient light damped down, the bright spot overhead was intensely white, outshining the planet's sun. For a horrified second he thought some other, nearby star had gone nova. *That* would be a milking hot story, except that he wouldn't be around to report it.

He heard shouting, cries of shock and alarm, from behind him. Someone was standing beside him, looking up—Tolk, the Lorrdian nurse. "What happened?" she asked.

"Looks like the bota transport blew up."

As if to confirm this, the sound of the explosion crashed down, vibrating the bones of those who had skeletons. Den felt his teeth chatter in response to the low-frequency waves.

A nearby clone trooper—a lieutenant, according to his blue chevrons—whistled in awe. "Yow. Their field must've gone critical. Probably slipped a superconductor coupling."

"No way," an Ishi Tib tech engineer—Den recognized him as the one dancing in the cantina during the rain on his first day planetside—said. "My crew went over the housing this morning," he continued. "Checked the seals three times—those vacuum bubbles were *tight*. A greased neutrino couldn't have squeezed between the plates."

The trooper shrugged. "Whatever. How many aboard?"

"Two loaders," a human, whom Den didn't recognize, said. "And the pilot."

The trooper shook his head and turned away. "Freaking shame."

You could call it that. Den glanced around. The open compound was full of onlookers now, all squinting upward even though there was nothing more to see. "What about debris?" a Caamasi nurse asked nervously.

"Debris?" the tech engineer snorted. "Only 'debris' from this gonna be gamma rays." He waved one arm overhead, indicating the sky just above the base. "Don't worry—energy shield over the whole place, remember?"

Others began to weigh in with their opinions on what had caused the transport's destruction. Den walked away, thinking.

One thing was for sure—Filba was going to have his own meltdown over this, if he hadn't already. Den pursed his lips thoughtfully, then changed his direction.

* * *

Den approached the Ops building, which housed the supplies and the comm station, with a little trepidation. Though he'd only been on Drongar for a few days, he knew Filba of old; they'd first crossed each other's paths on the rainy world of Jabiim, during one of the Republic army's last stands. Den had been reporting on the battle, and Filba had been a requisitions officer who was dabbling in the weapons black market. The Hutt was, like so many others of his kind, willing to use anybody's back as a vibroblade sheath, and had nearly gotten Den killed trying to curry favor with the rebel Alto Stratus.

Den's dewflaps tightened at the memory of it. Filba was a craven opportunist, with dreams of being a criminal overlord, just like his hero, Jabba. Perhaps ultimately even a Black Sun vigo, from the few slurred hints he'd dropped now and then when in his cups. Den's opinion was that the Hutt didn't have much chance of being a big noise in the underworld. All Hutts were invertebrates, but in Filba's case a backbone was sorely needed. Despite all his bluster, Filba was the first one under the table when *"Incoming!"* was heard—*And, given his size, usually the only one who fits,* Den thought.

Filba's primary assignment was as quartermaster. As such, he was responsible for ordering and keeping track of any and all medical equipment, drugs, munitions and matériel, wetware, cybernetics, droids, sensors and communications gear, transport parts, food, and whatever latest spore-fighting chemicals the Republic think-tanks had come up with—and these were just the tasks Den knew about. The Hutt also monitored the holo-comm station, sending and receiving orders and messages, usually between Admiral Bleyd and Colonel

Vaetes, but occasionally combat instructions from the fleet admiral to clone troop commanders. These jobs would seem to be more than enough for any six beings, but apparently the Hutt insisted on keeping track of the bota harvesting and shipments as well. Den wondered when Filba found time to sleep.

If I know Filba, the reporter thought—*and, Mother help me, I do—his interest in the bota is more than just a job.*

Filba's office was about what the reporter had expected: neat and organized, but also crammed to the ceiling struts with shelves, receptacles, and cabinets. These in turn were crammed with all manner of things, but mostly held various media for data storage. Den saw racks of holocubes, flatscreens, plastisheet files, and so on . . . it made his head itch just to look at all that information.

The Hutt was facing a holoproj, conversing with someone in the reception field. That was all Den saw before a trooper stepped in front of him, his blaster rifle at port arms. "State your name and business," he said.

This clone was a noncombatant, no doubt detailed as part of Filba's security. His armor was clean and white. "If you don't have a good reason for being here, your head's coming off."

"Den Dhur. Reporter, *Galactic Wave.* Just wanted to get Filba's take on the—"

The Hutt's bulk loomed behind the clone guard. "It's all right," he said. The guard nodded and stepped away. Filba glared down at the Sullustan, raising himself up to his full, enormous—to Den, anyway—height. Behind him, Den could see that the holoproj Filba had been speaking with was now gone.

"What do *you* want?" Filba growled.

"Don't try to intimidate me, slug-face, or I'll let some hot air out of you." Den had already pulled his recording rod from a pocket, and was posed to record Filba's words; now he poked it in the Hutt's belly as he spoke for added emphasis, regretting his action instantly when he pulled the rod, now dripping strings of slime, back.

Filba slumped nearly half a meter. He looked—if Den was reading the expression on the huge, toadlike face right—very nervous. Den wrinkled his nose, noticing that the Hutt's bodily secretions now smelled sour.

"I just spoke with Admiral Bleyd," Filba said. "Or rather, I listened while he spoke. He spoke quite loudly, and for a long time."

"Let me guess. He's not happy about the transport being vaporized."

"Nor am I." Filba wrung his hands; his fingers looked like damp yellow Kamino spongeworms. "More than seventy kilos of bota were lost."

"Along with three lives," Den reminded him. "What do they call that? Oh, yeah: 'collateral damage.'"

His sarcastic tone made Filba glance sharply at him. The Hutt drew himself up and away, leaving a glistening, wide trail of mucosal ooze. Den was just as happy to have some space between him and Filba; the huge gastropod's fear-scent was making him queasy.

"People die in wars, reporter. What do you want?" Filba's tone was cold; obviously he regretted the Sullustan seeing him in a moment of weakness.

"Just a quote," Den said in a conciliatory tone. No point in antagonizing him further; Filba might be a coward, but his jurisdiction over Rimsoo Seven's shipping and receiving station, as well as much of the intel datastream, made him a powerful and influential individual—and a bad enemy once your back was turned. "Something official about the disaster that I can file with my story."

"Story?" Huge yellow eyes narrowed suspiciously. "What story?"

"Naturally I'm going to mention this in my next uplink. I'm a war correspondent. It's part of my job." Den realized he was sounding defensive. He closed his mouth.

"I can't allow that," Filba said primly. "It could damage morale."

Den stared at him. "Whose morale? The troops'? Nothing bothers them; cut off both arms and they'll kick you to death. And if you're talking about the base personnel, anyone who isn't in a coma or a bacta tank knows about it already. It was kind of an attention-getter."

"This conversation is over," Filba said, gliding away over his patina of slime. "You will not file any story on this incident." He made an offhand gesture, and Den was suddenly yanked upward from behind. The clone guard had picked him up by his collar and was now carrying him, feet dangling, out of the chamber.

Once outside, the guard set Den down—not forcefully, but not particularly gently, either. "No more dropping in unannounced," he told Den. "Filba's orders."

Den was trembling with anger. "Tell Filba," he said, "that he can take his orders and—" He described graphically just how the Hutt could use his cloacal flap as a file folder. The clone guard paid no attention; he simply went back inside.

Den turned and stalked toward his cubicle, keenly

aware that several clone troopers and a few officers of various species were watching. Some were smiling.

You will not file any story on this incident.

"Wrong," Den muttered. "Watch me."

8

The explosion had drawn Jos outside the cantina, as it had most of the other occupants. His vision was just a bit hazy—somehow, those two drinks had multiplied into four—but the transport's disintegration helped sober him up dramatically.

He saw Zan and one of the other surgeons, a Twi'lek named Kardash Josen, and joined them; they, like everyone else at the base, were speculating as to the disaster's cause. The prevailing theory was that the spores had mutated into something that could cause some kind of catastrophic reaction in the lift engines. And wasn't *that* a pleasant thought . . .

As they talked, Jos noticed Den Dhur striding across the compound toward his office, his dewflaps quivering with indignation and anger. Intrigued, Jos moved to intercept him. The reporter was muttering to himself, and probably would've walked right by Jos if the latter hadn't blocked his path. "Is there a problem? Anything I can do?" he asked, feeling a sudden rush of affection for the little guy; after all, he'd introduced Jos to Coruscant Coolers.

"One side, Vondar. I'll show him who he's dealing with . . ."

"Whoa, whoa," Jos said, backing up in front of Dhur

with his hands up until the latter finally came to a halt.
" 'Him' who?"

"That ambulatory clot of rancor phlegm, that's who!
That condescending, officious sea scum! That—"

"Ah," Jos said. "Sounds like you and our esteemed
quartermaster aren't getting along."

"When I get through with him, he'll be getting a *long*
stretch of duty on the backside of Raxus Prime, or
someplace even worse, if I can think of one." Dhur's
dewflaps were vibrating so fast Jos could practically
feel the breeze.

"Look," he said, "I'm the chief medical officer here,
and you're our guest. If you have a problem with Filba,
or anyone else—"

"It's Filba who's got the problem, Doc—he just
doesn't know it yet." Dhur dodged around Jos. "Now,
if you'll excuse me, I've got some work to do." He disappeared into his cubicle.

Jos watched him go, slightly nonplussed. While Filba
wasn't the easiest sentient to get along with, Jos had
never seen the Hutt inspire this kind of anger in anyone.
Usually the best Filba was capable of inducing was irri-
tation. He wondered if Dhur's earlier preoccupation in
the cantina had anything to do with this.

He decided to go ask the Hutt for his side of it. Usually he was inclined to let the principals in these matters
work things out by themselves—as a doctor he had
learned very early that often the best way to effectuate
healing was to just get out of the way and let nature, or
the Force, or whatever determined such outcomes, work
its way. But, as he had told Dhur, one of his duties was
to help Vaetes keep the peace.

He turned to head for the Hutt's sanctum when he

noticed the Jedi healer emerging from her quarters. He changed course.

"Not shaping up to be a very good morning, is it?" he asked as he drew near.

She looked up at him from within her hood, and he was shocked at her pallor. "Padawan Offee, if you don't mind my saying so, you look like you either just saw a ghost, or just became one. You need a shot of cordrazine stat—"

"I'll be fine," she said. "It's just a momentary reaction." She smiled sadly. "Your colonel was right—one gets used to all this very quickly. Too quickly."

Jos's puzzlement must have shown on his face, because Barriss added, "I—felt the destruction. Through the Force. Not the agony of their deaths—that was almost instantaneous. But the *recoil* in the Force, the reaction to whatever motivated this heinous act—*that* was . . . intense."

"'Heinous'? Are you saying that what happened to the transport wasn't an accident?"

She looked into his eyes; though her flesh was pale, her eyes were bright and intense. "Yes, Captain Vondar, that is exactly what I'm saying. It was not a malfunction caused by spores, or system failure, or anything like that. It was sabotage. It was murder."

Admiral Bleyd received the news while taking his daily sauna. His secretary droid delivered it, because none of the other organic beings on board the MedStar could comfortably enter the steam-filled chamber. Bleyd kept the temperature so hot it would blister the skins of most of the officers and staff. To him, however, it was comfortable.

He read the flimsi, then crumpled the thin sheet. When he opened his hand, the sheet's molecular memory immediately re-formed it, without even wrinkles. This did little to improve the admiral's mood.

Dressed and back in his office, he paced angrily. Who was responsible for this? He did not for one microsecond believe that it had been an accident. It was sabotage, subversion, and no doubt the beginning of a covert campaign to promote demoralization. Was it a ploy of the Separatists? Though the popular front promulgated by the HoloNet was that this was a war to stop the madman Dooku from spreading anarchy throughout the galaxy, in reality it was about commerce and capitalism, as most wars—even "holy" ones—were. The Confederacy and the Republic had not fielded armies and navies across the galaxy in the service of lofty ideals and sentients' rights. It was all about economics. The Separatists and the Republicans on Drongar were fighting over bota and the potential riches attached to it, whether they knew it or not. Therefore, it didn't make a lot of sense for a Separatist to sabotage a shipment of the only precious commodity that the planet had to offer.

But there were other players in this game; players of stealth, who moved pieces even more transparent than a dejarik holomonster.

Players like Black Sun.

Bleyd cursed himself for a fool. He had, perhaps, let his greed and his eagerness to achieve wealth and status spur him into a rash alliance. The plot had been simple—too simple, no doubt. Filba, in charge of the shipping orders, had been skimming a few kilos here and there of the processed plant. Because of its adaptogenic qualities, bota was in even more demand than spice in some corners of the galaxy. Its potential value was so great, in fact, that its use as a medication by the Rimsoos here on Drongar had been strictly interdicted—a rich bit of irony, that.

But transporting bota, even at hyper lightspeeds, was difficult because of its extremely limited shelf life. And that was where Filba had outdone himself. The Hutt had discovered a way to ferry the contraband across the galaxy without loss of quality. How he had come across this knowledge, Bleyd was still not sure. Filba was many things, but definitely not a scientist, so it could not have been born in the Hutt's scheming brain. Most likely he had found and followed a trail on the HoloNet, or bribed someone for the information. The important thing was that, as far as they knew, the process had not yet been discovered by either the Separatists or the Republic.

Bota's decay process stopped if it was embedded in blocks of carbonite.

Preserved this way, it could be shipped anywhere—if the blockades of both sides could be dodged. That was where Black Sun had initially come in. Filba had connections to the interstellar criminal organization, and they had struck a bargain: for a percentage, Black Sun would provide a YT-1300f freighter, with a modified hyperdrive, that could slip past both Republic and Confed blockades and smuggle blocks of carbonite carrying bota to the far corners of the galaxy.

But it was now quite apparent that Black Sun was not satisfied with just a cut of the illegal profits they were making. They wanted the nexu's share. Bleyd assumed that this calamity was some kind of a warning shot. No doubt they would be contacting him and Filba soon to—

Bleyd stopped pacing as a new thought struck him. Was Filba double-crossing him? It was no secret that the Hutt wanted to be a vigo. And what better way to ingratiate himself with the crime cartel than opening the way for Black Sun to take over a profitable smuggling operation?

Bleyd nodded. Yes. He had to consider that possibility.

He stepped over to the observation port, looked down at the planet. The terminator line was just reaching the peninsula where RMSU-7 was based. The thick transparisteel showed his reflection, overlaid on the planet below him. *An appropriate image*, he thought. *Because if Filba has betrayed me, there's no place on this world or any other where he can hide . . .*

9

Not all of the troops' medical problems were traumatic. There was a section at the Rimsoo that housed patients who had illnesses or infections not related to battle, but which were bad enough to require monitoring. Allergies, idiopathic fevers, and a fair number of respiratory sicknesses—not surprising, since the air was full of spores, pollen, and other as-yet-unknown agents. Every planet had its own particular set of medical problems—bacteria, viruses, and, as here, spores. The state of galactic medicine was such that most patients on most planets could be healed, or at least kept alive, most of the time—but not always. And sometimes the side effects of the treatment were as bad as the cure.

Barriss Offee had agreed to do a rotation in the ward because her use of the Force was particularly well adapted to this kind of medical treatment. The Force could not in itself close a gaping wound—at least she did not have that kind of control—but it could help a sick person's weakened immune system overcome attacks from pathogens.

As she scrubbed down, the Padawan had other things on her mind. That the transport had blown up had not been an accident—this she knew with certainty. Was that sabotage somehow connected to her mission regarding the bota? There was no logical reason to assume so, but she felt that it was. Was that the Force prompting her? Or was it simply intuition, or even mere imagination?

Her contacts with the staff on Drongar had not produced any dark undertones in the Force thus far. The doctors, surgeons, nurses, and support people all seemed to be more or less what they claimed. Yes, there were things going on behind their facades, tensions that they hid, passions that they suppressed, but nothing that smacked of espionage or thievery.

Of course, she hadn't met everyone yet, and there were some species that she simply couldn't read at this point in her training. The minds of Hutts, for instance. Hutts' inner selves were very slippery; when she reached for the core of one, it felt as if she were trying to pick up a transparisteel ball covered in ramjet lube. She was best with her own kind—so much so that at times during the last couple of years she had felt hopelessly provincial.

An FX-7 med droid handed her the flatscreen chart of the patient in the Green Bed. Because the clones all looked exactly alike, each wore a Rimsoo ID tag around his right wrist. The staff had also taken to putting little colored pulse-stickers on the beds, and so, it had been explained to her, most of the nurses and doctors tended to refer to them as the Red Bed, the Blue Bed, the Purple Bed, and so on.

The man in the Green Bed had an MUO—malady of unknown origin—that somehow caused his blood vessels to dilate suddenly, as if he were plunging into deep shock. The causative agent had not yet been found. The result kept his blood pressure so low that if he tried to stand, or even sit up quickly, he passed out from lack of blood feeding his brain. The planetside specialist in xenobiotics, a human woman named Ree Ohr, called it orthostatic hypotensive syncope of idiopathic origin—which, translated, meant: "somebody who faints every time he tries to stand or sit up quickly, and we don't know why." Doctors put great store into labels, as if naming an illness were in itself somehow going to cure it. The Jedi healers tried to be more holistic in their approach to treating the ill.

Let's see how well it works here, she thought.

She went to his bedside. The trooper—his designation, according to the chart, was CT-914—seemed fine as long as he was lying down. They had just put him on a histaminic retardant whose side effect was to decrease blood pressure. If they could not cure the illness, they would treat the signs or symptoms as best they could.

"Hello. I'm Padawan Offee. How are you feeling today?"

"I feel well," he said. He did not amplify that.

"Sit up, please."

He did so. Two seconds later his eyes rolled up to show white, and he collapsed back onto the bed, unconscious.

So much for the new medication.

After a few more seconds, the trooper recovered. He opened his eyes.

"Tell me what just happened," Barriss said.

"I sat up and blacked out. Again."

She had not been on this world very long, but she had learned that the clone troopers tended to be somewhat literal and taciturn in their communication. When asked a question, they responded with precision, but didn't generally volunteer things.

"How long were you unconscious?"

"Thirteen seconds."

The confidence in his voice surprised her. "And how do you know this?"

"There's a chrono on the wall behind you."

Barriss looked over her shoulder. So there was. Feeling slightly foolish, she said, "I'm a Jedi healer, CT-Nine-one-four. I have certain abilities that might be helpful. I will, with your permission, try to help you."

A small smile appeared on his face. "Is there another choice for me, Jedi Offee?"

That brought a smile to her face, as well. A joke. The first one she'd ever heard a clone make; not that she'd conversed with all that many.

She exhaled, pushing as much air out of her lungs as she could, then relaxed, letting them fill again. She repeated the action. *Tidal breathing,* her mentor had called it. It always worked; she felt herself relaxing, moving into a state of mind more receptive to the Force. A clear, calm place, unburdened with recollections and anticipations. A place where she was no longer Padawan Barriss Offee, no longer anyone at all; merely a conduit for the living Force.

It was there for her, as it always was. She reached out with it and into the trooper's energy field, seeking the *wrongness.*

Ah. There it was. A disturbance in his neural net, centered in the hypothalamus. There did not seem to be any pathogenic cause—she sensed no forms of microscopic life except those that should be there. Yet somehow, the man's hindbrain had been injured. She could "see" a glowing red malignancy, and, using the Force, she soothed the injury, "stroked" it with etheric ripples until the glow faded.

Then she withdrew. Returning was always slightly

disorienting. She centered herself, then opened her eyes. CT-914 was watching her.

She said, "Sit up, please."

The patient did so. After a few seconds, he was still conscious.

"Let's see if you can stand."

He swung his legs over the edge of the hardfoam bed, put his feet on the floor, and stood.

"Do you feel faint?" she asked.

"No. I feel optimal." He bent, knees locked, put his hands flat on the floor, raised up on the balls of his bare feet, stretched his arms wide. "No dizziness or disorientation whatsoever," he reported.

"Good. Please get back in the bed. Someone will check on you in a little while. If the affliction doesn't come back, you'll be released."

He got back into the bed. "Thank you, Jedi Offee. It'll be good to get back to my unit and my mission."

"You're welcome."

As Barriss turned and started toward the next patient, she noticed the chrono on the wall. Its reading surprised her; a little more than an hour had passed since she had first spoken to CT-914. She had stood there for an hour, immersed in the Force, and yet it had felt as if only a few seconds had passed.

Such things still amazed her.

The Indigo Bed was next . . .

The call had come much sooner than even Bleyd had anticipated. In fact, it had come in person.

Seated across the desk from Bleyd, Black Sun's representative was more than simply self-confident—he was obnoxiously smug. And why shouldn't he be? He was a career criminal, a delegate of the biggest gangster syndicate in the galaxy. In addition to that, Mathal, as he called himself, was large and very muscular, with a blaster strapped low on his right leg and a vibroblade sheathed on his left hip. *And he looks like he knows how to use them,* Bleyd thought. *Good.*

Mathal had just delivered Black Sun's offer. It was more like an ultimatum. They didn't want more bota.

They wanted it *all*.

"We can get top price for as much as you can deliver," he said.

Bleyd would have raised an eyebrow, had he one. As it was, he smiled and nodded, all the while thinking that the human was a fool. Did he think that there were no safeguards on the planet at all? Even for the commander of the Republic med units here, there were steps too risky to take, and bleeding off any more of the precious crop than he and Filba were currently doing would surely be noticed.

Mathal and his bosses didn't care. They were greedy, they wanted to make a killing, and if that left Bleyd a wisp of smoke drifting from a crater—well, too bad.

"So, the deal is, you up your production and shipments. We set up a big transport outside sensor range— we got a Damorian Nine Thousand, carry half the planet, forget about that milking YT-Thirteen-hundred-f they've been using—you ferry the stuff up, fill the hold, we pay you and space. Everybody makes massive creds, everybody gets happy."

Bleyd wanted to laugh. *Right. And my face goes on every criminal-wanted holocast from here to Coruscant, while you remain anonymous.* There's *a deal.*

Even if Black Sun let him live after the transaction— and he wasn't betting his *yithræl* on that—even if he came out of it with a fortune, it wouldn't be enough to make life on the run worth it. Always looking over your shoulder for Republic peace officers? Never able to relax, never able to watch moonrise on Saki again? No, thank you. Bleyd knew that the only way to be a successful criminal was to commit a crime that nobody knew about. It didn't have to be perfect—simply one that couldn't be traced to your door. Buy an unregistered blaster, zap someone with whom you had no discernible connection on some starless night, run far and fast, and chances were excellent that they'd never attach you to the murder. But hijack a freighterload of high-profile contraband like bota? Might as well start getting used to prison food now.

But to Mathal, he said, "All right. It might take a little while to arrange it."

The man smiled, showing his puny teeth. "We can have a transport here in, say, a local half month. Should be plenty of time, don't you think?"

Bleyd smiled in return. *Observe* my *fangs, human.* "Why, yes, that should work fine."

Of course, it doesn't matter what I say, since it isn't going to happen—and you aren't going to carry the tale back to your masters.

"Then I guess our business is done," Mathal said. "Except for your, ah . . . helper. Is the slug still involved in this?"

"Filba is a loyal and trusted employee," Bleyd said, offering the lie up easily. The truth was that he trusted Filba as far as he could throw him one-handed in spitting distance of an event horizon.

"Excellent. I'll get back to my vigo and we'll set up the operation."

Wrong again, my friend, Bleyd thought. *The "opera-*

tion"—in which I take out your viscera—begins right now.

Aloud, he said, "Yes, yes. Oh, one other thing—I have a small, but particularly good batch of bota cast in carbonite, extremely high-grade product. I would like to send it to your vigo as a gesture of goodwill."

"High grade, eh? How much?"

"Not much." Bleyd shrugged self-deprecatingly. "Five kilos or so."

"Excellent," the human said. "My vigo will be pleased."

"And I am pleased to hear it." Bleyd stood. "I've had to hide it, of course. Would you care to accompany me? It's on the quarantine deck."

Mathal looked uncertain. "Quarantine? As in contagious disease?"

"No, no, nothing like that. Anything that comes up from the planet has to be sterilized—irradiated—purely as a safety precaution. Drongar, as I'm sure you know, is a positive sump of exotic pathogens. The deck is clean now, and I'm keeping it off-limits to make sure nobody happens across some items I don't want noticed—such as the one I have for you."

Mathal nodded. "Smart. You know, when this war is over, you might consider coming to work for Black Sun, Admiral. A being like you could do all right there."

"You are too kind." Bleyd politely gestured for the other to precede him. "Shall we go and collect your vigo's gift?"

"I'm game," Mathal said.

This time Bleyd really had to fight to contain his smile.

*   *   *

Den Dhur waved at the tender, got his attention, pointed at the nearly empty glasses on the table, and held up two fingers. The tender, a different one than the taciturn Ortolan, nodded.

Den turned back to the being across from him, a stubby Ugnaught med-mechano specialist named Rorand Zuzz who was a head under his own height.

"Fascinating," Den said. "Tell me more."

Zuzz drank the rest of whatever foul-smelling concoction he was using to alter his brain chemistry and set the empty glass down. The odor—some kind of carboxyl-based intoxicant—reminded Den of week-dead mellcrawler, and he did not consider himself fortunate to know that stink as a reference. The bottle, which the droid had left on the table, was labeled TYRUSIAN RED ALE, and the slogan read: BECAUSE YELLOW DOESN'T LOOK GOOD IN SPACE. *What does that mean?* Den wondered.

"Well, yar, I kin tell ya t' job is one o' t' toughest in t' service, you bet, yar."

His Basic was rough; Ugnaughts didn't generally bother to learn the common language of the galaxy unless they had to, but Den had heard and understood a lot worse.

"Dem docs alla time yellin' 'Fix dis! Fix dat!' like they 'spect me t'pull t' spare parts outta m'backside! Supply ain't deegle dung on dis world, you bet. Docs," he muttered, staring moodily into the dregs of his drink.

The server droid rolled over and put the fresh drinks on the table. It cheeped something, and Den impatiently waved it off.

"Yes, yes, on the tab."

The droid beeped acknowledgment, then rolled away.

"You work with Filba, is that right?"

The tech picked up his new drink, gulped a third of it. "Ah. Dis good. What was I sayin'?"

"You were telling me that you work with Filba."

Zuzz shook his head. "Dem 'utts 'r worse'n humans. Fussy no-crèche-fecal-retents, y'know?"

Den nodded. "Oh, I hear you, brother. Know one, know dem all."

The Ugnaught cocked a bleary eye at him. *Easy, Den. He's not drunk enough for you to start talking like you're clade-breds quite yet.*

Zuzz belched. "I mean, I'm tryin' to zero-reset t' whole biosensor array for Recov'ry, every single milkin' machine, and I can't get t' 'utt t'spring for a decen' calibrator!"

"I can't believe it," Den said. "What scum."

"Got dat right, bloodline." He glanced around, then leaned forward. " 'Tween you 'n' me?" he said in a low, slurred voice. "D' 'utt's got somet'in goin' on t' side. I t'ink dem creds went into Filba's pouch, y'know what I'm sayin'?"

"Really?"

"Oh, yar. I bin keepin' an eye on 'im. 'E's collectin' sweetsap from somewhere, y'know what I mean?"

"Oh, yar, bloodline," Den said. He smiled. Filba was going to be milking sorry he had gotten in Den Dhur's way. You could scan *that* and zap it to the bank.

10

It was a little thing that did it—it often was a little thing. In this case, it was a female human lab tech laughing at something the guy sitting at the next table with her had said. It wasn't loud, but it was a happy sound, the sound of someone forgetting, for a blessed moment, the grim realities of the Rimsoo. All of a moment, Jos remembered a girl from primary school, the first one he had made laugh. True, he had accomplished this by hopping about, pretending to be a Selonian with a hotfoot, but they'd both been seven years old at the time.

He stared at the food partitioned into the various compartments of the meal tray that sat before him. Though he knew he should eat to keep his strength up, he was finding it hard to work up an appetite. Oh, the food was okay—the powdered hawk-bat eggs did have a slightly gritty texture, but the shroom steaks weren't bad, since they were local. Still, overall, it wasn't one of the more memorable meals of his life.

Jos sighed. If not for this war, he would probably be at home, starting a practice with his father or perhaps one of his aunts or uncles—there were a lot of doctors in his family, and several surgeons—and maybe, after a hard day in the operating theater, going home to his impressive conapt in the swank Golden Beach area of Coronet. His spouse would meet him at the door; a bright, funny, sexy female companion with whom he could share his life and love. Maybe even children . . .

Apruptly, the food on his table held no appeal. What he wanted to do with his few precious minutes of free time was to go back to his cubicle and crawl into his cot, pull the thin syncloth sheet over his head, and sleep for a week. A month. However long it took for this blasted war to be over and done with so he could go home.

Yeah, he was a surgeon, and yeah, you couldn't slice without seeing blood, but being up to your ankles in it? Every day? *That* was hard.

It didn't matter that the vast majority of the troops were clones, all stamped from the same press, and all programmed not to fear war. Even though they weren't quite individuals, they still suffered and died, and the ones who didn't die he and his colleagues had to put back together any way they could, desperately jury-rigging and cobbling procedures, swapping out organs and patching up wounds, and then send them back out to suffer again. And maybe, this time, die.

There were days when he hated the talent in his hands and nerves that made it possible for him to slice and plastistrip and heal. Perhaps, if he'd been trained in something else—genomics, maybe, or bio-robotics—he wouldn't be on this stinking planet, mired in this stinking war. Of course, he'd rather be behind the lines in a Rimsoo than in the thick of things. His genetic programming didn't include immunity to fear, after all. But he didn't really want to be here in any capacity.

Jos thought of Barriss Offee, of the attraction he had initially felt for her. It was just as well that it hadn't continued, he told himself, since she was not *permes*.

The fact that she was off-limits, however, did nothing to assuage his loneliness. He wanted someone for a life mate, someone to be close to, to cherish. But he would have to wait until he was back in his home system for that to happen.

He stared moodily into the depths of his tanque tea, as if some answer might be divined from the root fragments bobbing in the murky liquid.

"Stare any harder and it'll evaporate."

He glanced up and saw Tolk standing there, in her off-duty whites. The light from the chow hall door was behind her, putting her in partial silhouette, but not so much that he couldn't still see her features. Everything went out of his head except for one thought:

Son-of-an-ibbot! She's gorgeous!

It wasn't as if he hadn't been aware that his chief nurse was human, and quite attractive; that was obvious to anybody with one working eye. But the same problem that existed with the Padawan also applied to Tolk: she was not *permes*. The Vondars and the Kersos—his father's and mother's clans—were very solidly enster; disciples of a long and traditional sociopolitical affiliation in which Jos had also been raised. A big part of an enster's core belief system was that no marriage could be made, much less consummated, outside the inhabitants of one's own planetary system. The more extreme zealots restricted it even further, refusing to allow any affiliations offplanet. No exceptions were made.

Yes, a young man or woman could go offworld, and yes, even the staunchest Ensterites might turn a blind eye if a son or daughter somehow managed a temporary alliance with one of the eksters—the "outsiders"—but when you came home, you left your wild urges behind. You did *not* bring an ekster home to meet your parents.

It was simply not done—not unless you were willing to give up your clan and be renounced and ostracized for the rest of your life. Not to mention bringing shame and contempt on your immediate family.

All this flickered through his thoughts at lightspeed. He hoped none of it showed, given a Lorrdian's uncanny ability to read expressions and body language. Tolk wasn't an empath, like Klo Merit was, but she could pick up and decode the smallest physical clues to just about any species's mood.

"Tolk," he said casually. "Sit. Have some tea. In fact, have mine."

Tolk sat, took his cup and sipped from it, looked at him closely, and said, "Who died?"

"About half the troops in the Republic military forces, seems like lately."

"We're keeping eighty-seven percent of those who rotate through our surgery alive."

He shrugged. She took another sip of his drink. "Okay, thirteen percent of a big number is still a lot. But it could be worse."

She had a nice scent about her; something slightly musky, yet fresh. He'd never noticed that before. Of course, the glare of the operating theater's UVs and the overlapping sterile fields tended to wipe out odors, which was generally a good thing, given what gases sometimes escaped when a vibroscalpel pierced body cavities.

"What's *really* wrong, Jos?"

For a moment, he was tempted to tell her. *What's wrong? I'm lonely, a long way from home, and sick of death. I'm sitting next to a beautiful woman I'd like to get to know better—a lot better—but there's no future in it, and I'm not the kind of man who wants a quick*

connect–disconnect, even though that seems like a ter-
rific idea at just this moment.

It took no imagination at all to picture her on his cot,
with her hair spread out on the pillow . . . and *that* was
a bad lane to be spacing down, he quickly realized. So
instead of speaking the truth, he said, "Just tired. Bio-
rhythms are off. I need a vacation."

"Don't we all." But she gave him a look, and for just
a second he was certain she knew exactly what he was
thinking.

Exactly.

Jos and Zan watched as the supply drop ship lowered
on invisible repulsor waves. "They'd better have those
biomarkers," Zan said. "I only ordered them half a
standard year ago. A Tatooine Sarlacc moves things
through its system quicker."

Jos mopped his brow and nodded, waiting for the
ramp to lower. There were a number of things he'd
ordered that the base needed desperately: bacta tanks
and fluid, bioscan modules, coagulin, neuropreno-
line, provotin cystate, and other first-line pharmaceuti-
cals . . . the list was practically endless. One of the most
important things on the inventory, however, was more
droids. The order had been mostly for FX-7s and 2-1Bs,
but he had also requested a couple of new office work-
ers; two of the four CZ-3s originally supplied had succumbed to rust and overwork months ago, and the
others were becoming eccentric. He suspected spore-
rot.

The ramp lowered. Filba, of course, was there to inspect the manifest, meticulously checking to see that
every last synthflesh strip and chromostring reel was
accounted for. The two surgeons, along with several

nurses and scrubs, watched the duraplast containers as they passed, trying to read the photostenciled content lists.

"Yes! Got the biomarkers at last," Zan said with a hiss of satisfaction. Then his tattooed jaw dropped. "What, only one case? They'll be gone in a month! Typical . . ."

Jos was also disappointed as the last canister autorolled past them. "So where are the droids I ordered?" He looked at Zan. "Did you see any droids come off? Anything that even *resembles* a droid?"

Zan glanced over his friend's shoulder. Before Jos could turn around, he heard a voice say, "I've been told *I* resemble one, sir." The words were precisely articulated, with that slight mechanical hollowness that comes only from a vocoder. He turned and saw a droid standing halfway down the ramp.

"Of course," the droid added, "those who said it might only have been trying to be kind."

Jos looked at the droid. It looked like one of the protocol models that were ubiquitous all over the galaxy. If so, it had been refurbished a few times; the powerbus cables weren't the standard models, if he remembered correctly. The recharge coupling was different as well. The light pewter armor had more than a few nicks and dents. Jos looked back at Zan. "I ask for office models," he said. "Anything, even an old CZ model. And they send me a *protocol* droid."

"It'll come in handy at all those fancy state dinners and diplomatic summits you're always being dragged off to," the Zabrak said with a straight face.

"Oh, yeah. I don't know *how* I've managed to survive here without my very own attaché droid."

The droid muttered something behind him that sounded very much like: "Blind luck, I'd say."

Jos and Zan both turned and stared at him. "What was that?" Jos asked.

The droid came to attention, and even though his face was an expressionless metal mask, Jos felt that something—fear? resentment? both?—somehow flashed there for a moment. But when the droid spoke again, the voice was emotionless, even more so than most 3PO models.

"I said, 'I'm instructed to stay—' here, that is. On Drongar. I think you'll find me more than competent to assist you, sir. I've had extensive medical programming, including access to the database files of Sector Gen—"

"What's your ID classification?" Jos interrupted.

"Eye-Fivewhycue, sir."

Zan frowned. "I've never heard of a Fivewhycue line."

The droid glanced at Zan and hesitated a moment before answering. Again, although the rigid features did not change, Jos felt somehow that the droid was momentarily unnerved by Zan's appearance. But when the I-5YQ answered, it was politely.

"A modification of the Threepio series, sir, with certain changes in the cognitive module units. Its design borrows somewhat from the old Serv-O-Droid Orbots model. The line was discontinued by Cybot Galactica not long after its inception, due to litigation." The droid hesitated, then added, "I am usually called I-Five."

The two surgeons looked at each other. Jos shrugged and said to the droid, "Okay, I-Five. You'll be doing double duty—data storage and secretarial as well as assisting in the OT. Think you can handle that?"

I-Five hesitated before answering, and Jos felt again, for just a fraction of a second, that the droid wanted to respond in kind to his sarcasm. But I-Five simply said,

"Yes, sir," and followed them as Jos and Zan started across the compound.

Strange, Jos thought. *The heat must really be getting to me if I start expecting* droids *to mouth off . . .*

11

The man from Black Sun couldn't believe it.

"This is a joke, right? You're tapping my buttons."

Bleyd said, "Not in the least." He had disarmed Mathal at blasterpoint, and the man was nearly having a seizure in his disbelief.

"You're insane!" Mathal's tone was truculent, but his eyes were darting about nervously, and Bleyd could already smell the man's fear-sweat.

"In your position, I might think so, too. But I'm afraid it's not that simple. Now listen carefully. The hatch is locked. The code that opens it is here, in my belt pocket. If you want to leave this vessel alive, you'll have to collect it from me. There is a large knife in plain sight somewhere on this deck with which you may arm yourself for your attempt."

Mathal glared. "Yeah? What's to stop me from breaking your neck right now?"

"You could try, even if I didn't have a blaster, but I wouldn't advise it. I am stronger than you, and my heritage is . . . somewhat fiercer. Your chances of victory would be exceedingly small. Even with the knife and me barehanded, the odds are probably no better than fifty–fifty."

"When I get back to my vigo and tell him about this, he's going to have your skull for a drinking cup."

"That may well be," Bleyd said. "But only if you get past me. I'll give you two minutes before I come for you. Next time we see each other, one or both of us dies." Bleyd flexed his hands, feeling the tendons in them moving like oiled cables. "You'd best hurry." He nodded in the direction of the spinward corridor.

The human knew a real threat when he heard it, Bleyd gave him that much credit. He tucked his bluff and bluster away and took off, fast. In ten seconds he was out of sight around the corridor's curve.

Bleyd gave him the rest of the allotted time, enjoying the slight, lingering, sour odor of the man's sweat, then started down the corridor opposite the direction Mathal had taken. The weapon was closer this way, and there were several places wherein he could hide to watch it and wait. He would allow the man to collect the knife—that was only fair, since a Sakiyan's muscles and ligament-attachment angles were mechanically superior to those of a human's, making Bleyd at least half again as powerful as a strong man, and a good deal quicker as well.

Had he been hunting for food, if there had been a mate and younglings to feed back home, he would have pulled a blaster and shot the man dead without a second's hesitation. Then dressed him out, shouldered him, and started home. Survival demanded efficiency, and you did not give food-prey any chance—you did not risk yourself if you had a family to feed. If you died, so would they, and then both *monthræl* and *yithræl*—personal honor and pride honor—would be forever stained.

Ah, but sport hunting, when there were none depending on you . . . well, that was completely different. If you were stronger, smarter, and better armed than your prey, where was the challenge? Any well-armed mindless drone could kill. The quarry of a *real* hunter should have a chance to win. If you made a mistake hunting a predator, it should cost, and if that cost might be your life, that was the spice that made the game taste best.

Mathal might be only a messenger boy now, but Bleyd knew that Black Sun operatives usually began their careers at the basic levels. Once upon a time, before he had been recruited by Black Sun, Mathal had been freelance muscle, paid for his ability to offer violence or even death. He was not a grass eater, Bleyd knew. He was a predator.

Hardly in Bleyd's class, of course. Bleyd was a firstrate hunter. Armed with naught but a lance, he had stalked Shistavanens on Uvena III. He had taken a rancor with a pulley bow and only three quarrels. He had tracked and killed unrepentant Noghri with a pair of hook-blades whose cutting edges were no longer than his middle fingers.

He could not remember the last time he had made a potentially fatal error on a sport hunt. Of course, it took only one . . .

He reached the knife a few minutes before Mathal could possibly circle around the length of the torus. There were three places that afforded a good view. One was at deck level, three steps away, in a shadowed corner. The second was behind a massive heating/cooling coil across the corridor, at least a dozen steps away. The third hiding spot was inside a ventilation shaft almost directly over the weapon's location, and, while two body-lengths in distance, it was a straight drop.

There was no real question of where he was going to hide. His ancestors, like those of the humans, had originally come from the trees and the high ground.

Bleyd gathered himself, squatted low, and sprang. He caught the edge the ventilation shaft, pivoted aside the grate covering it with one hand while clinging to the edge, and pulled himself into the shaft feetfirst. He turned around, rotated the grate back into place. Supporting himself by the strength of his arms upside down in the narrow shaft, he began to breathe slowly and evenly, dropping his heart rate into hunting mode. A tense hunter could not move fast.

He did not have long to wait. Two minutes, three . . . and here came the human, stomping along and vibrating the deck loudly enough for a deaf old pride elder to hear.

Mathal arrived in the vicinity of the knife. He looked around warily, then snatched the blade up. Bleyd heard him sigh in relief, and his grin became wider.

The knife was a good weapon, one of Bleyd's favorites. It had a thick haft; the blade as long as the man's forearm and nearly as wide as his wrist. It was made of hand-forged and folded surgical stain-free flex-steel, a drop-point fighter with a circular guard of flex-bronze and a handle of hard and pebbled black rass bone, so it wouldn't slip in a sweaty or bloody grip. After all, it would hardly be sporting to provide one's prey with a poor weapon. And his research had told him that Mathal was an expert knife fighter. Bleyd knew he would need skill and strength to prevail. Luck was not a factor.

He took a final breath, pivoted the grate cover aside, and dived for the man, headfirst. He screamed the blood cry of his pride:

"*Taarrnneeesseee—!*"

Mathal looked up, terror on his face. Too late, he raised the knife. Bleyd brushed it aside and reached for the man's throat.

Then they were joined—

The spy had less trouble with this kind of thing. After all, anyone could blow things up and assassinate targets. While it was true that a certain amount of skill was required to do such acts without being caught—and the spy had more abilities in that direction than anyone here could possibly know—the real challenge in this project was in a different arena. The labyrinthine ways of bureaucrats and the military could be slow, but just as certain to accomplish the desired results when manipulated properly. As the spy had been taught from childhood, any job could be done with the correct tools. In order to undermine a military organization or a government hundreds of thousands strong, subtlety was a must. One thought of armies and navies as giant Sauropoda—huge beasts that lumbered ponderously along their paths, crushing anything that got in their way, often without notice. A single person could not hope to stop or even turn such a beast by him- or herself, no matter how physically strong or adept. Hence the old saying: "If a ronto stumbles, do not stand under it to break its fall."

No, the way to move something so massive in a new direction was to convince the monster that the change of course was its own idea.

In theory, this was also simple. One planted the idea in the right place at the right time and waited for it to take hold. In practice, it was somewhat harder—a complex game of wits.

The recent transport destruction had created concern

and not a little paranoia. But the threat was still too nebulous to turn the monster from its path so that it could be overwhelmed. A bit of mystery was all to the good, but military leaders were not swayed overmuch by the unseen. They lived and died by facts—or what they could be convinced to believe were facts.

The threat had to become more real. What Vaetes and his people needed to see at this point was an actual villain. And there existed on the base someone who fit the bill perfectly. Too bad he would have to suffer, but it was what it was.

12

Zan sat on the backless folding stool he favored for playing his quetarra, tuning the instrument. When he wasn't playing it, it rested in a spun-fiber case that was light, but strong enough to support him jumping up and down on it without damage to the instrument. After a few drinks one late evening, Zan had demonstrated this with considerable gusto. Watching a Talusian Zabrak hopping around on an instrument case like a giant, demented Geonosian leaf-leaper, his cranial horns nearly puncturing the low ceiling, was a sight that Jos was fairly certain he could have charged credits for people to see.

Jos was stretched out on his cot, reading the latest flatscan update of the *Surgica Galactica Journal*. Some hotknife thorax chopper had posted an article on microsurgical laminotomy revision for spinal injury on the battlefield, and it was all Jos could do to keep from laughing out loud. "Use the pemeter scope to check for nerve impingement." Or: "Application of sthenic field and homeostatic phase induction is critical at this juncture."

Pemeter scopes? Sthenic fields? Homeostatic phase inductors? Oh, yeah, right. Outside of a twenty-million-credit surgical suite in a first-class medcenter, your chances of finding any of these, much less all of them together, were about as good as reaching lightspeed by flapping your arms. It was obvious this guy had never been in the field. *Love to see what the wonder slicer could do with just a vibroscalpel and a hemostat on a patient with a ruptured aorta . . .*

Zan finished tuning his quetarra and strummed a chord.

After a moment, he began plucking the strings, softly at first, then a bit louder. Jos didn't mind listening to Zan play, despite what he said sometimes just to get a rise out of his friend.

The piece Zan played was fast, had a good beat, and after a few seconds Jos gave up reading and listened. Was that leap-jump? Was Zan actually playing something written in the last hundred years? Wonders, it seemed, would never cease.

Jos didn't say anything. It wouldn't matter if he did, because when he was really into it, Zan tuned out all distractions. Once, about six months before, a fumble-fingered Gungan harvester who ought not to have been issued any weapon more dangerous than a stick had somehow activated one of the pulse bombs he carried on his hopper. The hapless amphibian had turned himself, his vehicle, and a goodly section of the local landscape into a smoking crater. He'd been three hundred meters away from their cubicle when it had gone off, and even at that distance the blast had been enough to knock over glasses, rattle the furniture, and shake a few pictures from the shelter's walls. Zan, who had been in the middle of some concerto or another, didn't miss a note. When he was done, he'd looked around, puzzled, at the mess. "If you don't like the music, just say so," he'd said to Jos.

Besides, Jos didn't want to interrupt the music, which had gone from the driving beat of leap-jump right into the heartbeat bass and melody of heavy isotope. Amazing how his friend could make a single stringed instrument suggest the sounds of omni box, electroharp, and all the other instruments of a six-piece band . . .

After another minute or so, Zan stopped.

Trying to act casual, Jos said, "Interesting. What, uh, was that?"

Zan grinned. "That? 'Etude for Dawn,' the Sixteenth Vissëncant Variation. Good to see you've become a classical music fan at last, my lead-eared friend."

Jos stared. "Didn't your mother ever tell you your horns would grow if you told a lie?"

"I admit I speeded it up a hair. And shifted the timing in a couple of places, brought up the bass line, but essentially . . . well, judge for yourself."

He began to play again, looking not at the fret board but directly at Jos, a small smile on his lips.

Jos listened. Sure enough, it was the same piece of music, but with an entirely different tone and mood— definitely classical now.

"How'd you do that? One minute it's good, the next it's lift-tube music."

Zan laughed. "You're pathetic. A space slug is less tone deaf."

Something about the way Zan was watching him, as if waiting for something to sink in, sank in. "All right," Jos said. "Fire the second round."

Now Zan really laughed. "If you had any education past the end of your scalpel, you'd know there were only *fifteen* Vissëncant Variations. What I played was Duskin re Lemte's 'Cold Midnight,' a leap-jump/heavy isotope fusion just out on the HoloNet. I downloaded it a couple of days ago. Slow it down, add a little contrapuntal line, and it isn't bad. Re Lemte obviously had some classical education on his way to the mass market. Not that *you* would know."

"You'll suffer for this," Jos said. "My revenge will be terrible. Maybe not swift or particularly inspired, but definitely terrible."

Zan chuckled and started playing again. "Couldn't be any worse than your musical taste."

Alone in her cubicle, fresh and clean from the sonic shower, Barriss Offee sat naked on the floor. Her legs were crossed and knotted, ankles over thighs, her back straight, in the position called Repose. Her hands rested, palms up, on her knees; her eyes were open, but unfocused. She breathed slowly, drawing the air in through her right nostril and whirling it deep into her belly, then expelling it slowly through her left nostril.

Floating meditation was, for her, one of the trickiest of the Jedi exercises. There were days when it was as smooth as mercury on a transparisteel plate: she would sit, and breathe, and be *there*—gravity would fall away, and she would rise like a balloon, to hover weightless half her body-length in the air. But at other times her mind refused to clear, and no matter how long or hard she concentrated, her rear stayed firmly on the floor.

Today was one of those times. Thoughts chased each other through the corridors of her mind like Tyrusian butterfly-birds, chittering inanely. Master Unduli would be shaking her head, Barriss knew, if she could see her Padawan now.

The thought of her Master released a flood of mixed emotions. Back on Coruscant, Barriss had thought of herself as an average Padawan, a little more adept than some, a little less so than others. Not brilliant, but not particularly stupid, either. Her Master had told her this was part of the limitation Barriss had put upon herself. She could remember that lesson well. It had come after a long hand-to-hand combat workout at one of the training centers, followed by lightsaber practice that had left her arms sore and burning. They had moved to a high-walled balcony, two hundred flights above ground level, beneath the constant stream of traffic going to and from the nearby skyhook way station. The balcony had been shielded, but Master Unduli had dropped the fields so that the sounds, the smells of burned fuel, the winds funneled by massive buildings, and the glare of passing advertising banners were a multisensory assault. Along with the slightly sour odor of her own sweat and the physical exhaustion she felt, it was nothing less than overwhelming.

"Sit," her Master told her. "Do your Rising Meditation to a height sufficient that you can see over the wall to observe the small bakery directly across the way. For the purpose of this exercise, consider that it is vitally important that you be able to tell me how many pastries are visible in the window."

Barriss tried, but, of course, the balcony's floor held her fast.

After a few moments, her Master said, "Is there a problem, Padawan?"

"Yes, Master. I am trying, but—"

"By saying 'try,' you limit yourself. Jedi do not limit themselves by choice."

Barriss had nodded meekly. "Yes, Master."

"I need to know how many pastries there are in that bakery window. This is of primary importance. Continue. I will return later."

And so saying, Master Unduli left.

But, of course, the pressure was too great. Barriss had not been able to levitate even a hair's thickness from the floor. She was still trying, her rear and thighs numb from the cold ferrocrete, when Master Unduli finally returned, hours later.

"I failed, Master."

"Yes? How so?"

"I could not manage to levitate."

Her Master smiled. "But was that the lesson, Padawan?"

Barriss stared at her, confused. "What?"

"One can fail at a task but still learn the lesson, Barriss. The first time I sat on this balcony trying to do Rising Meditation, all that happened was that I got sore. A Jedi does not put limits on herself, but there *are* limits, and you must find them, and understand how to *deal* with them. Have you ever heard the story of the old man's river crossing?"

"I do not recall it."

"At the bank of a wide river on this world, long before it was as it is today, an old man sat by the water, meditating. A second, younger man came along and saw the older one. 'What are you doing?' the younger man inquired.

" 'I am working on the ability to walk on water, so that I may cross the river,' the older man said.

" 'Ah. And how is it going?'

" 'Pretty well. I have been at it for forty years, and in another five or ten I believe I will have it.'

" 'Ah,' said the younger man. "Well, good luck to you.'

"He bowed, then walked to a boat tied up nearby, climbed in, cast off, and rowed across the river." Master Unduli looked at her. "Do you understand the meaning of this story?"

Barriss thought about it for a moment. "If the important thing was crossing the river, then the younger man was wiser than the older one."

"Precisely. Why spend decades learning how to walk on water when there is a boat moored right next to you?" The Jedi paused, then asked, "What was most vital in this exercise with which I tasked you?"

"How many pastries were in the bakery window."

"Exactly."

Barriss felt incredibly stupid as she suddenly understood what her Master meant.

Master Unduli smiled. "I see you comprehend at last."

"I could have simply stood up and *looked* over the wall," Barriss said. "What was important was not *how* I got the information—only that I got it."

Master Unduli nodded. "There is hope for you yet, my young Padawan . . ."

Barriss smiled at the memory. Then she took a deep breath, exhaled, and let her mind clear. A second later she floated upward from the floor, and hovered, weightless and free, in the air . . .

13

Jos had to admit that the formchair was comfortable. Ergonomically speaking, it did exactly what it was supposed to do: relax him somewhat, but not enough to make him drowsy. He had heard that the chair was equipped with biosensors that monitored heart rate, pulse, beta and theta wave activity, and so on, and relayed the information to Merit, to better help him help those sitting there. Jos doubted it. Not that it couldn't be done, but he really didn't think Merit needed it. The Equani minder seemed always to know the right words to say, the right questions to ask, and the right times to be silent.

Like now.

Jos had been staring at the floor; now he looked up and met Merit's eyes again. They were large for the fur-covered face, slate gray in color; an Equani's eye pigmentation always matched his fur, Jos had read in one of the many medicrons he'd had to study while a resident. And right now they were fixed on him.

"Explore, for a minute, your feelings for Tolk," he said gently.

Jos leaned back, and the formchair obediently flowed, like warm mercury, into a new configuration to accommodate him. *Of course,* Jos thought; *it has to be able to adapt comfortably to any species. Even Hutts, probably.* He suppressed a shudder at the thought. *I sure hope someone wipes it down afterward . . .*

"Jos," Merit said. His voice was quiet and noninsistent, but somehow it penetrated the surgeon's thoughts like a particle beam. "You're not trying very hard," the minder continued.

"You're right. Sorry."

"It's your time," Merit said. "You're allotted one hour a week to get things off your chest—or to 'upchuck gizzard trichobezoars,' as the Toydarians so colorfully put it. How you spend that time is up to you. You can talk to me—in which case I might be able to help you work through some things—or you can sit there and enjoy the furniture."

Jos grinned. "All right, Klo. I guess I'm going to talk about things whether I want to or not."

The minder smiled. "It's always hardest to help yourself." He waited a moment, then prodded gently, "About Tolk . . . ?"

Jos sighed. "It's like I just noticed her yesterday. Before that, she was just another pair of hands at the table—smart, don't get me wrong, she's an excellent nurse—but no more than that. Outside the room, she was someone to have a drink with, someone to complain about this pit of a planet with . . ."

"And now?"

"Now she's . . . more. But she *can't* be."

Merit said nothing, but his expression said, *Go on.* So Jos explained briefly about the beliefs of his family and his clan, about how he couldn't flout them by marrying an esker.

"They're your family's beliefs," Merit said. "But are they *your* beliefs?"

Jos opened his mouth, then closed it. He was making an honest effort to find the answer to that question, but his mind was having none of it. He found himself thinking about the formchair again. *Wonder how much one costs* . . .

After another fairly fruitless ten minutes, Merit glanced at the chrono and said, "We have to stop."

Jos felt relieved, and then felt irritated at himself for feeling relieved. "I guess I'm just not a very introspective sort," he told Merit at the door. "My family and clan are big on tradition, not communication. My dad's idea of a revealing moment is forgetting to lock the 'fresher."

"All you need to know about yourself is in you," the minder replied. "You may have to dig a little deeper and a little harder, but it's there."

"Maybe the Padawan could help me," Jos mused. "Can't Jedi read minds, that kind of thing?"

"I wouldn't know. The Equani species is—was—by nature rather resistant to the powers of the Jedi. But I think you need to find your own answers instead of looking to others for them."

The multiple-repulsor drone of incoming medlifters filtered into Barriss's sleep, and the siren that sounded almost immediately afterward meant that everybody within earshot needed to get to the OT. *Now.*

She dressed hurriedly and headed for the triage area. It was only twenty meters from her cubicle, but the humidity was so high today, she felt that she was wading through a pool of heated fleek oil.

When she got to the building, she stopped, momentarily unable to believe her eyes. Thirty-five or forty wounded troopers lay on stretchers, on gurneys, on the floor itself, being tended by doctors, nurses, droids, techs—anybody, in short, who could help. Most of the troops were bloody, and many were burned, with weeping red blisters and scorched black patches. Some were missing arms and legs.

Some were all of those things, and more.

Still more injured were incoming. She could barely hear the whine of the lifters' repulsor fields over the cries and groans of the wounded. Barriss swallowed, nauseated. Even doctors could be overwhelmed by too much gore. Nothing she had ever seen in her wartime experience so far had been anything close to this.

Tolk was calling triage, and it was short and to the point. Barriss watched her for a moment. To anybody outside the medical field and the battlefield, triage would seem remarkably cruel, but she knew it was the most efficient way to save the most patients.

"This one won't make it," Tolk said, rising from the side of a sergeant whose legs had been blown off above the knees. His skin was chalk white, and from the red, ragged stumps the last of his life's blood was dripping slowly. Following behind Tolk was a droid, which attached a pulse-sticker to the dying clone's shoulder. A large, red x glowed rhythmically.

Tolk moved quickly to the next patient, examined him briefly. "Shrapnel wounds to the belly and groin. Surgery, category three."

The droid put a sticker on the man's shoulder. The number 3 throbbed on it.

Barriss bent to examine the trooper closest to her— a lieutenant. He was awake and alert; his only injury seemed to be that his left arm was gone, blown off in a ragged stump just above the elbow. A constrictor around the stump had stopped the bleeding. His gaze met hers.

"I'm good," he said through clenched teeth. "Take care of my men."

"He can wait," Barriss said to Tolk. "Five."

Tolk nodded at the droid, who affixed a number 5 pulse-sticker to the man's good shoulder.

When there were fewer doctors than patients, one had to rank the injured as to survivability and the time necessary to keep them alive. Rimsoo category numbers ran from 1 through 6; category X was reserved for injuries that appeared mortal or very time-consuming to treat. The rating system was more complex than it appeared. The injury, survival chances, and need for immediate treatment all had to be taken into account. A severed artery might bleed out in a minute and all it would take to save the patient would be a simple staple or suture tie, so it would be best to treat him first, whereas a man with his leg blown off but heat-cauterized from a blaster bolt could be left until more life-threatening injuries had been dealt with. Making these decisions, the Padawan knew, was often as much intuition as science.

A 6 meant a patient might survive if treated, but indicated treatment could consume a lot of time and effort, and there were no guarantees he would make it. But 6 could also mean that the injury was not likely to be fatal if not treated right away. Either way, a 6 waited. A 5 meant survival chances were higher and treatment less time-intensive, and so on down the count. The triage caller had to use experience to make the decisions, and thus had to be knowledgeable in treating the kinds of injuries coming in.

A droid stepped up to Barriss. "I am to assist you,

Padawan," it said. In one hand it held a pad of pulse-stickers.

Barriss nodded, turned to the next stretcher, and gasped. Before her was a terrible sight: a trooper with all four limbs burned down to stumps, and nothing but red, suppurating tissue where his face had been. On Coruscant, or Corellia, or any of the other hundreds of civilized worlds, technology could attach cybernetic limbs and reconstruct his face—he would be a strange hybrid of machine and man, but at least he would be alive and relatively functional. But here on Drongar, they had no facilities even remotely capable of such things. She bit her lip and turned to the droid assigned to her. "Category X," she said.

The droid applied the sticker, then looked at her. "A purgation of fire," it said. Barriss thought it was an odd comment for a droid to make, but she had no time to wonder about it. The wounded were being brought in so fast that she had to keep moving or be overrun.

She had damped down on her connection to the Force as much as she could; extrasensory experience of this much agony at this close range carried a real possibility of synaptic overload. Even closed down as she was, she could still feel the pain, the fear, the horror of it all pounding and scrabbling at her mind. She swallowed dryly and kept moving. There were some here she knew she could heal with the Jedi arts she had learned, but it would take too long. Not even the Force could mitigate the cold and brutal equations of triage.

Ahead of her, Tolk continued moving through the maze of dead and dying, followed by her droid, designating who would live and who would almost certainly die. The fact that they were clones, all identical in appearance, in no way lessened the horror; in fact, in a strange way it increased it—at least that was so for Barriss. Seeing the same body wounded and traumatized in a thousand different ways gave the whole scene a surreal aspect, as if it had no beginning and no end, a perpetual loop of pain and death.

She knew she had to focus, had to utilize the resources at hand wisely.

Tolk moved to the next patient, slipped in a patch of blood, recovered her balance. She veered toward Barriss, who was looking at another wounded trooper. The Jedi shook her head.

Another x, its red glow waxing and waning like the flow of lives all about them, was applied by the droid.

They were dying like wingstingers hitting a zap field, and nothing Jos did seemed to matter. A repaired artery held without leaking, but the patient was too far into shock to come back, even with his blood volume pumped to the max. Another patient, without a mark on him, was smiling one second and dead the next. A scanner showed that a sliver of metal, thinner than a needle, had pierced the corner of his eye and gone deep into his brain.

Despite the floor-level pressor fields, those working in the OT were at times up to their ankles in blood, urine, feces, lymph and spinal fluid. The air coolers and dehumidifiers were still not working, and the stench, combined with oppressive wet heat, overwhelmed the scents of antiseptics and astringents. The surgeons cut and resected and transplanted with practiced efficiency, their nurses and what few droids they had at their sides, and yet the patients still didn't make it. Commands, both shouted and whispered, filled the reeking air:

"—need twenty cc's coagulin, stat—"

"—rotate the bacta tanks, no one gets more than ten minutes—"

"—keep that field going, even if you have to hand-crank it—"

After two hours' work Jos was five for five—none of them had lived. He was beginning to reel with exhaustion—it was taking nearly all he had just to keep his hands steady.

"Get a pressor on that, stat!"

He worked like a man possessed, exerting every bit of his skill, every trick he had learned in the day-to-day war against Death from the day he'd hit dirt here, and Death laughed at him at every turn, ripping the fading lives out of his and the other doctors' grasps with insulting, infuriating ease. The law of averages said things like this would happen, that there would be bad days and nothing to be done for it. But still Jos raged against life's dark foe, fighting it for all he was worth.

The sixth one died on the table and couldn't be revived.

Time blurred. He looked through a long and dark tunnel, with nothing visible in it except the patients before him. He passed through exhaustion, through his second and third winds—and still the wounded and the dying kept coming, their eyes beseeching him under the stark, unforgiving lights.

His life was painted in red and white. He had been born here doing this, had lived all his life here doing this, and would die here doing this . . .

And then, as Jos sealed the latest patient, a double-lung and liver implant who would probably die, too, Tolk touched his arm.

"That's it, Jos. That's the last one."

He didn't understand what she was saying at first. It

made no sense—how could there be an end to something that was endless? He blinked, as if coming into the light from a great darkness. Slowly, her eyes above the mask came into focus. "Huh?"

"We're done. We can rest now."

Rest? What was that?

He stumbled away from the table. Tolk moved to help him. "Careful," he mumbled. "Someone turned up the gravity." He peeled his gloves off, his hands fumbling, and tossed them at the waste hopper. They missed. He thought about going to pick them up, but the idea of bending over was too much to bear. He might never get up.

He looked around. Others were finishing, or had just finished working on injuries, and they, too, had the look of stunned exhaustion—the same look that had been on the common face of all those who had come under his knife.

"How—how bad was it?"

"Bad." He saw streaks of moisture along the top of her mask, where it had soaked up her tears.

"Did we save any?"

"A few."

He tried to walk, staggered. She grabbed his arm, steadied him. "I don't want to know the percentages, do I?"

"No. You don't."

Jos felt himself slump even more. "I feel like I just went ten rounds in an arena on Geonosis." He wanted—*needed*—a drink, but that was far too much effort to contemplate, too. All he could think of now was finding a flat spot where he could collapse. It didn't even have to be flat. A pile of rocks would do . . .

He looked across the tables at Zan. His friend managed to lift his hand in a half salute or wave. Jos returned it, then staggered toward the door.

And once outside, he heard the sound of more incoming lifters.

Jos started to laugh. And, for a long, frightening moment, he couldn't stop.

14

Want to see something interesting?" Dhur asked.

Jos, Zan, Tolk, and Barriss were in the cantina, all drinking some form of alcohol, except the Jedi. It had been four days since that hellish influx of wounded. These days *interesting* was a loaded term, as far as Jos was concerned. But, as long as it didn't involve slicing into wounded troopers, he decided he was up to it.

"Have a seat," Jos said. He waved at the tender, who nodded and started mixing. He knew who Dhur was and what the Sullustan drank by now.

Dhur sat and pulled a small device from his pocket, a stressed-plastoid and metal sphere, about the size of a human child's fist. He held it up.

Jos squinted at it. "Can't say I'm overly enthralled," he said. "Wait—" He took another drink, set the mug down, and squinted at the device again. "Nope," he said. "Still not enthralled."

"Looks like a spiceball," Zan said. "*That* would be interesting."

Jos raised his mug in silent agreement.

Barriss said, "It's from a cam droid. Military grade, looks like."

"Give the Jedi first prize," Dhur said. "I got this from a harvester, who happened across it in the field after a recent sortie by the Separatists. Apparently it was pretty much destroyed in the battle except for passive functions—couldn't move, no weapons online . . . even its comm was out."

"Still not exactly front-page news, now, is it?" Jos said. "There are pieces of blown-apart droids all over the place."

"Think I broke a tooth on one in my grainmush this morning," Zan added.

The server arrived with Dhur's drink. "Put it on Vondar's tab," Dhur said. He looked at Jos. "Money back if you don't think it's worth it."

Jos nodded at the droid, which registered the transaction and moved off. It wasn't as if he had anything else to spend his pay on here.

"Just a wild guess," Zan said, "but I'm thinking it's not the sphere itself we're interested in here."

"Can't get anything past you, can I? Watch." Dhur set it on the table and activated it.

The holoproj rezzed up from the sphere, one-sixth life-sized. There were some broad-leaved trees, a lot of burned-out or blown-up droids, and a few clone troopers lying about. Everything was canted, at an odd, low angle, as if recorded from a few centimeters above the ground.

"I've seen dead troopers, too," Jos said. "Lots of them. Don't even have to go into the jungle for that, we've got a service brings 'em right to your door."

"Shut up, Jos," Tolk said, without any heat in her voice.

After a moment, a trio of humans appeared, working their way through the downed machines and bodies. They wore black-and-purple thinskins and jump boots, with slugthrower carbines slung over their shoulders.

"Those are Salissian mercenaries," Barriss said. "I had heard that Dooku had some working for him here."

Dhur said, "Yep. Some are mechanics, some run the harvesters—not many battle droids are programmed to pick the local produce, which is why, ultimately, we are all here on this fetid dungheap of a world. A few are special troop, recon, like that, who can go places and do things droids don't do too well—climb trees, covert recon, those kinds of things. Sometimes only a humanoid will do. And Salissians will do just about anything as long as there's a few credits at the other end of it. Ugly bunch of folks, just as soon shoot you as look at you. Probably rather shoot than look at you," he added to Jos.

Jos smiled indulgently and glanced at Zan. "They're so cute when they're that size, aren't they?"

The three mercenaries were scavenging, picking up tools and weapons from the battle site and checking the clone bodies. There was no sound, and the image occasionally wavered a bit, breaking into digital blocks and then steadying again.

"Droid was on its last power reserves," Dhur said. "Cam went dead a few minutes after this was captured. Just sheer luck it happened to be pointing the right way."

Suddenly the three Salissians froze. They dropped their weapons and raised their hands, then backed away from their fallen blasters.

"It seems somebody has caught our mercenaries off-guard," Tolk said.

A moment later, a man walked into the cam's frame, a blaster rifle held on the trio.

Jos looked at the human. The odd angle made recognition difficult, but still, he felt he knew this guy. He leaned to one side, studying the holo from a different perspective. Of course—it was—

"Phow Ji," Barriss said. Her voice was soft.

As they watched, Ji smiled—then threw his gun to the ground. It struck in a silent splatter of mud.

Tolk, Jos, and Zan reacted in surprise. Barriss did not. "What's he think he's *doing*?" Zan said.

Tolk was watching the holo closely. "He knows what he's doing," she said. Jos said nothing. As far as he knew, neither Zan nor Tolk had seen the combat teacher in action, although Tolk's cold-reading skills had obviously told her Ji was no one to trifle with. Jos looked at Barriss. She shook her head, but Jos was pretty sure she, like Tolk, knew what was about to happen, because he was pretty sure *he* knew as well.

And Zan was about to find out . . .

The holo flickered again as Ji moved in and the three Salissians went for him—

A moment later, all three mercenaries were on the ground, and darned if Jos could tell what had happened.

Maybe he'd had enough to drink for today, after all.

Dhur said. "Let's look at the replay on that." He touched a control on the sphere. Everyone sat up and watched carefully as the scene began again at one-quarter speed.

Even slowed down, it wasn't easy to see exactly what Phow Ji did, but Jos knew enough anatomy to recognize what damage had been inflicted as the three mercenaries fell. One had a crushed larynx, one a broken neck, and the third had taken an elbow to the temple that had surely cracked the skull. All three injuries were apt to be fatal if not treated, and he didn't see any Separatist medics in the jungle clearing.

Phow Ji went to each in turn, squatted next to the body, and appeared to take something. The image froze as he squatted next to the last one.

"Not sure what he was doing at the end," Dhur said, "but I'd guess he was taking some kind of trophies. Separatist troops use sub-Q implants for ID, so it's probably pieces of clothing, or . . . something."

Looking around the table, Jos knew everyone was thinking the same thing—the "something" Ji had taken could have been a chevron or some other adornment—or it could have been a finger, or an ear.

"The droid's power kicked out about then, 'cause that's all there is." Dhur looked at Jos. "Worth the drink, Doc?"

"Worth several," Jos replied quietly. "However many it takes to forget it."

"He *killed* those three mercs," Zan said, outrage in his voice. "With his bare hands. He could be court-martialed and sent to prison for that!"

"Not likely," Dhur said. "They were mercenaries, pretty much the scum of the galaxy, on a battlefield, and it was three against one. Except for this recording, there were no witnesses, and who would trust an enemy cam droid? Everybody knows how easy it is to fake such things. They could have left this here for just that purpose, for all we know."

"Cold-blooded murder," Zan said. His voice was thick.

"People die in wars, Captain," Dhur said. "If Ji had shot them down, nobody would blink twice at it. Enemy troops, on a field of battle, looting the bodies of our dead? Even though he killed them with his bare hands, there are a lot of Republic officers who would say 'More power to him!' and put him up for a medal."

Zan finished off the last of his drink and set the glass down carefully. "I *hate* this war," he said. "I hate everything about it. What kind of people are we that such things can go on and nobody is outraged? What does that say about us?"

Nobody had an answer to that.

Zan stood, carefully, for he had drunk enough to make him unsteady. You couldn't tell unless you knew him, but Jos could see it. "I am going to bed," the Zabrak said. "Don't wake me until the war is over."

After he walked away, Dhur sipped at his own drink. "There's a good story here, though I doubt the censors will let it by. The citizens back home might find it . . . disturbing." He paused. "Your friend's too sensitive to be here. He's an artist. They never do very well in wars."

"Does anybody?" Jos asked.

Dhur nodded at the frozen holoproj image. "Some do. Where else can you legally beat people to death and get paid for it?"

On her way back to her quarters, Barriss thought about the recording she had seen. It was night, warm and muggy, and wingstingers and scavenger moths swarmed the glow lamps, casting giant, ghostly shadows. A late thunderstorm grumbled in the distance, heat lightning flashing in the darkness. The rain would be welcome if it got this far—it would cool the smothering, sticky air somewhat, and the sound of it on the foamcast roof of her cubicle would be comforting. She could certainly stand some comfort—there was little enough to be found on Drongar. Tropical worlds had their beauty, and humans were at their core tropical, or at least temperate, creatures, but she preferred cooler worlds. A walk in the snow was, for her, far more invigorating than one in broiling sunshine.

The Jedi part of her had been impressed by Phow Ji's efficiency as a fighter. His moves had been fluid and powerful; against an opponent unaided by the Force, he would be formidable indeed.

But the part of her that lay deep beneath her Jedi training was repulsed by the violence. It had been murder, for it was obvious that the three mercenaries had not had much, if any, of a chance of defeating Ji. Even three against one and barehanded, the odds had still been in his favor—and, of course, he had known it.

How many trophies did he have hanging on his wall? She did not really want to know, but again, a part of her was curious. Back in the Temple, she had once listened to Mace Windu tell a group of students that killing somebody was easy—you could do it with a single swipe of your lightsaber. But living with the knowledge that you had killed somebody would change you forever. The Jedi Master had been right—it had certainly changed her. Killing was not a thing you did lightly, not if you had any kind of compassion, or even minimally decent moral and ethical codes. Sometimes, to protect the innocent, or one's own life, justice and survival demanded a Jedi strike with enough power to lay an attacker low. But the fact that it was necessary did not absolve you from seeing the faces in your dreams, or hearing the anguished cries of the fallen late in the silent night. How could a person with any humanity at all deliberately go out and stalk victims, kill them with his bare hands, and then take trophies to remind himself that he had done it?

As if he could possibly forget?

The Force allowed you to be a powerful fighter, but it

also leavened your impulse to do violence. When you knew what you could do with your lightsaber, knew how deadly you were, it gave you pause. Because you *could* do a thing did not mean that you *should* . . .

She shook her head. Phow Ji was a killer, a seeker and savorer of violence, and whether he did it as some personal challenge or because he enjoyed it really didn't matter—it was a sickness. If she could touch his mind, bring the Force to bear upon his psyche, maybe she could cure him of this sickness.

Or maybe he could infect you with it.

She shook her head again, this time against her own thoughts. The constant pressure here, the intensity of the work, the lack of real rest . . . all these things took their toll. A Jedi who was worried that the Force couldn't protect her against a trained thug was definitely overfatigued. She should get to bed and sleep— she needed it.

In the distance, the thunder grew louder. Good. Maybe the rain would wash away some of these dark thoughts along with the spores and rot in the air . . .

15

Getting rid of the body on board the MedStar would have been easy. A little messy work with an industrial vibroblade, then a trip down to the waste station with a bulky, liquid-proof bag, and *hatoo*! Mathal, the dead human, would be no more than garbage by now, indistinguishable from the rest of the all-purpose trash that was sieved from waste disposers and eventually spaced. But Bleyd knew that to have an agent of Black Sun mysteriously disappear, especially when he could be traced as far as Bleyd's ship, would be bad. They would automatically suspect him—rightly so in this case—and having Black Sun turn a quizzical frown in his direction was not even remotely appealing.

The problem was, there was no flunky Bleyd could trust to help him. The troops owed their fealty to the Republic, not to him personally. Droids' cognitive modules could be probed, and even after extensive reprogramming their data banks might retain residual quantum imprints. Some of the ship's personnel might be amenable to bribes, but there was no way to know if their loyalty would stay bought.

Which meant he had to do all that needed to be done himself.

Fortunately, he had considered his actions for some time and in detail; this left only the actual execution of his plan. It entailed some risks, but Bleyd felt it could be managed, with sufficient attention to each element.

The admiral first treated his own wounds—Mathal had been skilled enough with a blade to mark him. Bleyd had known that would be the case going in. It was the way of knife fighting—only a fool believed that facing an opponent with a knife would end without bloodshed. In his case, the injury was not serious—two long, shallow cuts on his right forearm. The pressure of his thumb for a few minutes on the proper nerve ganglion had stopped the bleeding temporarily, and an application of synthflesh would finish the job.

His injuries attended to, Bleyd then put Mathal's corpse into one of the carbon-freezing chambers in the quarantine section and sealed the body into a rectangular carbonite block big enough to show no sign of what was contained within. This he then holostamped with markings indicating that the block contained a set of defective harvesting enzyme converters. Sealing such volatile and active catalytical components for transport was normal enough. Then, with the help of a small antigrav generator, he moved it via the service lift tube to the aft cargo hold's trash lock.

In theory, he could have shipped the dead agent to a chemical storage warehouse and had him shelved. As long as he paid the pittance of a fee, the block of densely interlaced carbon and tibanna atoms containing Mathal's remains would sit stacked there forever, unmolested and uninspected.

But the body itself was of no consequence. The trick was to convince a skeptical Black Sun that their human agent had left Bleyd's ship in his own vessel, and that the ship had subsequently been destroyed by forces unconnected to Bleyd.

That next part would be a bit trickier, because on *this* vessel, everyone knew who Admiral Bleyd was—by sight, or, if not blessed with that sense, then by smell, taste, touch, or hearing. In order to continue his plan, Bleyd had to be disguised.

He had pondered this aspect at some length, and had decided that a simple disguise was better than an elaborate one.

He returned to his quarters. There he packed into a small case a long, white robe, hooded with an osmotic veil that would completely conceal his features. The robe was identical to the ones worn by a meditative caste of siblings-in-service called The Silent. There were usually a few of The Silent to be found on any large medical ship, since the order's universal mission was to aid the sick and injured. They did not speak aloud, even to each other. They took their meals in private and wore their hoods up in public, effectively hiding their identities at all times. A few days ago Bleyd had surreptitiously caused microtransmitters to be placed in their food—tiny devices no larger than grains of sand, which enabled him to track those few of The Silent who were on board, at least for a while. He would not run into one of them by accident, and no one else would be able to sense who was under the ersatz robe.

The refresher next to the library was empty, and it was one that was not covered by surveillance cams. Admiral Bleyd entered the 'fresher; it was a nameless, faceless member of The Silent who emerged.

None of the people he passed on the way to the starboard docking bay did more than nod or smile at him, and he, of course, did not speak. He walked in a slight stoop, aware that he was taller than most of the robed ones he had seen on the ship.

The Silent would not have the codes, nor the keycards for security doors that were locked, but Admiral Bleyd did. That part could be adjusted later—all traces of those security recordings would have to be altered or erased, leaving nothing that even the most diligent search might uncover. But there would be no such search, because there would be no reason for it. A person might remember one of The Silent passing through these doors, but it was unlikely in the extreme that anybody would ever ask about it. And even if someone did, there would be no way to connect that shrouded figure to Bleyd. He was covered.

He smiled at that thought as he strolled, unhurried, about his task. He *was* covered, wasn't he? The osmotic veil passed air freely, and allowed him an unimpeded view, but no one could see his face. It was pleasant. He found himself rather enjoying the novelty of being anonymous.

Mathal had been directed to park his small KDY Starspin in the darkest, least-used corner of the subflight deck, where a light had burned out only moments before, courtesy of a tiny timer that had, not coincidentally, vaporized with the electrical flare that killed the lamp. The ship had been precleared—on the admiral's orders—to leave at any time.

Bleyd smiled again as he approached the vessel. Yes, he had thought of everything. The key to a successful hunt was proper preparation. If you knew your destination before you took the first step, you saved yourself endless amounts of grief.

Once in the ship, he informed the controllers that he wished to depart, and was granted immediate clearance.

He taxied the vessel through the double sets of pressure doors and onto the launch pad, waited for the green lights, and put the craft into space.

Now came the hard part.

Timing was of the essence, if he was to pull this off. He looped under the multistoried keel of the medical frigate and headed aft, staying close enough to the hull so that the sensors couldn't see him. He rocketed past a few open portholes and smiled; anybody looking out would likely have gotten a sudden and considerable fright as he blew by them almost close enough to touch. In theory, however, that was good. If anyone ever did ask—not likely, but if they did—then the recklessness of the Black Sun pilot would surely be remarked upon.

Yar, I saw him. Freaking fool near broke the transparisteel port, he was so close—!

As he headed for the aft trash lock, Bleyd began to seal the robe. Under the cloth was a thinskin emergency vac suit, complete with gloves and boot seals, a flexicris head shroud and face cover. The emergency air tank held but five minutes of life—thinskin vac suits were designed to work inside a ship during a sudden atmosphere loss, and then only long enough to get to a pressurized section or a full vac suit. But five minutes would be more than enough, assuming everything went as planned . . .

The trash lock was just ahead. Bleyd triggered the remote control, and the hatch dilated. A second remote activated the antigrav unit on the carbonite slab and pushed it out the lock.

Expertly, for he was a good pilot, Bleyd pulled the Starspin to a velocity matching the slow-moving slab's, then used a grapple arm to grab it and pull it against the ship's body. He locked the arm in place.

He took a deep breath. This part wouldn't be pleasant, but he could not tarry. He sealed the vac suit, activated the airflow, and cycled the ship's canopy open. Then he maneuvered himself out of the cockpit, aimed at the open trash hatch, and pushed off.

Since the MedStar's orbital position was currently over the night side of Drongar, it was *cold* out there, a biting, harsh chill that stabbed him through the robe and thinskins like a thousand needles of frozen nitrogen impaling him all at once. But he ignored the cold, refused to accept the shock it threatened to plunge his system into. Bred into him was the stamina and strength of a thousand generations of hunters, an armor woven from his ancestors' ancient DNA. His resolve was icier by far than the void through which he floated.

His aim was a hair off, but not so much that he missed the hatch. As soon as he was in the ship's gravity field, he dropped, but he had been expecting that, and he landed on his feet, his balance firm. He slapped the hatch control, and the hatch constricted and closed. The chamber, even unpressurized, was still considerably warmer than the raw vacuum outside.

He activated the pressurization cycle and moved to the viewport to look at Mathal's ship, triggering the remote for it as he did so. The Starspin's ion drive lit, and the little vessel, its carbonite load still firm in its grasp, shot silently off into space.

Bleyd watched for a moment. The course was laid in—there was nothing more to be done now.

He unsealed the vac suit and headed for the inner lock door. In a matter of a few minutes, an unidentified vessel would violate Separatist orbital space on the far side of the planet. The ship would not respond to queries, nor would it deviate from its course. There would be warnings given, and finally the Separatist batteries would open up, and the ship would be blown to bits.

And alas, Mathal, the representative of Black Sun, would be vaporized as well, and nobody would ever be able to tell that he had been dead before it happened, for the thermonuclear explosion that destroyed the Starspin would not leave enough of the slagged carbonite to fill a wingstinger's ear. There would, however, be just enough trace molecular residue to establish that an organic body, probably humanoid, had been vaporized along with the ship.

No one would be particularly surprised, either. While the rules of war forbade one side attacking the other's orbiting medical frigate, no such injunction held against the invaded side defending itself.

As he stripped off the robe and thinskins to change back into a spare uniform, left there earlier for that purpose, Bleyd went over it yet again. He was no fugue master, but he was adept enough at dissembling to pull this off. When Black Sun came to call, as eventually they would, and when they asked him what had become of Mathal, as eventually they would, he did not doubt that he would be able to pass a truth-scan, if he worded his reply carefully enough.

Mathal? He left here in his ship, but for some reason he flew into Separatist space. They shot him down. Most regrettable, but this is, after all, a war zone, and Mathal did not have the proper clearances . . .

Which was all technically true.

There would be records in the ship's systems to show just that. Controller's logs, sensor logs, maybe even an eyewitness or three who saw the ship fly past, obviously piloted by an idiot, given how close he had been to the hull . . .

And nothing to show anything else.

Of course, it was a temporary stopgap at best. Sooner or later, Black Sun would wish to reinstigate its demands, but by then Bleyd would have another plan in place. Perhaps he could use Filba to buy more time. In any event, he would continue to smuggle the bota and add to his fortune . . .

16

Barriss would not have sought out a confrontation with Phow Ji—Jedi were trained to deal with conflict, not to go looking for it when there was no compelling reason to do so. What she had seen of Ji's action in the field had been reprehensible, in her opinion, but her mission was not that of military security. It was not her job to demand restitution for the mercenaries' deaths.

But the next morning, as she had gone out into the dawn's relatively cool light to do some stretching exercises, the Bunduki fighter had swaggered into view and stopped to watch.

"Up early, eh, Jedi?" There seemed always to be a sneer in his voice. She didn't bother to reply to the obvious comment, but instead continued her exercises.

"You don't look to be in bad shape," he commented. "Good to see that you don't rely entirely on your 'magic.'"

There was still no reason to engage in conversation, as far as Barriss was concerned. She was sitting on the damp ground, her legs extended to either side in a full split. She leaned over first one knee, pressing her cheek against her outer thigh, then did the same for the other side, feeling her hamstrings and back muscles warm with the effort.

"I wasn't aware that the Jedi took vows of stillness," he said. His voice was clipped, now, and there was an edge of steel underlying it.

She stood and extended her hands straight over her head. "We don't," she said, bending to put her hands flat on the ground, keeping her legs straight. "We talk when we have something to say—not simply to hear our own voices."

"You're angry. I thought Jedi kept their emotions under control." Ji smiled. "Something I said?" His tone was taunting.

Barriss raised herself from the front bend, brushed a strand of sweat-soaked hair back, and turned to look directly at him. "No. Something you did. You murdered three mercenaries."

If that surprised Ji, his face didn't show it. He gave her a small, bland smile. "And what makes you think so?"

"Someone recovered a crippled cam droid. It was all recorded."

"Really? I'd like to see that."

She could hear the interest in his comment; she did not need to use the Force to know the truth of it.

"Taking trophies wasn't enough?"

Ji made a gesture probably intended to be self-deprecating. "Well, I can only see things from my own viewpoint. A holorecording from other angles would be useful in self-critiquing my moves. Besides, I have a wall full of trophies. But a holo? That would be a first."

Barriss shook her head. "It doesn't bother you at all, does it?"

"What?"

He was baiting her, that she knew. *Be ever mindful of the living Force*—that had been the advice of Qui-Gon Jinn. She had been quite young when the Jedi Master had died in the Battle of Naboo, but she still remembered hearing that—one of the first bits of Jedi wisdom imparted to her. *Rise above this,* she told herself. But she could not help answering him.

"That you beat three people to death."

He looked surprised. "Is that how you see it?"

"Is there another way to see it?"

Ji smiled and spread his hands in a gesture of innocence. "I was unarmed, one against three, on a battlefield in a war, my dear Padawan. I was but utilizing the skills that I am paid to utilize. I'm a soldier. It is not considered murder to kill the enemy."

Barriss had stopped stretching; now she stood, arms folded against her chest, looking at the Bunduki master. "You're an expert fighter, and your hands and feet are as much weapons as a vibroblade or a stun baton," she told him. "Those men had no more chance than they would have had you used a blaster on them. Pretending otherwise is disingenuous."

"Are you calling me a liar, Jedi?"

There was no mistaking the danger in his tone now. *This is exactly what he wants you to do. Ignore him. Turn away.*

She faced him squarely. "Yes."

He smiled again, a cruel, triumphant smile. "Such an accusation presupposes the willingness to back it up. Would you care to demonstrate the efficacy of your mystical Force against my expertise?"

With the greatest of difficulty Barriss held her anger in check and kept her mouth shut. She conjured up before her mind's eye the disapproving visage of Master Unduli. It helped, a little. She had known when she'd first spoken that this was the road down which she'd started, had known it was the wrong path for her. And yet, here she was . . .

After a moment, he laughed. "That's what I thought. I beat one of your Jedi Knights in a hand-to-hand match, and it wouldn't really be fair for me to pick on a lowly Padawan, now would it? Enjoy your exercise, Jedi."

He turned contemptuously and started to walk away.

Barriss couldn't stop herself. She raised her hand, concentrated, and closed her open fingers into a fist.

As Ji took another step, time seemed to slow for Barriss. Ji's left foot came forward, and as it approached his right, his boot twisted inward, no more than a few degrees—just enough to catch the heel of his forward boot.

He tripped.

A man of lesser skill would have fallen flat on his face upon the wet ground. And, despite her knowledge that it was wrong, Barriss would have enjoyed that sight.

But even as he fell, Ji tucked into an ovoid shape, one arm curving, hand turned inward slightly, so that his motion looked like a deliberate action: he dived, rolled on his arm, shoulder, and back, coming up and turning slightly, a neat gymnastic move that left him standing in balance and facing her.

"Careful," she said. "The ground is slippery from the heavy dew."

He stood there for a moment, glaring. The sense of menace hung heavy in the air, the currents of it swirling about in the Force like a dark whirlwind. But even as angry as he was, he maintained control.

He turned away.

Once he was gone, Barriss shook her head at her action. What had she been thinking? One did not use the

Force for such childish, trivial things. It was wrong to take such petty action, even against a villain such as Phow Ji. Yes, it *could* have been an appropriate demonstration, designed to teach, to show that the Force was valid, but she knew this had not been the case. It had been a personal response, driven by anger, and she had known better from the beginning. Great power had to be wielded with great care, and taking an obnoxious character down a level because you thought he deserved it was simply not sufficient justification. It was chasing a fire gnat with a turbolaser. Her Master would have been *extremely* displeased.

She was never going to become a Jedi Knight by behaving thusly.

Barriss sighed and went back to her stretches. Her road was hard enough already. Why did she keep strewing boulders in her own path?

17

Den Dhur had seen a number of odd sights in his years on interstellar assignments. To the best of his memory, however, he had never seen a droid sitting alone in a cantina.

When he walked in out of the syrupy heat of midday, it took his eyes several moments to adjust, even with the droptacs' aid. As his vision cleared, he saw that the bar was mostly deserted. Leemoth, the Duros amphibian specialist, was seated in a far corner nursing a mug of Fromish ale, two clone sergeants sat at the bar, and at one of the nearer tables was the new protocol droid, I-Five.

There's something you don't see every day, Den thought. First off, droids rarely sat at all. Most of the more humanoid models were capable of the posture, but since they never got tired, there was no real reason for it. But I-Five was sitting there, albeit somewhat stiffly. His photoreceptors were trained at the plasticast tabletop. Even though there was no expression in the metal mask of a face, Den got a distinct feeling of melancholy from the droid.

On impulse, he pulled up a chair, sat down across from I-Five, and raised a by-now-well-practiced finger to the cantina's tender. "We don't see too many droids in here," he said to his companion.

"At these prices, I'm not surprised."

Den's eyebrows went up. This *was* something un-usual—a droid with a sense of humor. The tender brought the reporter his drink—Johrian whiskey. Den sipped it, watching I-Five with interest.

"I heard you were helping Padawan Offee earlier in the OT."

"True. It was—quite an experience."

Den took another sip. "If you don't mind my saying, you seem rather—unusual for a droid. How did you come to be assigned here?"

At first it seemed that the droid was not going to re-ply. Then he said, " 'I am cast upon the winds of space and time, like a planetesimal spun eternally between suns.' "

Now Den was shocked. "Kai Konnik," he said. "*Beach of Stars*. Winner of the Galaxis Award for best novel last year, if I'm not—"

"Two years ago," I-Five corrected him.

Den stared at him. "You have an impressive knowl-edge of literature for a droid."

"Not really. My memory banks are programmed with more than two hundred thousand novels, holo-plays, poems, and—"

"I wasn't talking about memory," Den said. "Most protocol droids have the capacity to store that much in-formation. And most droids, if asked to quote from a particular work, can access it as easily as you just did. But," he continued, leaning forward, "I've never met any kind of droid yet who could use the material *meta-phorically*. Which is what you were doing."

Silence for another moment; then the droid emitted something that sounded remarkably like a human sigh.

"At times I wish I were a carbon-based being," he said. "The concept of intoxication is attractive."

"It has its advantages," Den agreed as he took another drink. "You going to tell me why you're in here?"

Again, I-Five seemed disinclined to speak at first. Then he said, "Nostalgia."

Den waited. He'd come into the cantina to see if he could dig up any more dirt on Filba, but so far this was more interesting. If I-Five hadn't been a droid, Den would have plied him with drinks to loosen his tongue. It seemed, however, that little loosening would be needed. The droid obviously wanted to unburden himself to someone.

"I used to spend a fair amount of time in establishments much like this one," I-Five continued. "Places like the Green Glowstone Tavern and the Dewback Inn, in the Zi-Kree sector on—"

"Coruscant," Den finished. "I know them both well. Nasty part of town; they call it the Crimson Corridor." He finished his drink and signaled for another. "I found a lot of good leads to stories there." He looked at I-Five in silence for a moment. "Most watering holes don't like droids; some old superstition, I believe. I'm surprised your master got away with bringing you in with him."

"Lorn Pavan wasn't my master," the droid said. "He was my friend."

The muscles in Den's forehead were starting to get sore from their strenuous workout. "Your *friend*?"

"We were 'business associates.' We traded underworld information, ran sabacc numbers, brokered the occasional minor government intel—that sort of thing. Not exactly the thrilling life one sees in the holodramas, but it did offer an occasional frisson or two."

"Colorful," Den commented. When the droid did not continue, he said, "Well, you're a long way from the big city now, as I'm sure you've noticed. Why are—?"

He broke off, noticing I-Five's sudden shifting of attention from him to a group of surgeons who had just entered. Among them was Zan Yant, who carried his quetarra. Den assumed there would be music later on, after the cantina filled up a little more; that was the usual way of it. He didn't mind; he liked Yant's musical choices, for the most part, although the Talusian's homeworld compositions sounded to him like two sand cats in a sack.

The droid, however, seemed a bit—nervous. *I'd swear he somehow shows expressions with that metal mug of his,* Den thought. The concept was surprising, but no more so than the idea of a droid having the emotions necessary to produce those expressions.

Den's second drink was set down before him, and he lifted it thoughtfully. "So, what motivated you to pack up and leave such a rewarding existence?"

I-Five said, "I have no idea. Lorn and I were being pursued by . . ." He seemed to be choosing his words carefully. ". . . an assassin."

"A Zabrak," Den said casually. He watched the droid's face carefully this time. His photoreceptors didn't get bigger, but they did get brighter, which somehow conveyed surprise just as well. *That's it,* he thought. *The eyes are the most expressive organs in most humanoid faces. You can read a world of meaning into their slightest movement. Somehow, I-Five gets much the same results by varying the intensity and angle of those optical sensors of his.*

He was so intent on figuring out how the droid

showed expression that he almost missed I-Five's reply. "Do I rummage around in *your* data banks without permission?"

"Sorry; reporter's instincts. It was obvious that something bothered you about seeing Yant come in, and since I'm assuming you're not a music hater—"

"Congratulations. The assassin was an Iridonian Zabrak. Quite deadly; a martial arts master skilled enough to make Phow Ji look like a drunken Jawa. He had . . . other skills as well."

Den nodded. "I see. Yant's from Talus, if that makes any difference."

I-Five didn't reply to that. "This assassin stole an item of value from us and fled Coruscant, into orbit. Lorn and I were about to go after him, and then—the next thing I knew, I was serving on a spice-smuggling freighter."

"Any theories?"

"I think Lorn deactivated me to keep me out of danger. By then this had turned into something very personal for him, you see. Someone he cared for greatly had sacrificed herself to save us, and—"

"Sounds like a great story," Den said. "Wish I'd been around to write it up."

"Trust me—you don't. This assassin was—" I-Five hesitated, then shook his head—another disturbingly human action.

"Black Sun?"

"Worse. Far worse. Besides," he said softly, "what's a story without an ending?"

"Every story has an ending."

"This one doesn't—not for me. I don't know what happened to Lorn. I suspect he's dead, but there's no way to know for certain. I've tried to find out, but this all took place more than a decade ago, and routes of inquiry are limited for droids, even droids that know how to hack past pyrowalls and other computer defenses. The entire thing seems to have been completely hushed up at an extremely high level."

"Now you're getting me interested," Den said. "Nothing like a good conspiracy story, although they tend to go over better when there's not a war on. I'll see what I can dig up."

"Dig too deep on this, and you may be the one who gets buried," the droid said darkly. "I have no idea how I escaped being mindwiped. All I know is one minute I was at the spaceport on Coruscant; the next I'm helping feed people's glitterstim habits across the Core systems.

"That's subjective, of course. According to my interior chrono, I was deactivated for about twelve standard weeks. From what I was able to learn afterward, I was part of some kind of barter arrangement. I was on the Kessel Run for six years; then the smugglers' ships were raided by a local system's solar patrol. I was confiscated and auctioned to a merchant captain—why, I'm not certain. There are still large gaps in my data banks I can't account for—several years' worth, in fact.

"When the war began to spread, the Republic confiscated as many droids as they could to keep them out of the Separatists' hands. I was serving as a house droid for a noble family on Naboo when the order came. My programming was augmented with medical training, and now here I sit in this . . . picturesque . . . establishment, telling you my life story." He paused. "I really do wish I could get drunk."

"Maybe you're lucky you can't. If you've been this forthcoming to everyone you've met," Den said, "It's a wonder you haven't been reprogrammed. Most folks have little patience with an uppity droid."

"Do tell. No, I've kept my sparkling wit and effervescent personality firmly in check until now, rest assured. It's been somewhat lonely, I must say."

"So why tell me all this? Do I just have that kind of face?"

"I'm tired of the charade," I-Five replied. "I'm tired of playing a meek little automaton to humans and their ilk, especially after watching the brutal results of organic sentients' inability or unwillingness to coexist. The more I see of all this carnage, the more convinced I am that a CZ-Three maintenance droid could do a better job of running the Republic."

Den couldn't resist a grin. "That's sedition, you know."

"Who, me?" The droid's photoreceptors projected innocence. "I am but a humble droid, built to serve." He sighed again. "Perhaps I just need my disgust damper recharged."

"Or maybe you just need to get drunk."

"That, too."

"Of course, in order to accomplish that, you'd have to be organic."

I-Five actually shuddered. "Perish the thought." He stood. "Excuse me. I have duties to perform; most of them involve changing dressings and administering spray hypos. Thoroughly fulfilling tasks for a being of my capabilities, I must say. Perhaps I'll occupy the ninety-nine percent of my cognitive module *not* engaged by my chores by solving Chun's Theory of Reductional Infinity. Or composing a light opera."

Den watched I-Five leave the cantina. A few moments later Zan Yant began to play, a slow, soulful melody. It seemed the perfect accompaniment to Den's bemused mood.

A droid that had been accorded equal status by his sentient owner? Den had heard of such things before, but always before they had been fiction. For a droid to actually be emancipated, even informally, was somewhat revolutionary. He wondered why he wasn't more shocked by the idea.

It did seem a good reason to have another drink, however.

18

Usually, whenever he had a few moments in which to try cutting through some of the caked sweat, spores, and grime that Drongar so liberally provided, Jos used the sonic shower, which was faster and more efficient than chem-wipe or water. Step in, click the foot switch on, and the dirt was vibrated right off—no muss, no fuss. At least the base had that basic level of technology working, most of the time.

Today, however, he stood under the pulsing beat of a fluid nozzle, and the water, piped and filtered from a deep aquifer, was cold. Cold enough to cause chilblains, cold enough to make breathing harder than usual.

The water was not cold enough, however, to chill his thoughts—and the problem of Tolk. Tolk, who had certainly discerned his interest in her. And who had apparently decided to have some fun with it.

The water thrummed against his head, sending icy trickles and rivulets into his eyes and ears, but it was not cold enough to drive the memory of what had happened just that morning from his too-warm thoughts . . .

He had stepped into the dressing room to change his surgical suit, the one he'd been wearing having become soaked from a bleeder that popped in the middle of a vein graft. The room was unisex, but there was an IN USE indicator on the door to keep people from being surprised. Jos had palmed the door switch and stepped briskly into the room, having seen that the IN USE diode was dark.

And there was Tolk, halfway through changing her own surgical suit. Which was to say, not entirely clothed. Or, to put it another way, mostly naked. Bare. Gloriously so . . .

As a surgeon, Jos had seen plenty of flesh in his career, male, female, and other. It was simply part of the job—you didn't have friendly thoughts about somebody whose liver you were resecting. But to step into a room and see your recently noticed and decidedly beautiful assistant nearly nude was an entirely different matter.

Even that wouldn't have been so bad—well, okay, it *wasn't* bad, it was just blasted embarrassing—since he'd gaped in slack-jawed shock for only a second, maybe two or three, before turning around, crimson-faced, and saying, "Oops, sorry!"

But what kept him staring for that extra second was Tolk's expression. That, along with the rest of her.

She smiled. Slow, languid, no-mistake-about-it. "Hi, Jos. Did I forget to thumb the diode on? How careless of me."

Jos managed to exit and shut the door, the vision of Tolk's mostly bare form seared into his memory—forever, he was pretty sure. But that smile . . . oh, that *smile* had been the stopper in the bottle. And as he thought about it later—at least two dozen times during the day as they worked together—he kept wondering: *Had* she forgotten to light the diode?

Even at its coldest, the water couldn't wash *that* question away.

"You've been in there half the night, Jos! How clean do you need to get?"

A very good question, that.

Seated at a table in the chow hall, Den Dhur was a happy diner. It didn't really have anything to do with what he was about to eat. He was savoring the taste of imminent cold revenge, for soon—very soon, now—he would slam the hatch on Filba, that no-crèche outling Hutt. He had just collected another rock for the Hutt's cairn from an unhappy corporal, and soon he was going to bury Filba like a battle dog does an old bone.

The thought made him smile. You do *not* mess with the press, no way, no how, especially if you are as crooked as a rancor's back teeth. Most everybody had something to hide, something they wouldn't want to see splashed on the evening holonets, but if you were a thief, it would be something worse. A lot worse.

And he'd found it.

Filba was going to be flensed and hung out in the hot sunshine to dry, and good riddance. Den chuckled to himself, and reapplied his cutlery to the food before him with gusto. Vengeance was the perfect spice for dinner.

Of course, what dinner was and how it was prepared was something he had to get used to when he spaced to odd planets. One of the first things Den had discovered as a young reporter was that if he didn't learn to eat and drink the local flora and fauna when he world-hopped covering the military, he got hungry and thirsty in a big hurry. Space on board an interstellar troop transport was at a premium, and it wasn't usually wasted on exotic foods. He'd heard the clone troopers had been conditioned to be happy with simple fare, but even so, given the number of different species in the Republic armies and navies, they couldn't begin to stock favorites for everyone. Especially since the officers, as usual, got preferential treatment.

The soldiers in the field got RRs—Ready Rations—which were reconstituted pap with essential nutrients for each species. They usually ranged in color from pustulent to putrid, and in texture and taste from old boot plastoid to something that would gag a Neimoidian. Given this, the first thing military cooks generally did when they got to a new planet was assign foragers to find and bring back anything that might be edible. Den had been on some worlds where there wasn't much local produce or game to be found, and a steady diet of RR meals made for a lot of thin troopers. He'd lost a little mass himself on those assignments.

Fortunately, one of the few positive things that could be said about Drongar was that there were plenty of things to be trapped, picked, tapped, or dug up, and, while it was not the best he had eaten, the Rimsoo chow hall wasn't bad as such things went. Den had ordered a plate of the local land shrimp, a hand-sized creature that, boiled with herbs and spices, tasted surprisingly like hawk-bat, although more pungent. It came with some bright orange mashed plant root that had a smooth consistency and a nice cinnamon flavor. Wash it all down with some of the locally produced ale and, well, he'd eaten a lot worse. Until someone finally figured out how to invent a gadget that could instantaneously assemble a meal from basic elements, like the adventurers in those future-fic holodramas were always using, military food would always be a chancy affair.

And besides, even eating an RR wouldn't have been so bad, feeling as he did today. All cynicism aside, a good story went a long way toward making a reporter feel like he was worth his paycheck—as little as that was . . .

He looked up and saw Zan Yant leave the serving line, carrying a tray. Den caught the Zabrak's attention and waved him over. "Hey, is that fleek eel?" he said, when he saw the other's plate. "I didn't see it on the menu."

"No. It's wriggler, a local species of giant worm, seared in redfruit juice and sprinkled with fried fire gnats."

"Ah. Sounds . . . tasty."

"Well, it's not the Manarai on Coruscant," the surgeon said, "but it sure beats RRs."

Dhur regarded Zan Yant quizzically. "You've eaten at the Manarai?"

"I wasn't born on this mudball, friend Dhur. One of my instructors was a professor at CU's School of Music. I went to visit him from time to time."

"Still, a spendy place for a student."

"My family is . . . comfortably well-off," Yant said, slicing off a big chunk of worm and popping it into his mouth. "Ah. That Charbodian cook really knows its stuff. Want a bite?"

"Thanks, no, I'm happy with mine." Den regarded the surgeon with curiosity. A rich medic and an expert musician—not the sort of person one expected to run into in the galactic hinterlands. Why hadn't he or his family been able to have Yant exempted from the military? Wealth and power had its privileges, everybody knew that. Could it be that Yant had volunteered? If so, Den's respect for him would have to be ratcheted up a notch.

Before he could pursue the subject, Yant asked, "And how goes the crusade to keep the public informed?"

"Good." Den smiled. "And about to get better."

"Ah. A hot story?"

"Yes, indeed. I can't talk about it yet—don't want to let the kreel out of the cage, you understand—but I'm pleased with it. I expect it will shake things up quite a bit in certain quarters."

"That's good, I suppose." Yant took another big mouthful of worm, chewed, swallowed, and smiled. "Not bad at all." He paused a bit, then said, "A question, if you don't mind."

"I'm all ears."

"I and the other medics here are conscripts. Left up to us, we'd be a dozen parsecs in any direction away from Drongar. But you're a noncom. You don't have to be out here—you could be reporting off a civilized planet, up to your dewflaps in relative comfort and safety. So why are you here? What calls you to this work?"

He hadn't expected that one. Nobody had asked that particular question in years. There were stock answers, of course—every reporter had a few. The adventure, the chance to be where the action was, the desire to serve the public. Maybe they even believed it—he had once, a long time ago.

And now?

Abruptly, without meaning to, Den found himself telling the truth. "Wars make for big stories, Doc. It's all about the important issues. Life, death, honor, love . . . it's the raw feed, the mother lode, the crucible. You watch people deep in this kind of fire, trying to get out, trying to get each other out, and you see what they're really made of.

"Listen—you interview a local politician after a public meeting, and he spins word webs like an educated spin-worm: all glossy and shiny, but without any real substance. Sure, he's working to keep his job—he might even be working for the public good and all, stranger things have happened—but he's not under any real *pressure,* so he's got time to sort out his lies and make them nice and neat.

"But you catch a commander whose unit has just been shot to bloody pieces, with no hope of rescue and enemy fire still incoming? *He* is going to tell it like he sees it, and forget the consequences. War is ugly, my friend, ugly and painful and cruel—but it strips away the cover, it flenses out truth—and *that* is what it's all about."

Zan nodded, thoughtfully chewing another bite of his dinner. "But you see so much death. Not to mention you could get killed yourself."

Den shrugged. "You see an epidemic of Rojo Fever, you see plenty of bodies. And you could get run over by some wet-head kid bringing his landspeeder to the city for the first time. When your name is called, you go— doesn't matter where you're standing, does it?"

Zan chuckled. "No. No matter where you are, you're always at the head of the line."

Den chuckled as well, and for a few minutes the two were silent, enjoying the rest of their food. At length the Sullustan drained the last of his ale, burped, and leaned back. "Let me tell you a story," he said. "A long time ago, I was assigned to cover a little insurrectionist brush war on some backrocket world in the middle of the Gordian Reach. I was hanging around the exit base—a prefab muster station where the troops shipping out for home were staged for lift into orbit. It was way behind the lines, a day's ride by crippled bantha from any shooting, as safe as your mother's lap—or crèche, or pouch, or whatever.

"So I'm talking to this human pup. Tall; I'm not even chest-high to him, even though he's real young. Seems he lied about his age to get into the army, so he's no more than sixteen standard years old, and by the maker's grace he's survived his tour without a scratch in the middle of some *very* heavy action. Seventy percent of his unit got fried blacker than carbonite, but he's still breathing, and on his way out. Just a child. A child who now knows about war.

"So I'm running my thumb cam, recording the kid, getting some basic how-does-it-feel-to-be-going-home? stuff for the viewers. All of a sudden, *braap-zap!* somebody cuts loose with a pulse carbine, just waving it back and forth like a pressure hose and cutting troops down, left, right, and center. One of the insurrectionists, undercover on a suicide run.

"The security guys come running, but they're not getting there fast enough. The shooter is walking right at us, he sees me, and I can see that he sees me, and I know I'm about to have my datachip pulled. Everyone's yelling, 'Run!' at me. Are they kidding? I'm so milking terrified I can't even breathe, much less run.

"But then this kid, who isn't even armed, steps in front of me, quite deliberately. He catches a bolt in the gut—it was meant for my head—and goes down. The shooter's carbine runs dry right then, the secs open up on him, and that's the end of that.

"I squat down next to this poor human kid and I see he's not going to make it. So I ask him, 'Why'd you do it?'

"And the kid says, 'You're so little.'"

Yant stopped chewing and looked at Den, puzzled.

"I think he knew I was an adult, intellectually," Den continued. "But at that moment, when danger threatened, he equated small stature with youth. He jumped in front of me because that's what humans do—they protect their young. I thanked him before he died." Den paused. "Know what he said?"

Yant shook his head.

"He said, 'It's okay. Would you tell my mother I love her?'"

They were both quiet for a moment. Yant ran one hand lightly over his stubby horns and sighed. "That's so sad."

"There's more." Den looked at his hands, saw they were knotted together. He unlaced his fingers, feeling them crackle.

"The shooter? He was also a human. He was fourteen. I didn't get to him before he died, but one of the secs did. The shooter's last words were, 'Tell my mother I love her.' Brothers in death, children saying good-bye to their mothers."

Yant shook his head again.

"These are the stories you get on the front, my friend. These are the stories that people need to know." Den shrugged. "Not that it slows war down a microsecond, but at least they know it isn't all grand fun—not when you have children killing each other, and mothers' hearts breaking over it."

Somehow, the potential skewering of Filba didn't seem as bright and shiny now as it did when Den had sat down to eat.

"I'm sorry," Yant said.

"Yeah," Den said. "Aren't we all?"

19

Jos sometimes—not often, these days—felt as if he could call a dying patient back to life; that by dint of pure will, he could keep someone critically injured alive, refusing to let Death claim him.

It helped, of course, if his surgical procedure went well. Sometimes, however, even when the operation was technically correct, something went sour, and no matter how hard he tried, no matter how much he wished it otherwise, the patient expired.

So it was with the clone trooper on the table now. The surgery had been relatively easy as these things went: a bit of shrapnel had nicked the pericardium, and there had been bleeding into the pericardial sac with associated cardiac tamponade. But the blood had been drained, the wounds repaired, and that should have been that. Instead, the trooper had ceased breathing, the repaired heart had stopped, and all efforts to jump-start things had failed. Had Jos been a religious man, he would have said the man's *essence* had departed.

This was the last patient, though, and he had managed to keep five others alive, including one who had sustained massive injuries to three organ systems that needed replacement: a multipunctured and deflated lung, a ruptured spleen, and a severely lacerated kidney.

Why had that one survived and this one died? It was totally unexpected, totally inexplicable, and totally frustrating.

Medicine was not an exact science, he knew—the patients often confounded things. You'd think that genetically identical clones would have pretty much the same reactions to physical stress, but that certainly didn't seem to be the case with these two.

Back when Jos had been a fairly fresh student in medical school, he had frequented a Bamasian restaurant that had become all the rage among his peers. The food was cheap but good, and the servings large; the place was within walking distance of the student housing complex, and it was open all day and all night—perfect for students. Bamasian cuisine was varied, spicy, and something of an acquired taste, but Jos liked it. At the end of each meal, the traditional complimentary dessert was a small, sweet, baked bread ring, about the size of a bracelet. Cooked into the treat was a protein-circuit onetime holocaster. When you broke the ring, the 'caster projected a bit of Bamasian wisdom that glimmered and hung in the air for a few seconds before the organic circuitry decayed. The aphorisms were amusing to the medical students, who tended to eat as a pack for the family-style discounts. Often they would all break the bread rings at the same instant, then try to read the homilies before they faded away. Some of them were real howlers: "Avoid dark alleyways in bad neighborhoods." Or "Being rich and miserable is better than just being miserable." Or "Beware smiling politicians . . ."

One evening, when Jos was exhausted from a long series of exams and tricky procedures he had mostly fumbled, and feeling overwhelmed by things he had never thought to see, never even considered might be a part of his training, he had cracked his sweetened bread ring open and gotten a message that had seemed personally crafted for him alone:

"Minimize expectations to avoid being disappointed."

At the time, it had struck him as oddly useful, if somewhat obvious, wisdom. If he didn't expect anything, he wouldn't be distressed if it didn't happen. He tried to plug it into his life, and found it helped. Sometimes he forgot, of course. Sometimes he *expected* to be able to save them all. He was a good surgeon; maybe, given the circumstances, even a great surgeon, and he never expected to lose a patient who had even the smallest chance of survival. When it happened, it was always a shock. And always disappointing.

It was hard to admit, even to himself, but there were times when he even caught himself feeling resentful toward the never-ending parade of wounded and dying troops. There were times, when they wheeled in a Twi'lek with a nearly severed lekku, or a Devaronian with one of his livers perforated, that a small part of him relished the opportunity to do something *different*. Because at this point it really did feel like he could build a stratosphere-piercing tower just from the sheer tonnage of shrapnel he'd pulled out of the clone troopers. Not to mention paint it red with their blood.

Jos sighed as he headed for the dressing room. It was too bad he didn't have a Bamasian bread ring now to offer him solace . . .

Barriss was on her way to the medical ward when she passed a trooper standing in the hall outside the main operating theater. He didn't seem to be doing anything other than simply standing there, staring at a blank wall.

To the unaided eye, they all looked alike, but to one who was connected to the Force, this was not the case. She knew this one. He had been her patient.

She stopped. "CT-Nine-one-four," she said.

He looked at her. "Yes?"

She could feel his question roiling in his mind, and she smiled. "You might all look alike, but you aren't all the same. Your experiences shape you as much as your heritage. The Force can recognize this."

He nodded. She regarded him. "You have no problems with your blood pressure," she said, and it was not a question—she knew it was true.

"No. I feel fine—physically."

"Why, then, are you here?"

She felt rather than saw Jos Vondar emerge from the OT behind her, was aware of him listening.

"I helped transport another trooper here yesterday. CT-Nine-one-five."

"Ah. And how does he fare?"

"I don't know. He's still in surgery."

Jos drifted over. "Nine-one-five? He, ah, didn't make it."

The wave of grief that broke from CT-914 and washed over Barriss was sudden and strong. To look at his face, however, it was hardly apparent that he felt this deep emotional chord. He said, "Unfortunate. He was"—he hesitated, just a heartbeat or two, —"a good soldier. The loss of someone so well trained is . . . regrettable."

Barriss could see that, even without the Force, Jos picked up on something either in CT-914's tone of voice or his body language, as subtle as both were. He said, "You knew him?"

"He was decanted just after me. We trained together, were posted here together, we were part of the same cohort." CT-914 hesitated again. "He . . . I thought of him as my brother."

Jos frowned. "But you're all brothers, in a sense."

"True." The clone trooper straightened. "Thank you for your efforts to save him, Doctor. I'm going back to my unit now."

He turned and strode away. Barriss and Jos watched him go. "If I didn't know better," Jos said, "I'd say that he was upset."

"And how is it that you know better? Wouldn't you feel upset if it had been your brother?"

She half expected him to answer with a wisecrack—his standard response under circumstances like these. He didn't, however. Instead, he frowned. "He's a clone, Barriss. Those sorts of feelings are bred out of them."

"Who told you that? True, they are standardized, trained, and toughened, but they are not mindless automata. They're made from the same kind of flesh and mind as are you and I, Jos. They bleed when cut, they live and die, and they grieve at the loss of a brother. CT-Nine-one-four is in emotional pain. He covers it well enough, but such things can't be hidden from the Force."

Jos looked as if she had just slapped his face. "But—but—"

"The clones are bred for combat, Jos. It's what they were designed to do, and they accept it without question. Were it not for war, they would not exist. A hard life as a soldier is better than no life at all. But even without the Force, you felt it," she said, her voice gentle. "Stoic as he tried to be, it came out. Nine-one-four grieves. He suffers the loss of his comrade. His brother."

Jos stood speechless. She felt emotion radiating from him as she had from CT-914. "It never occurred to you before, did it?"

"I—it—of course, I . . ." He ran down. No. It *hadn't* occurred to him, not like this. She could see that.

How blind those who did not know the Force were. How sad for them.

"Surgeons are notorious for their lack of bedside manners," she said. "They tend to view and treat injuries without worrying about the whole patient, even with 'real' people. Most beings consider clones nothing more than blaster fodder—why should you be any different?"

Jos shook his head, confusion still bubbling in his thoughts. She felt badly for him. One of the drawbacks to the ability to use the Force was that you sometimes learned things that you weren't expecting, things that you weren't capable of properly understanding, much less able to do anything about. Over and over again, Barriss had discovered that power brought knowledge, and that this was a decidedly mixed blessing.

"I'm sorry, Jos. I didn't mean to—"

"No, no, it's fine. I'll see you later." He gave her a patently fake smile and walked away. He looked as if the weight of the planet had just been dropped on his shoulders.

Jos walked across the compound, a damp heralding wind and suddenly overcast sky cooling the muggy afternoon somewhat as—big surprise—another storm approached. He had gotten pretty good at judging these things after all the months here. He knew he had two, maybe three minutes before the sky would open up.

"Jos?" Tolk said. "You okay?"

She had come up to walk beside him. He hadn't even noticed her in his preoccupation with this new and suddenly troubling knowledge.

"Me? I'm fine."

"No, you aren't. Remember who I am. What is it?"

He shook his head. "Just had a blindfold removed I didn't know I was wearing. Something I took for granted, never really thought about before. I'm . . . feeling pretty stupid."

"Well, how unusual is that?"

He looked at her, saw the smile, and appreciated her trying to cheer him up. He managed a small smile of his own. "Bet you scored 'sharpshooter' on your basic weapons tests."

"Actually, I rated 'master' with the pulse rifle, and dropped down to 'sharpshooter' only with the sidearm blaster."

"Figures. I was 'basic marksman' with both, which means I can't hit the side of a Destroyer—from the inside."

"You want to talk about it?"

He stopped. The rain was almost here. She put her hand on his shoulder, and, oh, yes, he wanted to talk about it. Later—when they were holding each other, kissing, and happier than he'd been since he had been conscripted. *Then* he'd talk about it. She'd be hard-put to shut him up, then.

But now . . .

"Not really, no," he said. The touch of her hand on his shoulder was almost hypnotic in its comfort.

The storm hit then. Big, fat drops, a few at first, pattered—and then the deluge. They stood together in the rain, not moving.

20

Jos had hoped that Klo Merit could shed some light on his newfound and uncomfortable knowledge about clones, but so far, the minder was more stirring up mud from the murky bottom of his thoughts than pumping in clarity.

Clarity seemed a forlorn hope right now.

"So, what exactly are we talking about here when you say 'expertise'?"

Merit said, "Well, you can tell a lot about how much somebody knows by listening. See this ring?" He held his hand up so that Jos could view it. The piece of jewelry was a deep golden band of metal with a thumbnail-sized stone inset into it. The stone glittered in the overhead light of Merit's office, flashing multiple colors—reds, blues, greens, and yellows in a kind of rolling pattern, as Merit moved his hand. It was quite impressive.

Jos nodded. "Very nice. Some kind of firestone?"

Merit smiled. "Yes. And your question marks you as somebody who knows a little about them, but not much. You recognize it as a firestone, but that's only a small step into the subject."

Jos shrugged. "I'm a surgeon. You want to know about kidney stones, I'm your boy."

"Somebody who didn't know anything about gems would say, 'That's nice—what kind of stone is it?' Somebody who knows a little more will comment as you did. A person with a bit more knowledge might say, 'Is that a Gallian firestone, or a Rathalayan?' They know there is a difference between those two and probably that this is one or the other.

"Now, a *real* expert will look at my ring and say, 'Ah, a black Gallian firestone, very nice. Is it a crystal or a boulder matrix?' Because he can tell that many specifics just by looking at it—that it is a firestone, that it comes from Gall, that it is a black. But the way it's mounted, he can't see the back of it, so he can't tell the matrix. It's a boulder, by the way, which denotes the kind of rock in which firestone is sometimes found, and the term *black* refers to the background colors upon which the flashes shine."

Jos shook his head. "So now I'm educated about gems."

Merit smiled broadly. "No, you aren't. You couldn't tell a real one from a fake, and you don't know anything else about them other than what I just told you. How valuable is it, do you think?"

"Even if you found it in the Jasserak Swamp, I still couldn't afford it."

"It's worth more than a blue-white diamond of the same size. And do you know about the curse?"

" 'Curse'?"

"Yes. Firestones are supposed to be unlucky. But that was a canard, started by diamond merchants who were losing business to firestone sellers. Only thing unlucky about them is not owning one."

Jos smiled. "Okay, I take your point. At least part of it."

"So take the rest of it. You weren't an expert on clones because you never tried to be. Other than knowing how to cut and glue them back together, which is sufficient for your needs, why would you bother? Before the war, there weren't enough clones around to make it a concern. Out of sight, out of mind. You deal with their physiology, not their psychology."

"That's true."

"But clones aren't the only beings you probably haven't thought much about. What about droids?"

"Droids? What about them?"

"Do you consider them people?"

"Only in the same sense that a tetrawave is. They're machines."

"But they think. They interact. They function."

Jos looked perplexed. "Okay, but . . ."

"Work with me for a minute," Klo continued. "Just for the sake of argument, have you ever met a droid that expressed worry, or fear, or that had, say, a sense of humor? That seemed . . . self-aware?"

Jos was silent. Yes. He had. I-Five came immediately to mind. "But they don't feel pain. They can't reproduce—"

"Aren't there people with neuropathic disorders who don't feel pain? And who runs the assembly line in a droid factory, building more droids?"

Jos laughed. "You can switch a droid on and off, disassemble it, put it back together, and it won't blink a photosensor. Of course," he added, "you can do that to me too, but only after a fourteen-hour shift."

"I'm not saying they are *exactly* like you and me. But if you stop and think about it, a self-aware construct that has an emotional content and a job isn't simply a dumbot welding seams on next year's landspeeder."

"You aren't helping here. I'm still trying to get my mind around the concept of clones as people, and now you're throwing droids at me."

"Life isn't simple, Jos. Once you start clumping cells into tissues and tissues into systems, the level of complexity goes up in powers of ten. I can't give you any easy answers—you have to figure things out for yourself."

"Whatever the Republic's paying you, it's too much."

Merit shrugged, a fluid and smooth gesture. "That's how the galaxy works. It's not my design; when I get to be in charge of everything, I'll fix it. Until then, we're stuck with this."

Jos sighed. When you wanted answers, more questions didn't exactly help.

Merit looked at his chrono and stood. "Our session is up—and I believe it's now time for the weekly sabacc game, is it not?"

"Raise," Den said. He tossed a ten-credit chip onto the table. The suspension field kept it from clinking too much or rolling away.

"I'll see that," Jos said, "and raise you two." Two more chips hit the growing pile.

Den glanced owlishly at his cards, then at the rest of the players surrounding the cantina table as each anted up in turn. Besides himself and Captain Vondar, there were five others: Captain Yant, Barriss Offee, the minder Klo Merit, Tolk le Trene, and I-Five. Den could glean no clues from any of them as to the hands they were holding; the four organics all had carefully noncommittal faces, and even though the droid was capable of subtle expressions, he apparently had no problem controlling them.

It had been said that sabacc was as much a game of

skill as it was of chance, and Den had no trouble believing that, especially with this crowd. Talk about a stacked deck: out of seven players, three of them were extremely adept at reading others. He was pretty certain that the Padawan would not use the Force to give herself an edge, but he wasn't so sure about Tolk and Merit. The minder might be able to sense feelings in the others that would betray their emotional state, and so gain an edge, but Tolk would have a harder time of it. Even though this group wasn't exactly at the same level of expertise as a bunch of card shooks working the Coruscant Crown Casino, they'd all, Den included, mastered fairly well the art of the "sabacc mask"—the completely expressionless face that did not betray by so much as an eyelash flicker any clues whatsoever. Not even a Lorrdian could read body language if the body in question was being utterly uncommunicative.

"Nobody calls? Great," Yant said. "Draw two." Barriss, the new dealer, handed him his cards.

From the camp's hypersound speakers, the voice of one of Filba's subordinates made an announcement, the focused sound beams making it seem as if he were speaking to each individual alone. "Attention," the voice said hesitantly, obviously reading unfamiliar copy. "At, uh, zero-six-hundred hours the scheduled inspection by Admiral Bleyd will take place. Let's make sure we give him a big welcome."

"Ah, yes," Jos said. "The visitation from on high. Think I'll start saluting now and avoid the rush."

A new round of betting began, starting this time with I-Five. Den had been watching the droid play with some interest. I-Five's cognitive module was no doubt capable of calculating all or nearly all of the myriad combinations possible in the seventy-six-chip-card deck, but not even the most advanced synaptic grid processor could anticipate the random order in which they might occur in any given hand. Still, the droid was an excellent player, calm and cool. "Raise three," he said.

Jos raised an eyebrow. "Maybe it's just the heat," he said, "but I could swear that durasteel skin of yours is starting to sweat."

"Must be a leaky lube node," I-Five replied imperturbably. "I might note, however, that my olfactory sensor is picking up a distinct whiff of fear pheromone with your genetic tag, Captain Vondar."

"How'd you get to be so good at cards, I-Five?" Den asked the droid.

"My partner taught me," the droid replied. "He could usually walk out of a game with more credits than he went in with. He's held more idiot's arrays than an asylum nurse."

"Do you consider yourself to be a sentient organic, like a human?" Jos asked abruptly.

"Only when I'm particularly depressed," the droid replied.

Jos made a wry face. Before he could reply I-Five continued, "Knowing what I do of organics, however, and of humans in particular, I must assume that your question is sincere, Captain Vondar. I can only answer that, due to a cognitive module superior to most droids of my category, as well as the lack of a creativity damper, I am more sentient than most of my colleagues. Does this mean that I qualify as a 'living' being? I suppose that depends on one's point of view. But most philosophers take the position that to be able to ask the question is to have already answered it."

Den saw a quick glance pass between the captain and

the minder, saw the latter smile slightly. Something sub-surface was definitely going on there.

"In the twelve years that I have ricocheted around this galaxy like the legendary Roon Comet," I-Five continued, "I have encountered a great many interesting personalities. Some of them have been droids. I still have gaps in my memory that seem to be connected to some kind of trauma occurring not long after my leaving Coruscant. My self-repair systems are processing these gaps, assembling the missing data from interior hologrammics, but my internal logic circuits won't allow synaptic linkage to proceed with less than seventy-five percent certainty."

Den glanced at Jos. It was his hand, but the surgeon seemed deep in thought, unaware of his turn.

"Jos," Barriss said gently after a moment.

Jos looked up. "I call," he said.

Everyone showed their hands. Den chuckled as he put down a full twenty-three. "Pure sabacc," he said, grinning and reaching for the two pots. "Scan 'em and sob, ladies and—"

Jos laid down his cards. Den and the other players stared in disbelief. It was an idiot's array: the face card plus a two of sabers and a three of flasks.

"*Nice* play," Tolk said.

"Thanks," Jos said as he gathered in the credits. But Den, watching the surgeon's expression, had the distinct feeling that right now, Captain Vondar could not have cared less about winning.

21

The night was, of course, warm. Wingstingers, fire gnats, and other hapless insects flew past and hurled themselves against zappers, adding little blue flickers to the camp lights and what little wan star gleam managed to penetrate the mostly cloudy skies. Drongar's two moons weren't even big enough to show disks, so, were it not for the Rimsoo lights, the swamp would be exceedingly dark now. As would the entire night half of the planet. On a rainy evening, the only light was from swamp rot, lightning flashes, and the intermittent glow of the fire gnats.

An unpleasant place in every aspect. Well, no, be honest—the enemy personnel were actually fairly decent beings.

There was a tendency, the spy knew, to identify with the people you found yourself among when you were working. There could come a time when you'd forget your original purpose, and start to think of those whom you were detailed to watch, or to damage, as real friends. It was called "going native." Many agents and spies had done it, in war and in peace. It was all too easy. Enemies were not faceless automata, or amoral monsters who got up every morning with a burning desire to rage forth and do evil. No, most of them were just like anybody else—they had hopes, fears, families, and they believed they were doing the right things for the right reasons.

It was hard to demonize such people.

To be sure, you could present it as such to a bunch of young troopers. You could indoctrinate them, visualizing the enemy soldiers as maniacal fiends who wanted nothing more than to slaughter innocent younglings, burn down your prime mother's house, and violate your drove father's grave. Modern soldiers rarely saw the enemy face to face at any event. Firing a missile at somebody ten thousand meters away was bloodless and uninvolving. But even a brief encounter at close range on the field was sometimes enough to ruin months of training: the first time one of your recruits saw a young being who looked a lot like him or her or it, sitting on a battlefield holding in his guts with his hands and crying for a drink of water—well, it was a shock. Your newly battle-trained conscript might suddenly realize that the dying young soldier had hopes and fears not all that different from his own—and maybe that all he, too, wanted to do was just serve his tour and go home. That realization was like an upended flask of liquid nitrogen, chilling to the core.

Thinking along those lines was not a good idea for a soldier. It might make him hesitate next time; might even get him killed. Best to try and ignore it.

But when you were a sub-rosa agent, you couldn't do that. You couldn't harbor illusions that your enemies were evil; not when you ate with them, drank with them, worked with them. You sometimes grew very attached to them. In a place like this, people lived in each other's pockets. You learned to know the one sitting

across from you at the chow hall table, almost as well as
you did your own reflection.

The staff at this Rimsoo were good people, almost all
of them. The spy knew this—judging beings was a big
part of an agent's business. If this war hadn't begun,
any of them could have been potential friends. There
wasn't a demon among them.

That made the tasks harder. When you weren't hurting some monster by setting events in motion, but instead were harming people who considered you their
friend—it hurt. You got up every morning and your life
among them was almost totally a lie. Everything you
said or did had to remain hidden behind a thick shroud,
kept secret for your own survival. Spies, after all, were
not well treated in times of war. You were seldom
traded when caught; generally, a quick military court
would be convened and you would be extinguished like
a switched-off glow stick, quietly and quickly, as soon
as they extracted whatever intelligence they could from
your soon-to-be-dead brain. Dead on some faraway
planet, unmourned in a shallow grave, detested by those
who thought they'd known you.

And even if you were successful—even if you com-
pleted your mission and returned safely—there was no
glory, no medals, no parades at home. If you were very
lucky, you got to live a quiet, low-key life without having extensive parts of your memory sponged away by
"your" side.

Spying was not a job for one with pale courage. You
had to be made of something stronger than the
strongest steelcrete to withstand the stress of being an
undercover agent, no matter which side you worked for,
no matter how strong and valid your reasons for doing
the job.

Valid? Oh, yes, the spy's reasons were certainly that. The reasons were old and far away, but undiminished nonetheless. Even so, it was impossible to smile at these people and not mean it, because they were good people. None of them had participated in the atrocity that had made all this necessary—all of them, in fact, would have been horrified at the event. Decent beings on any side of any war would be. But it wasn't the decent beings who caused such things. And it was the indecent ones who had to pay for their crimes. You had to resolve early on that the innocent might have to suffer, and you had to strive to make them suffer as little as possible, but suffering was unavoidable. People died in war, just as the spy's people had died, and there was little to be done about it, save to make it happen as cleanly and quickly as possible.

Some of them were attractive, bright, skilled . . . all the things the spy sought in friends and lovers. And yet they would die. That resolve had to remain steadfast. War was a cold business. The tears would have to come much later . . .

It was time for bed. Tomorrow would bring whatever it would bring, and rest, if allowed by happenstance, was always necessary.

At least once a month, Admiral Bleyd did a tour of the Rimsoos. It was a cursory inspection, to wave the flag and pretend he cared about the troops and medics toiling on this tropical mudball he had come to so thoroughly detest. When the next Black Sun agent appeared, it was not Bleyd's intent that there be anything unusual in his own routine. The inspection tour was scheduled and, without compelling reason to call it off, would proceed as normal. Business as usual.

It was largely a waste of everybody's time. They knew when he was coming, had had plenty of time to polish and prepare. He would not see anything amiss unless it happened by accident, and right in front of him.

He couldn't even take time off to go hunting—but then, there was nothing worthy of his skill on this sodden world.

Bleyd always used his personal lighter for the flight to the surface, a small craft traditionally called that because its namesake's original purpose had been to "lighten" vessels on planetary seas by moving cargo ashore. His craft, a modified Surronian Conqueror assault ship, was not the standard vessel for an admiral of the fleet. The vessel was small, less than thirty meters in length, and its cargo-carrying capacity was limited—it wouldn't lighten any ship of size to any noticeable degree, which was normal enough. It ran, however, a cluster of eight Surronian ion engines, four A2s and four A2.50s, and was the fastest thing in the atmosphere on this planet by far. Enemy guns set to track ordinary transport and starfighters would be shooting at empty air far behind the ship when Bleyd cranked it up. Exposure to the spores was also more limited than in other craft. On a good flight, with no local storms to slow him down, he could leave the flight deck and land at ground stations in half the time any other transport available could manage. The hyperdrive was a Class One Corellian Engineering Corporation H1.5, sufficient to carry a passenger back to the realm of civilized worlds. Bleyd had heard about the vessel after it had been captured from some pirate or other during a military engagement just before he was posted here, and with a bit of clever bargaining had managed to obtain it as his personal transport.

Aside from its other virtues, the ship had a pleasing aerodynamic shape, a kind of elongated figure eight. There was, after all, no reason an admiral's transport couldn't look as good as it flew.

This jaunt was a piece of dream cake. As he lanced through the atmosphere toward the surface, he was pondering his other problem: credits, and how best to amass as many as possible as quickly as possible without risk of detection.

"Please identify yourself," came the request from the main Republic ground battery control.

Bleyd smiled. They had to ask, but they certainly knew who he was. The sensor profile of his lighter was unique—there was nothing in twenty parsecs that looked even remotely like it.

"Admiral Bleyd here," he responded, his voice crisp. "On inspection tour from MedStar Nineteen." He rattled off the current identification code, which was changed daily on his order.

There was brief pause while the officer in charge pretended to check to make sure his commander wasn't some Separatist spy coming to bomb a poor Rimsoo unit squatting in a swamp. Then: "All fine, sir. Proceed to designated landing quadrant, and welcome, Admiral."

Bleyd shut off the comm without responding.

It was not the money per se, though that certainly had its appeal on some level. No, it was the recovery of honor, the prestige, the righting of wrongs—that was what a bank full of credits represented. He had already managed to build himself a nice sum, enough so that, if managed correctly, it would keep him fed and clothed and reasonably comfortable for the rest of his life. But the goal was not merely to retire in comfort; no, the goal was much more important than that. The goal was honor.

Mixed in with this was, of course, a degree of vengeance. There were beings who needed to be dealt with, old grudges settled, and a dynasty to begin. He had to find a mate, marry, produce heirs, and make certain that his sons and daughters would be sufficiently wealthy so as to guarantee their rightful places in the galaxy. This war would be over eventually. The Republic would prevail—he didn't doubt that, inconceivable that it would not—and life would go on much as it had before. A peaceful galaxy, with ample opportunity for the landed and wealthy to prosper even more—these were things to be taken for granted. No sane being wanted war, save that it served his own ends. There were fortunes to be made in times of conflict, power to be gathered, and when this one was done Bleyd and his descendants would be among the rich and powerful. Of that, there was no doubt.

The doing of it was not so easy, but he was both clever and resourceful. Small amounts of the bota could continue to be diverted and stored. His dealings with Black Sun would have to cease—a major theft was out of the question—but he could hide a lot of the valuable adaptogen on a ship the size of a MedStar, stack it in blocks of carbonite disguised as something else, and take it back to civilization himself, bold as you please. The material would never show up on a manifest, nobody would know it existed, and it would only become more valuable as time went by. A thousand kilos of pharmaceutical-grade bota stashed in some warehouse would eventually be worth millions all by itself.

But there were other things a smart admiral could do to enhance his fortune. A medical system necessary for a Rimsoo could be ordered in duplicate, and one of them could find its way elsewhere, perhaps to some world in desperate need of such a facility, and bartered for something of equal value but more portable. Precious metal or rare gems, say. And a couple of first-class medical droids misdirected to some frontier planet where doctors were in short supply would also be worth their weight in credits. Even a copy of a proprietary computer program, such as the one that ran the MedStar's operational systems, was a valuable commodity—if presented to the right customer. How many one-starship worlds would love to have one of those for its hospitals, with no questions asked, for the right price?

The ship's hull began to warm as it arrowed its way into the atmosphere. The sensors noted this and adjusted the environmental control systems. He was only a few minutes away from the ground medical HQ, traditionally called Rimsoo One. There didn't seem to be any fighting in this quadrant today, so he didn't expect any real trouble. Now and then, some pilot from the Confederacy would try a suicide run, braving the spores in order to get a chance to attack a Republic vessel outside his operational range. He had never been attacked himself, and the lighter was equipped with a pair of fire-linked ion cannons, as well as laser cannons he could use from the cockpit. He sometimes wished one of the Separatist fighters would try him so that he could demonstrate he was no rear-guard admiral, but such an opportunity had never presented itself. *Too bad.*

"This is Landing Control. We are assuming command of your vessel in thirty seconds, sir."

Bleyd nodded to himself. "Acknowledged, Landing Control." He would prefer to bring the lighter in himself on manual, but this was not standard procedure, and Tarnese Bleyd would not risk his future on pure ego-driven matters of such small consequence. Let them land the ship. He had bigger game to slay . . .

22

Bleyd liked to vary his inspections. Sometimes he would stick to one planetary sector; other times he would travel across an entire region. On one trip he might visit Rimsoos in numerical order; another time he'd hit only the even- or odd-numbered ones. There were a dozen of the emergency medical bases, one for practically every major battlefront, spread far and wide over Tanlasso. There was no way he could see them all in a single visit, unless he was willing to stay on the ground for a month of constant travel. Republic Mobile Surgical Units were technically able to pick up and move quickly, either to avoid danger or to follow the advance or retreat of the front lines. Once established, however, the units tended to stay put for weeks or months, and some of them were still in the same spot where they'd been initially dropped. There wasn't a lot of variation among them, since they all had the same primary purpose: the repair and maintenance of the clone trooper army and whatever other casualties might occur.

Not that it made any difference how he conducted his inspections; whichever manner he chose, the word would be there long before he arrived. Some leaders liked to drop in unannounced, but for him, surprise was not part of the process. He wasn't looking for something unpleasant to have to deal with. As long as nobody fouled up, he didn't worry about the day-to-day operations.

As the landspeeder ferrying him from the area's temporary hub spaceport approached the current location of Rimsoo Seven, Bleyd watched faint speckles of reddish spore dust glitter over the vehicle's transparisteel canopy. Even though the spores were much less dangerous at ground level most of the time, zipping along in a speeder with the top down was hardly a good idea.

The unit was just ahead; they'd covered the two hundred or so kilometers of marshland and bayous separating it from his landing pad quickly. His driver was a young, four-armed Myneyrsh male, which was something of a surprise. Most Myneyrshi had an aversion to technology, and Bleyd assumed that this applied to powered ground-effect craft such as this one. The driver also had an issue blaster on the seat beside him, though if attacked, Bleyd was fairly sure the trooper would reach first for the big garral-tooth knife he wore in a sheath strapped to his translucent blue leg. There was a Myneyrsh saying: "A knife never runs out of ammunition." Bleyd understood that well enough.

"Rimsoo Seven, Admiral, sir," the driver said.

Bleyd nodded. He had been here before, though it had been several months, at least. The place looked like all the others; only the location and the local graffiti marked it as different.

Well, that and the fact that his partner in crime, Filba the Hutt, was based here . . .

They approached the perimeter, were challenged by the guard, and admitted through the energy shield. The military-grade power shield kept certain things out, notably fast-moving missiles and high-energy spectra such as gamma and X-rays, while letting in radio waves and visible light. Unfortunately, heat, rain, spores, and insects were slow enough to some degree to pass through the osmotic shield as well.

Bleyd met Colonel D'Arc Vaetes, the commander, and each offered up the usual ordained and meaningless compliments and comments. Going through the motions, Bleyd was paying somewhat less than half his attention to the tour. Vaetes ran a tight ship, he knew, and the admiral would have been surprised to see anything really amiss.

As they passed the dining hall and cantina on their way to look at the main surgical theater, Bleyd saw a man leaning against a poptree twenty meters away, smiling.

A chill touched Bleyd's spine, for there was a distinct sense of danger emanating from the smiling human. There was nothing overt about it, nothing that might be seen as a gesture of disrespect, but the feeling was unmistakable. Here was a warrior—not just a soldier. A smiling killer who knew what he was and gloried in the knowledge.

Bleyd stopped. "Who is that?"

Vaetes glanced over and said, "Phow Ji, the Bunduki close-combat instructor. His workouts keep me in better shape than I'd like."

"Ah." That explained it. Bleyd knew about Ji. Like any good hunter, he always marked predators in his territory. Ji had had a reputation before he arrived here; his datafile had been flagged. And since he had arrived, he had done several things to add to that reputation. There was a rumor that a holo existed of Ji going up against a trio of mercs, and being the only one to walk away. Bleyd was very interested in seeing that.

To Vaetes, he said, "Let's go over and say hello."

As they turned and headed toward Ji, the admiral was amused to see the fighter's nostrils flare a little, and his relaxed pose become just a bit more tense. He smiled. It could have just been his rank, but Bleyd didn't think so. His file stated that Phow Ji had little respect for authority. No, Bleyd figured that Ji recognized in him the same thing that he had immediately seen in the Bunduki: a potentially dangerous opponent.

Ji came to attention, albeit somewhat slowly.

"At ease, Lieutenant Ji."

"By your command, Admiral." The fighter relaxed, bent his knees slightly, and shook his shoulders almost imperceptibly.

Getting ready to move, Bleyd thought. *Excellent!* This man could take on twenty Black Sun thugs like the one Bleyd had bested orbitside without breaking a sweat.

"You know me?" Ji asked.

"Of course. I have heard that you are . . . an adept fighter."

His tone, and the pause, were just enough to give his comment an archness that might or might not be sarcastic. So close that it could have been nothing—or a calculated insult. Impossible to tell.

The two looked at each other for a second, each gaze cool and measuring.

Ji said, "Adept enough for anyone on *this* planet. Sir."

Bleyd held a grin in check, though he wanted to show his teeth. The Bunduki was insolent. The comment was plainly a challenge.

There had been a time, when he had been much

younger, when Bleyd would have stripped off his skin-shirt at such a remark, and they would have danced right then and there. He wanted to do it now—and he could tell that Ji knew this, and was ready to go at it, too.

Three things stopped Bleyd from physically attacking the Bunduki who was standing there and inviting just that. First, he was an admiral of the fleet, and it was beneath him to be seen brawling in public. Such a match would have to take place behind closed doors and un-witnessed, were it to happen at all.

Second, Bleyd's plans to redeem his family's honor were still paramount, and a physical squabble with an-other officer, for whatever reasons, would draw un-wanted attention from uplevels. He did not want to risk that.

Third—and this reason came hard, but he could not deny it—he wasn't at all sure he could beat Phow Ji in a fair match. There was no doubt that he was stronger and faster, but the human was a combat champion, and his skills had been honed in dozens of matches, some of which had been to the death. Size and strength and speed all mattered, of course, but an opponent with enough skill could level that field. When two fully grown saber-fangs fought, the winner and the loser both came away bloody, and which was the victor was some-times difficult to tell. Bleyd was a predator, and as such was willing to risk death, but smart killers did so only when the reward was worth the risk. Bragging rights for beating a combat champion did not fall into that category—at least, not on this day, and not in this place.

What if, he wondered briefly, he were to turn Ji loose in the rain forest and make it a hunt? That would give Bleyd the advantage, but even so, it might not end with him victorious. Such risk would definitely spice the game, but it was not, unfortunately, going to happen now.

"I would like to see you in action someday," Bleyd said.

Ji nodded without breaking eye contact. Bleyd could see that he understood that the admiral was not backing down, but only postponing a possible confrontation. "I'd like that as well, Admiral. Sir."

The two stood there for a few seconds, neither of them blinking. Finally, Bleyd turned to Vaetes. "You were going to show me the operating theater, Commander. And I expect that the field commanders will want to display their troops, who will no doubt be getting warm in this weather."

Vaetes, who had kept a respectful distance from and a noncommittal expression about what must have seemed to him a very strange interlude, nodded. "Right this way, Admiral."

Bleyd could feel Ji's gaze on his back as he walked away. A pity, but it was true that a hunter without patience usually went hungry. There would be another time. Already, though, Bleyd felt better about his tour. There was nothing like a dangerous animal stalking you to get the blood circulating.

His enthusiasm dampened a bit as he remembered that there was other business to which he must attend at this particular Rimsoo, distasteful as it was. No rest for the being in charge . . .

It was time.

With the Rimsoo admiral planetside for his tour, there would not be a better opportunity, Den knew, to spring his trap for Filba. To see the larcenous Hutt's many crimes finally brought to light—the embezzlement and usury and countless other illegal appropriations that Den had diligently discovered over the past several weeks, both through the HoloNet and by skillful interviews with the staff, all revealed right under Admiral Bleyd's nose—what could be more fitting? Or more satisfying?

It hadn't been easy. The data trail had been as serpentine as the Hutt's own slime track after a massive cantina bender. The most incriminating indictment had come from one of the medical staff who had an uncle on the supply side. The uncle had in his possession encrypted data that implicated Filba in the rerouting of five hundred hectoliters of Anticeptin-D into the cargo hold of a black marketeer's freighter two months ago. It wasn't strong enough evidence by itself, and Filba had at least been smart enough not to bleed the same source twice, but coupled with the other infractions Den had discovered, it would be more than enough to take him down.

Den leaned back on his formcot and smiled. Payback would be sweet.

Over the hypersound speakers came the martial strains of the Republic Anthem's first stanza—the music traditionally played whenever a ranking officer or visiting dignitary was present. Of course, Den was a noncom, so he was not technically obligated to turn out with the others. Still, no harm in showing a little courtesy.

He'd only spoken to the Sakiyan officer once, and that briefly, before he'd made the drop to Drongar. But from what he'd heard around the base, Admiral

Bleyd was held in reasonably high regard. He ran a tight operation, and there seemed to be little question of his personal courage, pride, and honor. Den didn't know that much about Sakiyan culture, but he did know that the society was structured around complex family-political units, and that honor, dignity, and respect played a big part—so much so that there were a multitude of subtle, yet distinct, permutations, each with its own name and rules.

He emerged from the tent, blinking and, as always, slightly astonished at the stifling, sodden heat, and saw the officers, enlistees, and medical personnel lined up for inspection. The clone cohort was separate, their gleaming black-and-white-armored forms, all exactly the same height and body type, standing at attention in rows that, if not perfect, couldn't have been off by more than a millimeter at best.

Why you would bother to inspect clones was beyond him. Seen one, seen them all.

Admiral Bleyd stood before them. He was an impressive figure, surely enough—tall and lean, his dress grays showing nary a wrinkle, and somehow Den knew that he wasn't using an antistatic field generator. No wrinkle that knew what was good for it would come anywhere close to the admiral's uniform.

The bald, burnished head gleamed in the sun, its dark bronze shining like an insect's carapace. Den couldn't see any sign of the admiral sweating. Maybe Sakiyans didn't sweat. Or maybe it was just Admiral Bleyd who didn't.

The reporter came to a stop not far from the officers' line. He could see Filba—*Not exactly hard to miss, he looks like something a space slug sneezed out.* The

Hutt's yellowish skin was even more mottled than usual, and he looked particularly slimy today. *You don't know what suffering is yet,* Den silently promised the gigantic mollusk. *At least this planet has an atmosphere, foul though it may be. Not like a prison on an asteroid, where all you'll have to look at is rock . . .*

The best time to drop his bombshell would be during the inspection tour—out of Filba's earshot, obviously. Den tried to visualize the look of dismay on the Hutt's face when security came to collect him.

Somewhat to his surprise, now that this elaborate revenge scheme he had worked on for the past several weeks was about to pay off, he felt remarkably unenthused about the whole thing. Blowing the whistle on the Hutt suddenly seemed like more of an obligation, a duty, than savory retribution. He didn't feel the joy he thought he would.

It wasn't just payback for the Hutt's recent treatment of him. He'd nearly gotten Den killed on Jabiim, as well. No, Filba had had this coming for a long time. But now—and this struck him with something very close to real horror—Den realized might actually be feeling *reluctant* to do it.

You're getting soft, Den told himself. *Losing your edge. Must be the heat. You gotta get off this planet.*

Then he noticed the admiral pause slightly as he passed the Hutt. There was eye contact between the two—a very quick glance, something that, unless you'd been an investigative reporter with your sensors attuned by years in the field, was virtually unnoticeable.

But Den noticed it.

Most interesting.

Although he was aware that he might be reading a terabyte or two into that look that wasn't necessarily there, still, the implications were . . . unsettling. He would bet his droptacs that there was something going on between the Hutt and the Sakiyan, and that it would be, at the very least, highly unorthodox. What would an admiral of the fleet and a supply sergeant have to talk about?

It was a lot to read into a single, almost subliminal glance. It might be nothing more than distaste for Hutts in general that had caused Bleyd's look, but Den Dhur was adept at what he did, and he had learned to trust his reporter's instincts—maker knew they had been hard enough to come by. And the more he thought about it, the more sense it made. The deeper his investigations into Filba's malfeasance had gone, the more obvious it had become that the Hutt couldn't be handling a black-market operation like this by himself. He had to be getting help from higher up. Den just hadn't realized how high up the help was.

Of a moment, he did a fast revision of his plans.

Looks like I won't be acquainting the admiral with your iniquities after all, you sack of slime. Certainly not until he was more knowledgeable about Bleyd's involvement. The rot had spread higher than he'd thought. If he went tripping into the admiral's presence and began blathering about Filba's crimes to his partner in those crimes, who just happened to be somebody who could have him shot with a wave of his hand— well, that could be a fatal error.

Don't tell me you're surprised, his mind whispered mockingly.

The admiral dismissed the troops and personnel. Colonel Vaetes, accompanied by Captains Vondar and

Yant, joined Bleyd to walk him through the operating theater.

Sooner or later, Bleyd would find time to speak to Filba alone. And Den was determined that they wouldn't be as alone as they thought they were . . .

23

Back in his cubicle Den pulled a small box from under the bed, thumbed the recognizer lock, and opened it. It was time to bring out the big guns—or, rather, the small ones. The smallest one, in fact, and it wasn't a gun, though it did "shoot."

Den held the tiny device close to his eyes and admired it. It was a tiny spycam disguised as a flying insect, known as a moon moth. The entire thing barely covered his thumbnail, but its biomimetic design allowed it to fly about undetected, letting its operator hear and see everything its sensors could pick up, from up to ten thousand meters away. He'd used it a few times before. It had a built-in state-of-the-art confounder that would nullify tangle fields, sensor screens, or other electromagnetic obstructions either Bleyd or Filba might be wearing. And, with all the winged pests buzzing around the base anyway, one more would hardly be noticed. It had cost him three months' pay, but the first time he'd used it, back when he'd done the story on the Wild Space smugglers, it had paid for itself.

"Off you go," he murmured as he activated the device. The moon moth flew through the open entrance and vanished as Den slipped on the virtual headset that would allow him to control it.

He let himself enjoy the feeling of flying for a few moments, climbing high over the base for a panoramic view of the swamp, then swooping down low to buzz one of the many clones in sight. Then he leveled out and headed for Filba's domain.

The door was shut, but there were plenty of tiny openings where the heat-warped plasteel was joined with the duralloy framework. He squeezed the moon moth through one. Not a moment too soon—Bleyd was already there, facing the Hutt, and from the looks on both their faces Den didn't expect either one to whip out holos of the kids anytime soon. He steered the bug-cam to a landing on a nearby shelf.

What was that old Kubaz saying about wishing one were a buzz-beetle on a wall . . . ?

Filba had evidently prepared for this confrontation by finishing most of a keg of what looked like Alder-aanian ale. His skin folds had that rubbery look that Hutts got when drunk.

Bleyd, on the other hand, was not at all intoxicated, unless anger could be considered an intoxicant. He was speaking in a low, level tone, and seemed—to Den, at least—ready to slice and dice Filba.

Den turned the gain up on the sound enhancers.

"—things are too hot right now," Bleyd said through his fangs. "I don't want Black Sun coming back anytime soon. Until this affair with their missing emissary is settled, we have to lie low."

"Easy for you to say," the Hutt rumbled. "Your profit margin's far higher than mine." He took another mighty swig of the ale; despite his distended gut, he was evidently nowhere near capacity. "I'm taking all the risks, and you're getting all—"

"There'll be no profits for either of us if Black Sun

moves in, you bloated imbecile! If you've a brain buried anywhere in all that blubber you'd understand that."

"Insults," Filba sneered, waving his jug about. "All I ever get. I deserve more for my part in this. I deserve—"

Bleyd was suddenly across the room and at the Hutt's throat. He'd moved so fast that the moon moth had only registered a blur. "You deserve," the Sakiyan hissed, "to have your innards rearranged, you swamp-sucking—"

He stopped abruptly. Filba's eyes were even more bulbous and distended than usual. His wide gash of a mouth opened and closed, either questing for air or trying to speak, and apparently not succeeding at either. The small arms were waving about in panic. The jug slipped from his hand and shattered on the floor.

Filba lurched forward, drawing more and more of his bulk upright until it seemed impossible that he could maintain his balance. He swayed, a mottled tower of flab and slime—then toppled, crashing down to the floor. Bleyd had to leap out of the way to avoid being crushed as the Hutt's considerable mass struck hard enough to shake the building. It nearly vibrated the moon moth off its perch.

Maker's eyes! He's fainted! Or worse . . .

Den, watching, could not believe his eyes—or, rather, the moon moth's photoreceptors. What was going on? Had the admiral actually scared Filba into having heart failure—or whatever the Hutt equivalent was; hard to believe Filba even had a heart—by appearing to attack him?

Bleyd bent over the motionless form. He touched the Hutt's back, perhaps feeling for some kind of pulse. Then he turned to the broken ale jug, lifted a shard, and sniffed it.

A peculiar expression spread over his face—equal

parts understanding, anger, and bafflement. He stood frozen for a moment, then hurled the fragment to break against the wall.

The entrance chime activated. A muffled pounding was heard, as were concerned shouts. Filba's collapse had probably been noticed by everyone in the area— Den would have been surprised if the Separatists hadn't felt it as well.

Bleyd turned to the door. He smoothed his uniform, made sure no medal hung even slightly askew, and then opened it.

Den knew it was time to go. The moon moth was immune to most detection devices, but shortly techs would likely be going over this chamber with gadgets that could hear an electron shifting shells. He made the moon moth fly off the shelf, toward the entrance, which was already filled with confused and shocked faces—

A hand came out of nowhere, moving so fast it just seemed to *appear*. Den gasped as his point of view shifted violently. And then, suddenly, the moon moth was being held close to Bleyd's face. The admiral was staring, it seemed, right into Den's eyes.

A second later the hand closed into a fist. There was a flash as the piezoelectrics shorted out—and then blackness.

Uh-oh . . .

24

Barriss Offee was just finishing her meditation when she heard the commotion, and felt a simultaneous ripple in the Force. She settled to the floor, unlocked her legs, and stood.

Outside, several people were running back and forth. This in itself wasn't unusual for the base, but the reverberations she had felt were not the familiar ones of incoming wounded. She followed these new feelings, and the excited crowd, and saw a knot of people animatedly talking outside Filba's office in the large central admin-and-requisition center. Zan Yant was among them. She stepped up alongside him.

"Doctor Yant."

He smiled at her. "Healer Offee. Looks like we all felt Filba's passing, one way or another."

"The Hutt is dead? How?"

"Hard to say for sure. Apparently it was very sudden. I had a word with one of the techs, who sometimes sits in on our card game, and the indication from him was poison."

A tech emerged from the large cubicle with an anti-grav gurney, upon which was a large body sack, sealed shut and obviously filled to capacity. The lifter's gyros and condenser whined under the load as the tech guided it outside.

"That would be the late, and fairly heavy, Filba, unless I miss my guess. I wonder who's on medical examiner duty today? Whoever it is has got quite a job ahead of him."

Jos Vondar arrived just then, and the three of them watched the gurney head for the OT.

"Bad luck," Jos said. He didn't look happy.

"Filba was a friend of yours?" Barriss asked.

He looked at her, obviously surprised at the question. "Filba was an obnoxious, officious, tightfisted fatherless squat who would make his own pouch mother sign a requisition for water if she was dying of thirst."

"You've got to learn to be more open with your feelings," Zan said.

"Why the grief, then?" Barriss asked.

"Because I'm on ME duty," Jos said dolefully. "Lucky me, I get to do the autopsy. This war'll be over by the time I've cut him up. I'll dull just about all the vibroscalpels we have in stock. I'm saving the last one for my throat," he said to Zan in a mock-aside whisper.

"Word is, he was poisoned," Zan said.

"Won't help, and you know it. I still have to dice him and weigh each organ, even if he just had a simple cardiac arrest. I'll need a wrecker droid to help."

"Oh, well, look on the bright side," Zan said. "Maybe we can recycle him into lube—it'd be enough to keep all our surgical droids working smoothly for, oh, the next couple hundred years."

"It's good to see you two can maintain a sense of humor at the death of a fellow being," Barriss said, sounding slightly stiffer than she had intended. After all these weeks at Rimsoo Seven she was certainly not unfamiliar with the black humor; even so, it occasionally took her somewhat by surprise.

Jos looked at her and shrugged. "Laugh, cry, get tanked, or go mad—those are the options around here. I'll leave you to your own choice—me, I have a mountain to carve." He headed toward the OT, following the gurney.

After he was gone, Zan said, "It gets to you, after a while. You have to develop defenses. I have my music—Jos uses sarcasm. Whatever gets you through the hot nights."

Barriss didn't say anything. She knew he was right, but still . . .

Zan sighed. "You know what I regret?"

"What?"

"I just heard a brand-new Hutt joke, and now I can't use it to steam Filba."

She looked at him in surprise, and he grinned at her. After a moment, she smiled back and shook her head.

It was, other than Filba's demise, a quiet day. There was a lull in the fighting, and no medlifters arrived bearing wounded, a welcome rarity.

The activity around Filba's death was exciting enough. The plithvine carried rumors everywhere. As Barriss made her medical rounds in the ward, even the patients knew about it. She overheard the Ugnaughts gossiping: *Yar, the Hutt drank poison. Suicide, f'sure. He beed a spy—it war Filba who blowed up the bota transport, no lie, blood. They were closin' in on 'im, 'e sar it comin' . . .*

Hadn't Admiral Bleyd himself gone to see the Hutt just before Filba had croaked? No doubt it had been to

question him about his activities. He was also stealing
bota, didn't you know? That little reporter, Dhur?—he
was on the Hutt like sleaks on swamp scum, nosing
around, building a case, and Filba was on the verge of
being arrested, and he had taken the poison to avoid being court-martialed and executed . . . and so on.

Barriss didn't add to the gossip; she just listened as
she went about her duties. If the suicide rumor was true,
then it might mean she would be leaving Drongar soon.
Her mission to find out who had been stealing bota
would be over, if it truly had been the Hutt. And from
the talk, it seemed it had. How many thieves, after all,
were likely to be operating at the same time in a small
outfit like this? Filba had been a supply noncom—he
would have had the access. And, while Barriss didn't
like to make sweeping speciesist generalizations, it was
true that Hutts in general were not known for their
honesty and virtue. Filba was a good fit for the crime.

Perhaps *too* good a fit. She could not be sure, because
the Force was not quiescent. Something was still roiling
in its invisible folds, and she did not have the skill to determine exactly what the subtle vibrations portended.
She only knew that the matter was not yet settled.

She had mixed emotions about it all. This war was indeed a situation that called for heavy emotional response, and she had been on a lot more pleasant worlds,
that was for certain. But it was all part of her test, her
path to Jedi Knighthood—and if she was called away,
then what? What would her own future bring? She was
not afraid—her training did not admit many fears—but
it was . . . unsettling.

What would be, would be. It was not up to her.

The day faded into evening, and eventually Barriss
was finished with her medical chores. She decided to

skip dinner and go to her cubicle. Perhaps another session of quiet meditation and deep breathing would shed some light on whatever it was causing those small, but continuing, disturbances in the Force . . .

The camp was quiet as night crept over it. Few people were about; shift change was long past, and most were either eating supper, or resting, or doing whatever it was they did when they weren't working. For the most part, that didn't include taking in the fetid, hot night air.

As Barriss neared the mouth of the alley that led to her quarters, she felt a presence in the shadows. She saw no one, but the Force's prompt was clear and unmistakable—almost the psychic equivalent of a hand on her shoulder.

She stopped. Her hand moved slowly toward her lightsaber.

"You won't need that," a voice said. "I'm not going to do you any real harm. Just teach you a little lesson in humility. You Jedi are big on that, aren't you?"

Phow Ji.

She still couldn't see him, but she knew where he was. Just over there, in the dark shadow of a quiet power generator, a few meters to her right. He was an evil presence, a pulsing obstruction in the Force's smooth continuum.

Her voice was low and even. "What makes you think you are the person to give lessons in humility?"

Phow Ji glided from the darkness. "Those who can, do. Those who can't, don't."

"Very succinct. What do you want?"

"Like I said—a lesson is required. The last time we chatted, you tripped me. From behind. I owe you a return of the favor. I think a mud bath is only fair. Nothing serious, no broken bones or anything. This is an exercise in reciprocity, nothing more. If your Force can stop me, then by all means"—he held his arms wide in a beckoning gesture—"use it."

What an egotist he was! So convinced in his own mind that he was unbeatable. And that he was so good he could humiliate her without hurting her—there was a real challenge for a fighter.

She briefly considered touching his mind with a subliminal suggestion that he didn't really want to do this, that what he wanted was go back to his quarters and take a cold shower—but she could feel the discipline of his thoughts. They were a dense weave, as impenetrable as spin-worm silk. Ji was not weak-minded enough for a Padawan's ability to sway him easily, if at all.

Ji settled into a stance, legs planted low and wide. He raised his hands, beckoned with one in a flippant gesture. "Come, Jedi. Shall we dance a little?"

I shouldn't be doing this. I should refuse and walk away. Let him think I'm afraid—what does it matter?

But he should respect the Jedi, even if he didn't respect her. It sat poorly with her to hear the name of her Order coated with contempt.

She stayed where she was.

She shifted her weight slightly, not moving her feet, just balancing herself so that she could push quickly with either leg, forward or back.

The evening was muggy; everything was damp, even the air. Her perspiration had nowhere to go; it gathered and rolled down her face and neck, soaked into her jumpsuit, threatened to drip into her eyes.

Ji smiled. "Good move. You don't want to be committed one way or the other when facing a skilled opponent."

He circled to his right, and Barriss moved away from him, maintaining a wary distance.

The temptation to reach for the Force, to use it to flatten Ji, was almost overwhelming. She had no doubt she could do it. One gesture, and Ji would fly into the nearest tree like a rabid rockbat. No fighter, no matter what his physical strength, could pit muscle against the Force and prevail. Maybe she couldn't control his mind, but she could control his body. This she knew.

She would win the battle if she did it. But, she knew, she might lose the war. Ji had told her he had no plans to harm her. He wanted to knock her sprawling into the mud, to embarrass her, but that was the extent of it. She sensed no darker, baser purpose than that. Nothing would be greatly damaged, save her dignity—which was, of course, his point. Ji's driving energy was control, and right now, he wanted, needed, to control her.

To use the Force against an opponent when you were in no real danger was wrong. She had been taught so all her life. The Force was not something to spend like a token in a sweets shop simply because you could. Neither was it solely a weapon.

So what was left? Her own fighting skills. These were not inconsiderable—Jedi were trained in all manner of disciplines, both mental and physical, and the Masters knew there were times when use of the Force was not appropriate. Even without activating her lightsaber, she was someone to be reckoned with.

Of course, her self-defense skills had not been designed to deal with a champion martial artist—what were the odds of ever encountering such a situation? Especially when he didn't intend to seriously injure or kill her?

She would have smiled at that thought another time. The odds didn't really matter when the reality stood two steps away, facing you and ready to attack.

There was always the option of using the lightsaber. Ji would, of course, consider it a breach of combat rules. That didn't matter to her, but she was concerned that the drawing of the energy blade might spur him to attack more viciously. A Jedi Knight or Master would have the skills to stop him without injuring him, but as a Padawan, she was not confident in her ability to do so. She might wind up killing him—and she did not want that on her conscience.

She had already determined that his would be the first move. If Phow Ji was waiting for her to attack him, he'd be waiting for a long—

He leapt, covering the two strides separating them with phenomenal speed. Barriss barely had enough time to dodge, twist to her left, and block, so that his punch glanced off her shoulder, instead of connecting with her solar plexus.

She backed away, keeping her guard up.

"Excellent," he said. "You have very good reflexes. But you should have counterattacked. Pure defense is a losing strategy."

By acting as a teacher with a student, she knew, he was trying to show his superiority—as if he needed to demonstrate that.

Ji circled the opposite way, moving his hands up and down and around in an almost hypnotic weave, trying to draw her attention.

His hands didn't matter. It was his feet she had to watch. To get close enough to her to attack successfully, he had to step, had to move in. He could wave his hands around all day as far as she was concerned. When he moved his feet, then she would have to—

He came in again, and this time, instead of moving out of his path, Barriss slid forward to meet him. But she dropped very low, below his center of gravity, firing a hard punch at his belly as his strike sailed over her head. She hit him, but it was like punching a wall—there was no give. His abdominals were like ridged plasteel.

She scooted out of range as fast as she could, but not fast enough. She caught a slap on the left side of her neck as she retreated, hard enough to make her vision flare red for an instant.

She gained two steps away, and he turned to face her again.

"Very good, Padawan! Not the best target, but a clean strike. You'll need more than one, though. Think combinations—high, low, multiple attacks."

Her neck stung, but the pain was small, and no damage done. The Force sang within her, and she could barely keep from using its power. The dark side was always there, her Master had told her; always waiting for an opportunity to be set loose. Give in once, it would be twice as powerful the next time. Give in again, and you might be lost forever.

Oh, but she wanted to *show* him—wanted to knock that gloating smirk from his face and replace it with awe, with amazement, with . . .

. . . fear . . .

Too much thinking, she realized too late. Ji leapt in again and, in a fast series of open-hand techniques, slapped her head, her torso, and her hip. The last hit was coupled with a foot hooked around her ankle. Barriss went down, hard, and the wet ground was only a little forgiving as she slammed into it.

Whatever might have happened next, as she scrambled back up into a defensive stance, was interrupted by the too-familiar drone of lifters arriving. People came boiling out of their quarters, heading for their stations.

Those who noticed Ji and Barriss at all spared them little more than a glance.

"I think we're done," Ji said. "My point has been made."

Barriss said nothing—she did not trust herself to. Her rage enveloped her like the mud. She trembled under the weight of it. She could feel the dark side surging within her, whispering to her of how *good* it would feel, how *easy* it would be to let her rage fuel it and send it ravening for her enemy, to seize her lightsaber, leap after him and bisect him with a single downward slash of the singing energy blade . . .

Phow Ji had no idea how close to dying he was just then. Her rage was such that a flicker of a finger would suffice. *He'd never know what hit him*—and it would even be justice, in a fashion—was he not, after all, a killer?

Yes, he was—but Barriss Offee was not. It was one of the hardest things she'd ever done, but she did it—she resisted the dark side. She lost the battle, but won the war.

This time . . .

25

Admiral Bleyd paced. The chill he felt in his spine seemed as cold as interstellar space. He had immediately regretted crushing the spycam disguised as an insect; had he simply kept it, he might have been able to backwalk the guidance system memory and find out where it had come from. As it was, all he had for certain was the knowledge that somebody was spying on either Filba or him. Given the nature of the device, the operator could be anybody within ten kilometers of the camp. Maybe Black Sun had an operative here? Or maybe it was one of his own people . . .

Bleyd growled deep in his throat. *Somebody* had poisoned Filba, the autopsy had confirmed that, and Bleyd was not a believer in coincidences that large. The Hutt is murdered and there just happens to be a miniature spycam there to witness it? The probability of it wasn't quite as high as that of a rogue planetoid smashing into Drongar in the next five minutes—but it wasn't far behind. No, the two events were surely linked.

Filba had enemies, of course, and it could be possible that one had just happened to choose this time to repay an old debt, and then used the spycam to make sure it went down smoothly. But whoever had done it, and for whatever reasons, that person now had information linking the dead Hutt with Bleyd in a criminal enterprise. No matter how he scanned it, that was bad. He had to find out who it was, get whatever recording there might be, and eliminate it—along with whoever had it.

He considered the possibility that it might be one of the enemy, but quickly dismissed the notion. It did not seem likely that a Separatist spy had managed to sneak into camp, poison Filba, and then hurry back to hide out in the marsh among the slitherers and saw grass, and watch it happen via the spycam. And what spy would have any interest in the goings-on at a Rimsoo? Nothing strategic happened here, save for the occasional shipment of bota. It was true that one of the transports had blown up, and, while there was no reason to assume Filba had anything to do with it, the rumor floating about the unit was that he had. Filba had been as warped as an event horizon—a fact that had evidently been fairly common knowledge. That could serve him, since he had been keeping the Hutt in reserve in case something went wrong with their black-market operation. He could have blamed the big slug for everything, and then Filba could have had an "accident" before his trial. And now . . .

Now that he was no longer around, it would be even easier to make him the scape-Drall for any illegalities that might turn up.

Bleyd stopped pacing and smiled. Yes. This could turn out to be an advantage after all. Even a killer storm watered the garden.

But if the spycam's operator was in the camp, as Bleyd suspected, *that* was a bantha of a different color. He—or she, or it—might seek to use the information against Bleyd—and that, of course, could not be allowed.

So. The hunter had evidence of prey. Bleyd bared his teeth. Let the tracking begin . . .

*   *   *

Den Dhur went where he usually went to work out his problems—the cantina. But even sitting there in the semidarkness, feeling the damp sluggish air, reluctantly stirred by the circulators, sliding over him like hot oil, he barely sipped at his drink. Now was not the time to dull his perceptions or his wits. Such as they were.

Filba was history, and so was Den's story—nobody wanted to read an exposé about a dead Hutt on a one-rocket planet. The masses wanted their bread and circuses. A nefarious gangster revealed, captured, and punished—that was the good stuff, that was what sold newsdiscs. But Filba dying of pump failure, or even being poisoned by an old enemy, before he was brought to justice? That wasn't what the readers wanted, not at all.

As he'd suspected, Bleyd had been in on whatever skulduggery had been going with Filba. *That* was a great story—but one he couldn't dare file until he was at least fifty parsecs away, the enmity of angry, crooked, and feral admirals being generally bad for one's health. Still, the stone hidden in the stew was that the admiral knew somebody had seen and heard what had happened just before Filba was shuffled off back to the primordial ooze from whence he'd come. It wasn't the admiral who had poisoned him—Den was fairly sure of that, judging by Bleyd's reactions. Not that it mattered much, since black marketing during wartime was generally considered treason and was punishable by death. At best, even if Den had all kinds of outstanding favors due him from high places—which he didn't—his career would be ruined if this got out while he was still in the same sector as Bleyd; at worst, he'd be quietly executed and spaced.

The first thing he had done after he saw Bleyd crush

the moon moth was feed the receiver unit into a waste disposal unit that turned it into sludge and piped it off into the swamp with the rest of the sewage slurry. He had cursed at the necessity—the unit had not come cheap—but it wasn't worth his life. Besides, without the cam, it wasn't much more than a big flimsiweight while he was here.

The recording from the cam, a disc the size of his little fingernail, was now glued to the back of a wall brace of the south refresher, just a hand-span above the catalytic tanks—not a place where anybody would happen across it, and one where, even if by some miracle it was found, it wouldn't be connected to him. He needed the recording to verify his story, but he didn't need Bleyd finding it and having him shot. As long as he kept his mouth shut, he should be safe enough. Bleyd couldn't know who had been watching, and the admiral wasn't about to start an investigation that might reveal his own complicity in Filba's bootlegging activities.

The only problem was, this meant Den was going to be stuck here on scenic Drongar for a while. Any sudden move to fire thrusters now would certainly throw the hard glare of suspicion on him. If Bleyd were looking for the cam's operator—and you could take it to the First Bank of Coruscant that he was—then anybody from this Rimsoo who tried to leave quickly would probably find himself being brain-scanned, and a reporter would likely have to endure a harsher exam than most. Den had no desire to be turned inside out by a high-ranking official who knew his life was in the balance if his crimes came to light.

Too bad—it was a great story, far better than if only Filba had been implicated. The rabble did so love to see the mighty brought low, and a fleet admiral stealing was the kind of thing that could win a Nova Award, if done right. Poor troops in the field, dying because medicine or some equipment wasn't on hand due to a crooked admiral who was filling his vault? Ah, the teeming trillions would love that. They would scream for Bleyd's head on a force pike.

But if he moved too soon he could get turned into fertilizer, and if there was one thing this planet didn't need, it was more fertilizer. Not to mention how much *he* didn't need it.

No, he would just have to stick it out. Find another story to justify his being here. Maybe something with Phow Ji, that fighter who'd slaughtered the mercenaries? It wouldn't be too comfortable having him irritated at you, either, but at least Den could get some protection from the higher-ups, Ji being only a lieutenant. Yeah. That would keep the pot boiling long enough for him to eventually jet this swamp world. Once he was on the other side of the Core, then he could bring low the mighty Admiral Bleyd for his audience.

Black Market Admiral Revealed! Associate in crime dies mysteriously!

Den smiled. He *did* love a thrilling headline.

He took a bigger sip of his drink. Problem raised, problem solved. Another victory for crack reporter Den Dhur, speaking to you live from the Jasserak Front in the Clone Wars . . .

26

There were times, during her meditations, when Barriss slipped from her concentration, drifted from being-in-the-moment and into memory. In earlier years, she had never been sure whether this was a good thing or not; then she had learned to simply accept that it was what it was. True, it was not conducive to the purpose of achieving a clear mind, but sometimes the past offered insight into the present; therefore sometimes she went with it.

And so it was tonight. Because she was still troubled by the strong feelings she'd had during the fight with Phow Ji the night before, when the memory arose unbidden she let it take her where it would . . .

It had been a sunny but cool morning on Coruscant. No rain was due in this sector for another day, and the slidewalk leading to the park was busy, but not too crowded, as she and Master Unduli reached the designated greenbelt. The other beings also on their way to the large patch of nature represented an amazing variety of sentients: Nikto, Phindians, Zeltrons, Wookiees, Twi'leks . . . a fascinating glimpse of the galaxy's infinite diversity, all headed for Oa Park. There was much ferrocrete and metal on this world—some said too much—and parks were dotted here and there to help those who wished more contact with nature achieve it. Oa Park contained within its boundaries more than thirty different environments simulating various other worlds, each with its own atmospheric mix, solar spectrum, and gravity field, separated from each other by energy boundaries.

On such a bright morning, in the middle of smiling and laughing folk going to enjoy the multifarious flora and landscapes and streams, the dark side seemed far, far away to Barriss. But even as that thought crossed her mind, as she and her Master stood in the shade of a four-hundred-year-old blackneedle tree three meters thick and two hundred meters tall, Master Unduli had smiled and said, "The dark side is always at hand, Padawan. It is no farther away than a heartbeat, an eye-blink, side by side with the bright side of the Force, separated by no more than a hair. It waits to snare the unwary, wearing a thousand disguises."

Barriss had heard that before, many times, and she believed what her teacher said, but she had never really felt or understood exactly what it meant. She had not been tempted by the dark side, as far as she knew. She said as much, as they moved to a quiet spot where the grasses had been engineered to grow short and soft, like a living carpet. "We'll do the Salutation here," her Master said.

Barriss nodded. She moved to one side a bit to give her Master space.

"To answer your question, let me offer this: every conscious move you make, from the smallest to the largest, requires choice. There is always a branch in the path, and you must decide upon which turning you will tread. Do you recall the testings of your ability to sense a remote while wearing blinders?"

"Of course." This was among the most basic of Jedi

skills. A remote was a small levitating droid about the size of a goldfruit that could be programmed to zip about and fire mild electric bolts at a student. With a blast helmet on and the blinders down, the only way to know the position of the orb was to use the Force. As a student progressed in the use of his or her lightsaber, blocking the remote's bolts became a standard exercise. Since you couldn't use your eyes or ears to track the device, the only way to avoid being shocked was to let the Force guide your hands.

Her Master continued: "And were there not instances when your use of the Force was less than perfect and the training bolts got past your lightsabor?"

"Far too many of those instances," Barriss said ruefully. She shook her head. "At times, I felt like a needle cushion!"

"And did you ever feel during those times like destroying the remote? Reaching out with the Force and crushing it like a wad of scrap flimsi?"

As she spoke, Master Unduli began the Salutation to the Force, a combination exercise and meditative posture that started with a body arch upward, followed by a deep squat and leg-extended stretch to the rear.

Barriss copied her Master's pose. "I confess there were occasions when I had little love for the training device, yes."

"And did you have sufficient skill in use of the Force to have destroyed it, had you chosen to do so?" Master Unduli stood and repeated the pose, ending on the other leg. Again, Barriss copied her.

"Yes. Easily."

"Why didn't you? If the goal was to protect yourself from being shocked, would that not have been justifiable?"

Barriss frowned. "But that was not the goal. The goal was to learn how to attune my lightsaber with the Force so that I could stop the bolts from striking me. The shocks were painful, but without any lasting damage. In a real fight, with a full-charge blaster bolt coming at me, if I could not block that, I might not have the power to stop a shooter fifty or a hundred meters away from pulling the trigger."

"Precisely. But did you know that one student in eight does eventually reach out to destroy a remote? That they usually justify it by saying it is more efficient to stop the source of the damaging bolts than to endlessly deflect them? Laser Pose, please."

Her Master lay upon the soft grass, rolled up onto her neck and shoulders, and extended her body skyward, her hands on the ground at her sides.

Barriss also assumed the Laser Pose. "I can certainly understand how they might feel that way. And it makes a certain logical sense, especially given the premise in our hand-to-hand combat training that says pure defense is inferior to a combination of defense and offense."

"Indeed. Arch Pose."

Hands and feet on the ground, Master Unduli pushed upward and formed her body into a high, rounded arch.

"I hear a 'but,'" Barriss said as she followed suit.

"And I see that yours could be higher from the ground."

Barriss smiled and pushed herself into a more acute arch. Her Master continued: "Many of the exercises Jedi in training must learn—and Jedi are *always* in training, be they Padawan, Knight, or Master—involve determining what the true goal of the exercise is. You will recall the levitation drill and the bakery."

"As if I could forget that one."

"To destroy the remote is, in itself, not necessarily a wrong choice. If you have developed sufficient skill to block the training bolts and you arrive at the decision through logic and with a calm mind, then you can justify using the Force to stop the attack at its source. Some of the more gifted students do just that. But if you do it out of anger, or pain, or fear, or any emotion that you have allowed to control you, then you reach for the dark side. If you offer that the end justifies the means without mindful thought to determine that it indeed does, you have succumbed to the insidious energy. If you remember nothing else from this talk, Barriss, remember this: *Power wants to be used.* It must be kept under constant vigil, else it will seduce and corrupt you. One moment you're swatting an annoying training toy; the next you're paralyzing an offending being's lungs and choking him to death. You do it because you *can*. It becomes an end in itself. As a Jedi, you live always on this edge. A single misstep, and you can fall to the dark side. It has happened to many, and it is always a tragedy. As with an addictive drug, it's too easy to say, 'I'll do it just this once.' That's not how it works. The only thing that stands between you and the dark side is your own will and discipline. Give in to your anger or your fear, your jealousy or your hate, and the dark side claims you for its own. If that happens," Master Unduli said, "you will become an enemy to all that the Jedi stand for—and an enemy of all Jedi who hold to the path of right. Rocker Pose, please."

Barriss moved to assume the pose. She said, "And have you ever given in to the dark side, Master?"

For a few seconds, there was silence. Then: "Yes. In a moment of weakness and pain, I did. It allowed me to survive when I might have perished otherwise, but that one taste was enough for me to realize I could never do it again. There may come a time when you experience this, Barriss. I hope not, but if ever it happens, you *must* recognize and resist it."

"It will feel evil?"

Master Unduli paused in her stretch. She regarded Barriss with what seemed to be great sadness in her eyes. "Oh, no. It will feel better than anything you have ever experienced, better than you would have thought anything could feel. It will feel empowering, fulfilling, satisfying. Worst of all, it will feel *right*. And therein lies the real danger."

Now, on a planet many parsecs away from Coruscant, in a Rimsoo medical facility, Master Unduli's words on that sunny and cool morning came back to Barriss with renewed clarity and, perhaps, a better understanding. She had been tempted to destroy Phow Ji. He had been no real threat, save to her pride, and she had almost justified it by telling herself that his attack had been a threat to the honor of the Jedi Order. That would have been a lie, of course—the Jedi Order was not threatened by Ji's attack any more than she personally had been. But how close she had come to using that as her rationalization for taking a life!

In a very real way, she realized that she owed a debt of gratitude to Phow Ji. Ironically, his presence here in her life was instructive, was an opportunity for her to learn how to resist the temptation of the dark side. If there was a purpose to all things—if, as the core tenets of the Jedi Code stated, the galaxy was indeed unfolding as it should—then Phow Ji had his destiny to fulfill, even as she had hers.

Barriss took a deep breath, exhaled slowly. Master Unduli had been right—she did indeed walk a fine line

that had to be watched at all times. It was not an easy
path, but it was the one she had been raised from birth
to tread. Failure was unacceptable, unthinkable. To become a Jedi Knight was her life's goal.

Without the Jedi, she was nothing.

Jos waited until the afternoon shower tapered to
sprinkles before he headed to the refuse bin to dump his
and Zan's trash. Unfortunately, there weren't enough
maintenance droids allocated for that duty, so many
times he either carried his own garbage out to the bins
or it quickly filled up their living quarters. He and Zan
had a side bet for the chore going at the sabacc game,
and even though Jos had walked away the big credit
winner, he had lost the trash bet to Zan, so he was stuck
with the duty all week. And it seemed at times that all
he and Zan did was sit around and generate trash—the
plastiwrap bag he carried had to weigh five kilos and
was barely big enough to zip shut.

He skirted the larger puddles and deeper mud, and
made it to the bin without being drenched, hit by lightning, or attacked by killer Separatist battle droids. The
sensor on the bin dilated the input hatch, and he fed the
bag into the recycler, listened to oscillating power hums
and crunches as the trash was reduced to small bits and
then flash-zapped into greasy ash by the reactors. There
was something curiously satisfying about the process,
although doing it with regularity certainly didn't hold
any appeal.

Another exciting moment from the life of Jos Vondar,
crack Republic surgeon . . .

He turned and nearly bumped into a trooper arriving
at the bin with several bags of refuse. The trooper murmured a respectful apology; Jos acknowledged it and

started to leave, then stopped abruptly. He felt somehow that he knew this one. If he looked past the Jango Fett template, there was something about the eyes, the face . . . he could be wrong, but he was pretty sure it was CT-914, the one who had sparked the question that had, of late, threatened to overwhelm Jos.

"Hello, Nine-one-four," Jos said.

"Hello, Captain Vondar."

"On trash duty, are you?"

"That would seem self-evident, sir." He began to feed the bags into the dilated maw of the bin.

First a droid, Jos thought, *and now a clone, cracking jokes. Everyone's a comedian.*

For a moment he just stood there, unable to think of anything to say—which, for him, was a rarity. Finally, he said, "Let me ask you a question."

CT-914 continued to shove the bags into the bin, which ground and hummed as it ate them.

"How did you feel about the death of CT-Nine-one-five?"

Nine-one-four pushed the last of the bags into the hopper. He looked at Jos. "The loss of a trained soldier is . . . regrettable." Both his speech and bearing were stiff.

Jos knew CT-914 didn't want to pursue this, but he forged ahead anyway. He had to know. "No. I'm not talking about his value to the Republic. I'm asking you how it made *you* feel. You, personally."

CT-914 stood there for what seemed like a long time without speaking. "Were I a civilian," he said at last, "delivered naturally and not vat-born, I could tell you it's none of your business—sir. But since I'm bound to obey my superior officers, then the answer to your question is that I—personally—was pained by Nine-one-five's death. We're all of the same flesh and design, all equal in basic abilities, but he was my comrade in arms. I knew him all my life. We fought together, ate together, and shared our off-duty times like brothers. I miss him. I expect I'll miss him until I die.

"Does that answer your question, sir? I have more trash to collect."

Jos swallowed, his throat suddenly dry. "Yes, that answers it. Thank you."

"Just doing my duty, Doctor. No thanks necessary."

CT-914 turned and walked away, and Jos watched him go, unable to move. Inside his mind, the tiny voice he was growing to hate piped up again and said, *You ought to know by now not to ask questions you don't really want answered.*

No kidding. If they were all like CT-914, then clone troopers were much more mentally complex than Jos had thought. They had feelings, inner lives, maybe even dreams and aspirations that reached beyond the art of war. And *that* shifted things into a realm Jos didn't want to think about.

Blast.

27

Though the action was unusual, Admiral Bleyd found sufficient reason to delay his departure from Rimsoo Seven for a few days. He offered as a reason his belief that the matter of the murdered Hutt needed further investigation, and his desire to make certain his people were protected. It might have seemed a thin excuse to anyone with more than a few working brain cells, but that didn't matter—he was the admiral, and no one would question his decisions.

The real reason for him staying, of course, was to find the one who had dared to surveille him. Whoever it was, he would soon learn how dangerous it could be to spy on a predator.

They erected a command module for him, not much more than a bubble with some basic furniture and comm gear, but it was enough. For someone who had hunted many times on planets where there was nothing to sleep on but the cold, hard ground, a formcot was more than he needed.

The morning after Filba's death, Bleyd was on his way to meet a transport bringing in the head of his military security unit to take charge of the search for Filba's killer. The man was late, and Bleyd hoped—for his sake—that he would have a good reason. As he strode through the camp, the mud from the near-constant storms caking his boots, he noticed one of The Silent drifting in his direction. Even in the cloying heat and humidity, the figure had his cowl up, his face hidden in its shadows. There were a few members of this particular order on the planet at various Rimsoos, offering their presence for whatever good it might be. The Silent would pass close to him, though their paths would not quite intersect.

As the figure drew near, Bleyd noticed a peculiar odor coming from it. It was not unpleasant—in fact, it had a heady, almost spiceflower-like aroma, noticeable even over the fecund stenches of the nearby swamp. Offhand, he knew of no species that carried this particular scent. He filed it away for later consideration as The Silent passed. He had more important things on his mind.

The head of the security unit was Colonel Kohn Doil, a Vunakian human with a pattern of ritual scars on his forehead, cheeks, and depilated head. The geometric whorls and configurations of the raised cicatrices, which signified caste status, were amazingly intricate. Bleyd knew that Doil had not used a pain inhibitor during the scarification ceremony; it was one of the reasons he had hired the man. A unit commander with a high pain threshold was not a bad combination.

Doil alighted from the transport, saluted, and apologized for the delay in his arrival. "A vortex storm hit the main camp just before I was due to depart; the wind wrecked the transport on the pad, along with a goodly portion of the supply prefabs and trooper barracks."

"No need to apologize for the weather on this forsaken planet, Colonel. But let us waste no more time. I know you have the facts of the case, and the autopsy report showing the poison used, but since I was there when the Hutt died, I thought I should brief you personally."

"I appreciate that, Admiral," Doil said as they walked back through the camp. "If I might be so bold as to ask, how did that come to pass? That you happened to be there?"

"I had heard certain rumors about Filba that I found disturbing. I suspected that he might have been responsible for a black-market operation, and maybe even for the destruction of the bota transport not long ago. In short, I feared he was either an illegal entrepreneur or a Separatist spy."

"Ah. You think it was suicide, then? Fear of being caught and disgraced?"

Bleyd did not want to appear too eager to lay that hypothesis before the colonel. Doil was an adept security officer, and it would be better if he came to the conclusion on his own. "Possible, of course. It might also be that the Hutt had a confederate who saw that we suspected his partner and decided to eliminate him. Hutts are not well known for their bravery under pressure."

Doil said, "Sir. Hutts are not known for their bravery under any circumstances. It would seem most unusual, however, for there to be a spy in a medical unit in the middle of nowhere, much less two of them."

Bleyd shrugged. "As you say. Better to consider all the possibilities, however."

"Yes, sir."

"I expect you'll need to find quarters before beginning your investigation. I shall remain here for a few days, to offer what help I can. Feel free to call upon me as necessary."

"Sir." Doil saluted, then set off to find Vaetes and arrange for his new lodgings.

As Bleyd headed back to his own quarters, he considered the situation yet again. He knew that Filba hadn't poisoned himself. The Hutt had thought that Bleyd could protect him—that he *would* protect him—and he was too much the coward to ever snuff his own greasy flame. No, somebody had murdered the slug, and under the Rule of Simple Solutions, it was likely that whoever had done that was the same one who had been spying upon them. But why? Bleyd shook his head. That was another question. Better to first determine the "Who" and then worry about the "Why."

As he opened the door to his bubble, a spicy floral smell wafted over him. Without even thinking Bleyd drew his blaster.

"Move and I'll cook you where you stand," he said.

"I won't move, Admiral. Though I'm not standing at the moment."

The voice had a musical and amused lilt to it. Bleyd passed his free hand in front of the room's lighting control and the hut's interior lit up, revealing the figure of a Silent—obviously a disguise, since by speaking he had broken the siblinghood's most sacred tenet. The robed and cowled being sat on Bleyd's cot, leaning against the wall.

Bleyd did not lower the blaster. "Who are you? What are you doing here?"

"If I may?" The other raised his hands slowly to the sides of his head.

Bleyd nodded. "Slowly, and with great care."

The figure slipped the cowl back to reveal his face.

It was not the countenance of any being Bleyd had ever seen before, and he had been around the galaxy more than a few times. The face was vaguely birdlike, with sharp, violet eyes, a nose and mouth that could have been a short beak, and pale blue skin that might be either extremely fine fur or feathers; Bleyd could not tell which from where he stood. The head was smooth, the ears flat and set close against the skull, and there was a hint of darker blue at the base of the throat. Quite striking, the admiral thought; he had certainly seen more unattractive bipeds.

The being smiled—Bleyd assumed he was male—and there were at least several pointed teeth in the thin-lipped beak-mouth. The beak seemed to be formed of rubbery cartilaginous material rather than keratin, which gave it a limited range of expression.

There was also more than a hint of danger glinting in those eyes. This was a deadly creature, whatever its origins or intentions.

"I am Kaird, of the Nediji."

Nediji? Nediji . . . he had heard the name . . . ah, yes, he remembered it now. An avian species from a far-flung world called Nedij on the east spinward arm. Bleyd frowned. There was something else unusual about them . . . what was it . . . ?

"I didn't realize the Nediji traveled outside their own system. I seem to recall hearing that such journeying was taboo."

"If one is properly nested, yes, that is true," the Nediji replied. His melodious voice was as pleasant to hear as his scent was to whiff, but the cold, calculating look in those eyes was all Bleyd cared about. As in most species, the truth could always be found in the eyes.

"But there are some among us who, for one reason or another, cannot be of The Flock," Kaird continued. "No one cares where the winds bear us." There was no regret in the words; what Bleyd heard instead was amusement.

"Well, here, we *do* care if somebody breaks into our quarters. Explain yourself—quickly." He gestured slightly with the blaster.

There was a small *click*! behind him, as if someone was trying his closed door. Bleyd shifted his attention to the sound for a heartbeat—

The Nediji vanished.

No, that was not strictly true. The being had moved, but so fast that Bleyd couldn't believe what he was seeing. Of a moment, he was sitting on the cot, and then in an eyeblink he stood next to Bleyd, out of the blaster's line of fire, close enough to touch.

Bleyd started to shift his aim, but stopped. If the fellow could move that swiftly in a one-gravity field, he would never be able to line up on him in time if he had a weapon of his own and wanted to use it.

He lowered the blaster.

"Wise move, Admiral."

Bleyd caught a flash of light on something in the Nediji's hand, then whatever it was disappeared.

"All right," Bleyd said. "You've established that you're faster than a dirt-demon. Though if I hadn't been distracted by that noise—"

Kaird walked back toward the cot, a slow stroll that had definite elements of avian locomotion in it. When he reached it, he turned, flashed his teeth again, and said, "You mean this noise?"

The *click*! came again. Bleyd did not allow it to distract him this time.

Kaird held up a small device the size of his thumb—the thing that had caught the light a moment before. He had yellowish talons on his fingertips, Bleyd noticed. "A simple clicker, operated by this remote."

"Fine. You came prepared. What do you want?"

"The continuation of our mutual benefit, Admiral. Apparently our last agent was careless in his piloting. I am a much better flier. In the genes, you know."

Bleyd felt a small but definite surge of fear. *Black Sun!* He hadn't expected them so soon.

"Ah," he said.

"Indeed," Kaird said.

As it turned out, Kaird was a surprise on more than one level. Apparently, Black Sun did *not* want to change its former arrangement regarding the bota. It took Bleyd but a moment to realize that Mathal, the agent whom he had dispatched to the Realm Beyond, had been up to some "business" of his own. Kaird's purpose was to investigate Mathal's death, which he had done to his satisfaction while disguised as one of The Silent, and to assure that the flow of bota stayed constant. Supply and demand kept the value very high, and moving a small amount of material for a large profit was better than moving large amounts at a lesser rate, which was what Bleyd had figured all along. So Mathal's real intention had been to grab as much bota as he could, then flee before his superiors in the criminal organization found out. How interesting.

Had Black Sun known what its late agent had been up to, they would likely have taken care of him themselves, Bleyd realized. He'd done them a favor. But he wasn't about to volunteer how Mathal had met his end—that would be suicide.

Despite his resolve to avoid such daring ventures, Bleyd was immediately beset with the idea of testing himself against the new agent. The Nediji was much faster than he was, and tricky as well. No doubt he was well trained in many combat arts. Avian predators would have a different way of viewing prey than those

who were ground-bred. Here was a foe worthy of
Bleyd's mettle.

But—no. If he were to die with his family honor tar-
nished, he would have failed in his life goal. Not to
mention losing that palace on Coruscant. No matter
how tempting such a confrontation was, he had to resist. He could give the Nediji no more thought in this
regard.

Still, it would be a glorious fight . . .

"I will remain in the camp for a few days," Kaird
said, "pretending to be of The Silent, observing the doctors and patients, so as not to arouse suspicion by leaving too soon. This business with the Hutt—your
doing?"

Bleyd considered his reply for a moment. He did not
need a Black Sun operative poking around in his business any more than was absolutely necessary. If the
Nediji believed he had poisoned Filba, he would give it
no more thought. "Yes. He was becoming greedy. I
thought it best to remove him before he caused problems."

"Wise. We like prudent beings in our partnerships."
The bird-being turned toward the door. "We will be in
touch, Admiral. Until then, keep following the original
plan agreed upon by you and my superiors."

"Understood."

Once Kaird had gone, Bleyd felt a sense of relief. The
loss of Black Sun's hot breath on his back was one less
worry with which he had to deal.

Now, if he could just find the spy, all would be well
once again.

28

The spy was not surprised to see one of The Silent standing in the hard shade next to the medical ward. There hadn't been any assigned to the Rimsoo in the last few months, but where there were doctors and suffering, the presence of The Silent was always a possibility. They lived only to serve their vision of helping the sick or injured, simply by being there. There would seem on the face of it no scientific basis for their belief, but it was well known that when one of The Silent took up residence at a medical facility, mortality figures dropped more often than not, and length of hospital stays somehow shortened. Some said it was merely placebo effect, but there were cases in which ill patients did not know one of The Silent was about, and they still tended to get better faster. A strange phenomenon, no question about it. Perhaps it had something to do with the Force; perhaps it was something entirely different. But it had been documented too often to be dismissed.

While seeing The Silent there was not a surprise, hearing the whisper from the cowled figure: "We need to talk, Lens," *was* startling. Almost startling enough to draw a visible reaction.

The spy was too well trained to give anything away, and there was no one else around, in any event. The code name *Lens* provided all the information necessary to know what, if not who, the being disguised as a Silent was. The disguise was unexpected and clever.

The spy had two code names on this world—one for the Separatists, and the second for the underworld organization Black Sun. To the latter, the spy was known as "Lens."

Anybody who spoke that name aloud could only have gotten it from Black Sun, and they didn't give such information to anybody but their own.

"My quarters, ten minutes," Lens said, lips unmoving.

When the agent from Black Sun arrived, precisely ten minutes later, in the cubicle, Lens was there and ready to deal with him. That an agent had been sent here was also not a surprise. Lens had information he or she wanted.

The cowl lowered. Lens saw that the face belonged to a Nediji, and that brought a smile. Another good choice for Black Sun. Few knew of the outfar avian species, and fewer still all that they were capable of. They were fast, ruthless, and clever, and there were only a relative handful of them outside their own system, so their talents were unlikely to be well known. Lens knew, of course. A kind of kinship, albeit not one of blood or genetics, existed between the two species.

"I am Kaird."

Lens nodded. To the Nediji's credit, he did not seem worried that his being here might be a problem. He assumed that Lens would not have invited him to private quarters if that was the case. But Lens volunteered it, just to be sure they were on the same trail: "Unlikely that anyone will ask you anything, but if they ask me, I have decided to write a monograph on the effect of The Silent upon patients in a war zone."

The Nediji nodded, eyes bright and sharp. He said, "I understand there was a death in the family here recently."

Lens nodded. "The Hutt was more useful to us dead than alive." As Black Sun's operative on this world, Lens had been given information pertaining to their operation here. That included knowing about Filba, the deal he'd had with the admiral, and the recent loss of the courier sent here to check on the bota.

Kaird cocked his head to one side. "Your doing?"

Lens nodded. "Of course. Who else? You are aware that I have . . . other duties, and that these do not conflict with my responsibilities to Black Sun. Filba was becoming greedy and erratic. His death was only a matter of time, and by hastening it, a certain measure of protection for my position here was provided."

"Interesting," Kaird said.

"You disapprove?"

"Not at all. You are here because our organization has trust in your abilities. As long as things get done, how you manage it is not our concern. It's just that I had a chance to speak with our partner here a short while ago, and it is the admiral's claim that *he* had the Hutt rendered inert."

Lens frowned. "Why would he say that?"

"An excellent question. One I feel I should find the answer to before I leave this world."

Lens nodded again. "And what of my mission?"

"The same as before. How goes the charting?"

"Slow, but steady. I have locations for all the major bota fields in this quadrant, many of them in the adjacent quadrants, and several wild patches on the opposite side of the planet that so far have not been officially logged. Nor will they be, unless by accident. I have caused the records to show those locations scanned and found empty of the plant."

"Excellent. When the Separatists or the Republic finally triumph, we are prepared to deal with either one regarding the bota. If there are unknown sources, so much the better. The more information we have, the stronger our position."

Lens smiled. "You don't care who wins, do you?"

The Nediji smiled also, a thin-lipped, wicked expression. "This bothers you because you have chosen a side."

Lens said nothing.

Kaird continued, "There will always be vices that need to be fed. Wars come, wars go, but business continues. Political systems change; people don't. Ten thousand years ago, people drank or inhaled or ate intoxicants, gambled, and dealt in matters of the black market. Ten thousand years from now, they will still do these things, no matter who rules. Even if Black Sun founders, there will always be somebody who will arise to fulfill these desires."

"And to make a fat profit."

"Of course. You know the works of the philosopher Burdock?"

Lens did not and said so.

"Burdock said, 'Face it—if crime did not pay, there would be very few criminals.' "

"Most criminals wind up in prison," Lens said. "Because most are not very bright."

"True. Which makes the smart ones all the richer. Black Sun does not suffer the stupid." Kaird smiled again. "You have the new information encoded?"

"Yes. It's on an implant chip." Lens removed a dome-shaped nub the size of a man's fingernail from a drawer and held it up. Inside the clear plastoid nub, the chip was the size of a small, sharp-tipped eyelash. "Put the flat end against your skin and twist the other end for a subcutaneous injection. Remember where, because it is undetectable by anything short of a doppraymagno scanner."

"Always a pleasure doing business with a professional," Kaird said. He stood. "We won't speak again while I am here. Perhaps someday we will meet in another time and place, Lens. Until then, live well."

Lens nodded. "Fly free, fly straight, Brother of the Air."

That surprised the Nediji, as Lens knew it would. He raised a feathery eyebrow. "You know the Nest Blessing. I'm impressed."

Lens gave him a slow, military nod, a small bow. "Knowledge is power."

"Indeed it is."

After he was gone, Lens sat for a moment, thinking. Why Bleyd had claimed Filba's death as his doing was, as Kaird had said, interesting, but the Nediji would sort that out, and Lens need not worry over it. The admiral's fate was of no real concern. Lens had much bigger quarry to bring down. What, after all, did a single admiral matter when you were after the entire Republic?

29

As Barriss entered the main medical facility to make her rounds, she noticed that the droid on duty was the same one that had aided her during triage—the same droid that had been in the sabacc game a few nights ago. I-Five. The droid with which Jos had discussed the essentials of being human.

She watched him for a moment. He was changing the bacta fluid in a tank. He moved with the economical precision of a droid, and yet, something was subtly different. She'd noticed the same thing about his face—it seemed almost capable of expression at times. Curious, she reached out to him with the Force. Ethereal tendrils, unseen and insubstantial, but no less effective for that, enveloped the droid's form, seeking knowledge and relaying it back to her. There was no sensory analog to describe how she received and processed the Force's data—those who were not sensitive to it could no more comprehend it than one blind from birth could comprehend sight. But to Barriss it spoke loud and clear.

Initially there seemed to be nothing unusual about I-Five. She could sense the almost undetectable susurrus of countless quarks and bosuns shifting spin and polarity, providing the synaptic grid with nearly unlimited potential connections. She could feel the hum of circuitry, the smooth pulse of hydraulic fluid, and the restrained power of the servos. The droid was well made, even though some of his parts were old.

But there did seem to be something else . . . something too subtle even to be called an aura. The merest hint that somehow, in a way unexplainable by scientific methods, the sum of I-Five was greater than his parts.

"May I be of assistance, Padawan Offee?"

He had asked the question without turning around. He had sensed her somehow; the most probable way was with his olfactory sensor, which was many times more sensitive than most organics'. He had smelled her.

"Merely here to make my rounds," she said, stepping forward. "Some patients whom I have been able to help."

I-Five turned to face her. "With the Force."

"Yes."

"I knew a Padawan, a female human approximately your age, on Coruscant. Her name was Darsha Assant." He seemed disturbed by this recounting.

Barriss nodded. "I've heard of her. Obi-Wan Kenobi says she died bravely, battling an unknown foe."

I-Five was silent for a moment. "Bravery," he said at last. "Yes. She was very brave. You humans are known for your courage throughout the galaxy. Even the most warlike of species respect it. Did you know that?"

"I hadn't really given it that much thought. There are a great many species who are as brave or braver than humans, I should imagine."

"Yes. But there is a crucial difference between your kind and a Sakiyan, say, or a Trandoshan, or a Nikto. They are fearless, but not necessarily brave. Fearlessness is encoded in their genes. There are two ways that life ensures survival of the fittest—by producing war-

rior types fierce enough to conquer all in their path, or
by creating life-forms that have the sense to run away.
Those capable of both are rare. You humans have a
choice—fight or flight. Yet so many times you choose to
fight—and so often for the strangest reasons." I-Five
raised both hands, palms up, in a very human shrug.
"It's fascinating, at times baffling, and often infuriating.
Humans never cease to amaze me."

As they spoke, Barriss took her lightpad from the
rack and started walking down the rows of beds, checking the overhead monitor stats against the glowing figures appearing on the pad as she entered each bed's
information field. The droid walked alongside her.

"You and Jos were talking about what it is to be human during the game," she said. "Do you consider
yourself brave, I-Five?"

"Somehow I doubt that anyone who is really brave
considers himself brave. I don't believe Padawan Assant
did."

They walked down the narrow aisle between the two
rows of beds. Nearly all of them were occupied by
clone troopers; the same face multiplied over and over.
Only the injuries were different.

I-Five said, "I've been told that the troops have also
been genetically modified to feel little or no fear on the
battlefield. One can't help but wonder—does eliding the
'fear gene' make them less human?"

Barriss did not answer; she was suddenly occupied
with watching the last piece of a puzzle fall into place.
She knew that Jos had been wrestling with some sort of
existential conundrum for the past few days, and, with
the surety of those connected to the Force, she suddenly
knew that this was it. Jos, like most people—even some
Jedi—had compartmentalized those around him into

comfortable slots—comfortable for him, anyway. For him, clones had been dumped into the same category as droids—the only difference being that they were made of flesh and bone instead of durasteel and electronics. It had been convenient to view them with such detachment; it made it easier to accept it when he was unable to save one on the table, though he still took it pretty hard. He was not the sort to be callous or indifferent to any life, even that of someone most considered an organic automaton.

But then, along comes I-Five, a fully cognizant machine, or at least extremely close, and suddenly life isn't so easily dealt with. If Jos couldn't mentally segregate a droid into something less than human, then he certainly couldn't fit clones into that category.

No wonder he'd seemed shaken up lately. His view of life had been wrenched.

A hand with a vibroscalpel needed to be steady. She should speak to him. Or at least make sure he spoke to the minder.

And yet—what words of wisdom could *she* offer to quiet his turmoil? Was she so certain of life in all its manifestations that she could offer a real solution to his problem? Wiser heads than hers had failed to come up with a sustainable philosophy of everything that made the galaxy a neatly packaged place. Who are we? Where do we come from? What does it all mean? She had the Force, a constant upon which she had been able to rely since she could remember, and her knowledge of it had grown stronger over the years. Like the microwave hum of the universe, the Force was always with her. She had a certainty. Those who were unable to feel the comfort of the Force—what did they have?

What could she say to a man who had questions for

which there were no simple answers? And even if he could feel the Force, what did it say about the life of a droid or a clone, or, for that matter, anyone else? The Force was not an instrument of any but the most basic of ethics and morality. There was the light side and the dark side, and those were the choices the Force offered. Education as to the true nature of sentient life? That must come from elsewhere.

Still . . . she was a healer. She could, at times, ease the fury of mental storms. At the very least, a calm mind was a better tool for dealing with such issues. She couldn't answer Jos's questions, but perhaps she could help him find a quiet place in which he could find his own answers. That much she was willing—and happy— to do.

30

The spy was known by two aliases—*Lens* to Black Sun and *Column* to the Separatists. It was the latter identity that sat and frowned at the odd-looking squiggle on the computer's holoproj. To the uninitiated, the little mark might seem nothing more than a flaw in the projector's image resolver. To those in the know, the glitch meant something else entirely.

The spymaster on Drongar had sent yet another of a series of all-too-frequent communications. It was irritating. Of the dozens of coded messages that had been sent, none had yet offered anything of substance. The messages were trivial intelligence, along the lines of "Keep an eye on the bota" . . . useless in general, and a particular waste of time to a field agent in Column's circumstance. It took hours to decode the blasted things, which were Feraleechi onetime loops. In a dull, repetitive, manual process a cipher was partially decoded, using a keyword in the early-morning holonews. This gave a series of numbers that were then keyed to a particular textbook available on the library 'cast, always something so boring that reading it aloud could stop a full-scale cantina riot dead—*Aridian Procedures for Development of Agricultural Fertilizer on Lythos Nine* or some such mindless twaddle. Then it had to be translated from Basic into Symbian, a language dead, but unfortunately not buried, for thirty thousand years, and every sixth word transposed. The end of all this labor was usually a message along the lines of, "How's it going?"

The spymaster must not have much to do, and must be paranoid in the extreme to boot.

Which, Column thought, teetered on the edge of silly. Even if somebody managed to intercept one of the messages—unlikely—and even if they were the best slicer in the galaxy and somehow broke the cipher—unlikelier still—learning the number of cases of Phibian beer delivered to the military canteen at Prime Base last month would hardly be worth the effort.

Column sighed. It was how the Separatists chose to do things, and no there was no help for it. It would have to be done, but not right now. Later.

Much later . . .

Jos moved through the medical section, on his way to see a postop patient who had recently developed a nosocomial infection. The patient was a human male officer, not a clone, and one upon whom both he and Zan had worked for several hours to replace a shrapnel-riddled heart. They had been lucky; five minutes more and they would have lost the man. After such a brilliant surgical triumph, losing him to some waste-hopper secondary bug was simply unacceptable. Even though the Rimsoo was state-of-the-art in sterile procedure and environment, nosocomial infections—contagions picked up while one was hospitalized—still happened now and then. This particular one had been very stubborn, not responding to the usual broad-spectrum antibiotics, and so far they had been unable to culture out and identify it.

The prognosis was dire. Unless they could ID the cause, the officer wasn't going to survive.

When Jos arrived at the isolation chamber, he saw that Zan was already inside the airflow "walls" and sterile zap field that kept pathogens from entering or escaping. Next to the bed, just outside the field, stood a hooded figure, one of The Silent.

Jos had never put much credence in the mute siblinghood's supposed efficacy in aiding patients' recovery rates, but at this point he was not one to turn down anything that might help. And, whether it was some kind of placebo effect, spontaneous healing or remission, or something completely outside Jos's medical experience, the fact was that a Silent's presence at or near a patient's side seemed to speed recuperation. So he nodded at the figure, whose face was hidden in the cowl, as he passed. The Silent nodded back.

Jos stepped into the field, which crackled slightly. Zan started, as if somebody had poked a finger into his back. He looked around, saw Jos, and relaxed. "Oh, it's you."

"Nice to see you, too." Jos noticed that Zan was holding an empty skinpopper.

"Sorry. Just a little on edge."

"I can't imagine why. These days everybody's adrenals are stuck on full throttle." Jos looked down at the unconscious form in the bed. "How's our latest poster boy for the horrors of war doing?"

The patient, one N'do Maetrecis, a major in the army, looked somewhat better than the last time Jos had seen him. His skin had been pale and anhidrotic, but now it was taking on a normal, healthy glow. The flatscreen chart hung on the bed's foot, and Jos picked it up and scanned the stats. Blood pressure normal, heart rate normal, white cell blood count . . .

Hello? Look at this. The elevated white count that indicated the infection was *way* down. And the differentials—the spread and proportion of specialized white cells, segs, polys, eos, and so forth—were all within normal limits.

The patient had turned around.

"Well, well," Jos said. "Looks like somebody has the healing hands of a Jedi. Or the fingers, at least."

The skin around Zan's horns mottled a bit—the Zabrakian equivalent of a human's blush. He dropped the empty skinpopper into the pocket of his one-piece.

Jos frowned. "You develop a sudden sentimental attachment to instruments? Going to have it anodized and put it on the mantel?"

"Excuse me?"

"Since when do empty poppers not go into the trash?" Jos waved at the waste hopper next to the bed.

"Oh. Sorry—guess my brain's gone on leave." Zan pulled the skinpopper out and tossed it into the bin.

As it arced past him, Jos got a good look at the pneumatic injector. The clear plastoid cover was just that—clear. Blank. No identification denoting what kind of medication it had held. No batch number, either. Nothing.

That simply wasn't done.

The patient, who was now awake, mumbled that he was indeed feeling much better. Jos made polite doctor noises, automatically checked the man's vitals, then raised an eyebrow at Zan. "Doctor Yant, if I might speak with you in private?"

Outside the building, Jos steered Zan into a patch of

shade and relative coolness. "All right. What's going on here?"

"Going on? What are you talking about?" Zan didn't meet Jos's eyes.

"I'm talking about a patient who comes out of a life-threatening secondary infection so fast he leaves ion burns on his chart. I'm also talking about treatment with unmarked skinpoppers."

Zan hesitated for a moment, then sighed in resignation.

In that short pause, Jos suddenly knew what had transpired. "You didn't," he said.

Zan said, "I did."

"Zan, have you got an ingrown horn or something? You know what the risks are. If they catch you, you'll be court-martialed!"

"If you see a fellow sentient drowning and there's a rope lying right next to your foot, are you going to worry about being accused of stealing the rope?"

"If there's a good chance they'll hang me with it, yeah. This is *not* the same thing."

"It isn't? We're on a planet with the biggest supply of a flat-out miracle drug in the galaxy—you can walk to a huge field of it in five minutes. We tried everything else on this guy, Jos—macromolecular regeneration, nanocell implants, maser cauterization—nothing worked. The man was *dying*. You've read the *SGJ* literature touting bota—an adaptogen that can cure everything but a rainy day in most humanoid phenotypes. We've had patients who died from infections we could probably have cured with one scale of it." Zan raised his hands, a gesture of inevitability. "I *couldn't* just watch him die. Not when there was the slightest chance . . ."

Jos opened his mouth, but said nothing. What was

there to say? Bota was valuable—so much so that the
Republic deemed theft of it a crime to be severely pun-
ished. The plant was, ultimately, why both they and the
Separatists were on Drongar. And, ironically, the local
Rimsoos were forbidden to use it because of its poten-
tial offworld value.

Before Jos could speak again, Zan said, "Nobody will
miss a few plants. There are little pockets of bota all
over the lowlands that nobody even knows about. Pluck
a couple of scales, stick them in your pocket, hand-
process them later . . . who's to know?"

"Zan—"

"Come on, Jos, you know a lot of the xenos around
here sneak out and harvest the stuff for recreational use.
Filba used to bliss out with a hookah full of it most
every night. Everybody knows what it can do for them,
and everybody looks the other way, as long as no one
gets greedy. At least I'm using it to save lives—which is
what the Republic says it's doing, too. Is the life of someone a hundred parsecs from here more valuable than
one in the next room? Can I stand by and let people die
without doing everything in my power to save them?"

"You didn't start this war, Zan. You're not responsible for everybody who gets hurt in it."

"Oh, that's good. This from the guy who once kicked
a hole in a wall when he lost a patient to Drakñahr Syndrome—something that all of Coruscant Med and a
room full of Jedi *and* Silents couldn't treat."

At a total loss for words, Jos looked at his friend, and
saw nothing in front of him but a doctor who took his
job as seriously as he himself did. He sighed. "Okay.
But you've *got* to be more careful—there are a lot
sharper eyes than mine around here who could notice a
blank skinpopper."

"Point made. I'll make sure they're marked from now on," Zan said. "I can even use dye to color the serum so it looks like polybiotic or spectacillin. Nobody will notice, Jos."

"I hope not," Jos said. " 'Cause if someone does, your career could be smashed flatter than a mynock in a black hole."

Zan grinned and clapped a hand on his friend's shoulder, and the two turned and reentered the building.

31

Den Dhur was not a being to sit idle for long. Despite his facade of being supremely bored and cynical, of doing his job solely because it paid his drink tab, the thing in which he took the most pleasure in his life was his work. Even with the admiral hunting him, he could not simply camp in his quarters—in fact, he couldn't do that precisely because the admiral was hunting him. The first question to answer during an investigation, an old police officer had once told him, is: what looks different now than it did before? Any change in the behavior of a criminal suspect was cause for suspicion. If a bank is robbed and the guard on duty at the time suddenly decides to take an unscheduled vacation or begins driving a new and expensive speeder to work . . . well, unless his rich uncle just passed away suddenly and left him a bundle of credits, or a winning ticket in the dauxcat races, he's going to have company, to be sure. Company in uniform, carrying sonic pistols and stun batons.

Den Dhur the reporter did not usually spend his days alone in his quarters, and he surely wasn't going to start doing so now. So it was that he found himself out in the blistering hot day, shadowing the Rimsoo's combat instructor. Discreetly. Very discreetly. It wasn't a real good idea to come to the attention of a being who could, if he

wished, exterminate you without even raising his heart
rate. A being who had demonstrated his ability and his
willingness to snuff out lives and who had been
recorded doing it. A being who glorified in the hunt and
the kill.

A being like Phow Ji.

Den slipped into the shade of an outbuilding, happy
for the relative coolness there, and watched his quarry.
He focused a tiny recording cam upon the scene and
triggered it. A little more background material never
hurt. Better to have too much and have to cut it than too
little and have to stretch it. This device wasn't nearly as
sophisticated as the moon moth, but it would get the
job done.

Phow Ji had assembled a class of combat students,
maybe a dozen or so, mostly humans, and they were
limbering up their bodies on a patch of pink shortgrass
behind the cantina. Broad-leaved trees offered the martial arts trainees partial shade, but their exertions still
had those who shed heat by perspiring sweating pro-
fusely, while those who used other means of cooling
themselves were panting, waving their limbs, or ex-
panding rills and bulbae—whatever it took to bleed off
excess warmth.

"What is the First Rule?" Ji said. His voice was oddly
soft, but carried well enough in the damp morning air.

"Always be ready!" the class chorused in unison.

"Exactly. You don't hang your fighting mind-set on
the hat hook when you enter your cube. You don't leave
it on the counter when you shower, you don't set it on
the bedside table when you sleep. If it is not part of you,
it is useless and—"

Without a hint of what he was going to do, Ji took a

quick step to his left, swung his fist in a short arc, and punched a tall, thin human amidships.

The human went *"Oof!"* and staggered back a step, hands coming up in a belated defensive posture.

"Too late!" Ji roared, loud enough to put a cold finger on Den's spine, thirty meters away and hidden.

The human had sagged to one knee, his face congested in pain. When he saw Phow Ji watching him, he hastily rose to his feet.

"Duels are fun," Ji said. "Duels come when you and your opponent both know what's about to happen, at least in general terms. Duels are neat, clean, and have rules. A match in the ring might kill you, but you are prepared for it. You know who your enemy is, you know where he is, and you aren't surprised when he comes at you.

"In real life, you don't have those luxuries. You could be sitting in the 'fresher when someone comes for you. Showering, sleeping, or taking a class like this one. Now. What is the First Rule?"

"Always be ready!" they shouted in unison.

Ji took a step toward the group. The group, as one, took a step backward. Some of them raised their hands. One of them pulled a knife partway from a sheath.

Ji grinned. "Better. Now. First Posture!"

The students took a stance, one foot forward, one hand high, one low. Ji walked around them, touching an arm or leg here and there, correcting the poses. Everybody in the group watched him with what Den could see, even from his hiding place, was a tense wariness.

Den shook his head. This Phow Ji was a bad man, no doubt about that. He already had enough to file a story, but he allowed the cam to continue running. He knew what his slant was going to be: Phow Ji, a murderous thug who, in peacetime, would likely be locked away to protect the citizenry, instead was indulging his violent tendencies on the field of battle, allowed to kill and be thought a hero and not a villain. How did the public feel about that? Knowing that someone who was mentally deranged and violent, an assassin, a monster, was out there, and ostensibly on their side?

Den knew he could twirl it so that they would be horrified. A few more sequences showing the human's cruelty and violence, and civilized beings would turn away in disgust and revulsion.

He smiled. This was what he did, and he was good at it. Of course, one could never be sure what the public would do, but he knew a good story when he saw one, and whatever else he might lack in, he could tell that story well.

32

Tolk, Jos decided, was deliberately torturing him.

She *knew* how she affected him—it was in her nature and training, both as a species and as a female—and she was doing everything but giving him a handwritten invitation to join her in whatever his heart might desire.

In the preop surgical scrub room, Jos washed his hands, taking the customary ten minutes to do so, lathering, cleaning under the short nails, then repeating the process, even though the need for such had been unnecessary since long before he'd been born. With sterile fields and gloves, there was not much of a chance any pathogens were going to be transferred into a patient because he washed his hands for nine minutes instead of ten, but he'd been taught by traditionalists who valued the old customs. So he washed, and he watched the chrono, and he brooded.

Old customs. On his world it was acceptable—barely—that a young unmarried person might go forth into the galaxy and sample the pleasures of ekster company. It wasn't spoken of in polite circles, but it was done. Then the young, having gotten it out of their systems, were to return home, find a spouse from a proper enster family, and settle down.

But even in his younger and wilder days, Jos had never

been comfortable with the idea of brief liaisons. He'd done it, of course, but the essentially meaningless encounters had weighed heavily upon him. At the core of his being, Jos knew that there would only be one love in his life, and that he should not be unfaithful to her—even if he did so before he ever met her.

But now, here was Tolk. Beautiful. Sexy. Adept. Caring. Intelligent and, Jos knew, all too perceptive. She called to him. He wanted to get to know her, to explore her emotional depths, to find out if what he saw within was real. And, were he from another background, he would have broken landspeeder records to pursue her, to see if she was indeed the One. But she could not be the One for him; his family, his culture, and a lifetime of duty to both forbade it out of hand. She was not of his people. She was ekster. There was no sacrament, no ceremony, no ritual, that could change this. She could not become one of them.

Jos was indeed a man torn.

Tolk knew about his cultural background, of course. She could have politely backed away from any possible entanglements. But she hadn't.

And why is that, Jos, you simpleton? Hmmm?

Jos scrubbed hard at the backs of his fingers. How pink the skin was getting there. Clean. Very clean.

Tolk hadn't made herself scarce for a simple reason: he wanted her, and not just physically. And she knew it. And apparently, she was of like enough mind so as not to be offended by the idea. And therein lay the real problem—

"I wouldn't recommend scrubbing the skin off entirely, Jos. Get serous fluid inside the gloves and all."

Speak of temptation, and lo! there did she appear!

He mumbled something.

"Pardon? I didn't catch that."

Jos continued to meticulously wash his hands, like that character in the old holodrama who believed that, no matter how hard he scrubbed, he would never be clean of his father's blood. What was his name again . . . ?

He took a deep breath. Might as well get to it.

"Listen, Tolk. I . . . uh, I mean . . . uh . . ." Blast, this was hard! The term *mixed emotions* didn't begin to cover how he felt. It was more like pureed emotions.

She smiled sweetly at him, pretending, he knew, that she didn't have a clue as to how he felt. "Yes?"

He straightened, stuck his hands under the dryer. "Why are you making this so hard?"

"Me? I'm sorry, am I making something hard, Doctor Vondar?" The finest strands of spun Yyeger sugar would not have melted upon her tongue.

"You know my culture," he said, determined to see it through.

"Yes. And this knowledge disturbs you . . . ?"

"Blast it, Tolk. You know very well what I'm talking about!"

She looked at him with an innocent gaze, her eyes so wide they made a Sullustan look squint-eyed. "My talents aren't perfect, Jos. I'm not a mind reader; I can only see what's obvious to anybody who looks closely enough. Maybe you should just say what you mean so there won't be any confusion." She smiled again.

He wanted to scream and break things.

"I—you—we—we can't have a future together."

Tolk blinked, as innocent as a newborn. "Future? Who said anything about that?"

"Tolk . . ."

"We're in a war zone, Jos. Remember? Our protective field might malfunction tomorrow, we could take incoming fire from the Separatists, and we could all cease to be, just like that. Or the spores could mutate and kill us. Or we could be hit by lightning. In short, this is a dangerous place. Prognosis dismal. Any future for us is purely theoretical."

Jos stared at her. Somehow he retained enough muscle control to close his gaping mouth.

Tolk said, "You know the Bruvian saying, 'Kuuta velomin'?"

He shook his head.

" 'Seize the moment.' It's all we have. The past is gone, the future may never arrive. What exists is *now*. I'm not asking for marriage, Jos. I know that you can't travel that path with me. But we could share what comfort we might have together, here and now. Two people who care for each other. The future, *if* it comes, will attend to itself. As should we. Where's the harm in it?"

He shook his head again. "I'm—I wish I could do that. I'm just not wired that way. I need to commit to something this important."

"Am I *that* important to you, Jos?"

He looked at her, and she smiled again, a sad smile. "You needn't say it aloud. Your expression tells me." She paused.

"All right, then. I'll be your friend and your co-worker, because it seems that's all we are allowed. More's the pity." She reached out and touched his hand, and he felt an electric thrill run through his whole body.

She withdrew her hand. She wasn't smiling now. "Oops, I've contaminated you. Sorry. You'll have to wash your hands again. I'll see you in the OT."

When she was gone, he found that he was shaking.

He *hated* this. The war, the deaths, his culture, and in that moment, he was very glad Tolk had left and could not see the despair that he knew must be showing on his face.

He had to get out.

Not for long, and not far, but he could not face the OT right now, especially with Tolk in it. He'd sooner face an entire platoon of droidekas armed only with a trochar than see that look in her eyes again, at least today. He wouldn't be able to concentrate; likely as not he'd wind up replacing a kidney with a gallbladder or something equally bad.

He commed Zan.

"You owe me," the Zabrak said darkly as Jos watched him scrub up. "I just finished my own rotation two hours ago."

"Sleep's overrated."

"I wouldn't know."

"Just give me an hour or so," Jos said. "I've got to clear my head."

"So you're going for a walk? Have you been outside lately? The air's so thick you could swim to the cantina."

"One hour," Jos said. "I'll be back."

He left the building and struck out across the compound, angling away from the marshes and toward the relatively drier bota fields. Zan hadn't exaggerated— ten minutes of walking and his clothes were already sweat-soaked. He would have to decontaminate all over again.

He didn't care.

He stepped through a small stand of broad-leaved trees, waving away the wingstingers and fire gnats swarming around him, and saw the bota fields. Twenty or so parallel rows of growth stretching into the misty distance. Bota grew low to the ground; actually, the majority of the plant was underground, with only the fruiting bodies exposed. The rows were being tended by the usual assortment of droids; he didn't see any organic handlers at the moment.

He made no attempt to pinch off a bit of the plant, knowing that the rows were protected by a low-level zap field. This innocuous growth was a precious commodity—understandable, since its adaptogenic cells could serve a variety of purposes, everything from potent broad-based antibiotic to hallucinogen to nutrient, depending on the species. If it could be cultivated offworld, it would give the spice traders considerable cause to worry, because it could literally be all things to all people.

All things to all people. It suddenly seemed to Jos that he'd spent a goodly part of his life—entirely too much, perhaps—trying to be the same thing. As far back as he could remember, it had been assumed that he would be a doctor. It wasn't a decision he regretted—he was proud of his profession—but that was only one of many ways that he had endeavored to be the Good Son. He'd studied hard, always toed the line, been a child of whom anyone could be proud. And his family *had* been proud of him, no question of it. They had never stinted in their praise. He had no desire to hurt them or to see them hurt. And he knew that espousing an ekster would probably put them in early graves.

But—he seemed to be hearing the voice of Klo Merit in his ear: *Are they* your *customs?*

Are they?

It didn't take a Jedi to see that Tolk would shine out

amid an entire planetful of women. And he couldn't deny that her offer of wartime comfort was tempting, very tempting.

But he *couldn't*.

What are you afraid of?

"I'm afraid I'll fall in love with her," he said aloud.

"I think it's too late to fear that," a gentle voice behind him said.

Startled, Jos turned, expecting for an instant to see Tolk, to wonder if he should be delighted, angry, afraid, or something for which he likely had no name—

But it wasn't Tolk. It was the Padawan, Barriss Offee.

33

Barriss had been initially surprised to encounter Jos this far from the base. After a moment, however, she realized there was nothing to be surprised about. She had been wanting to talk to him, to offer him some solace for the mental and emotional turmoil she knew he was going through. It was not just her desire as a friend; it was her duty as a Jedi.

And now, here he was.

The Force does work in mysterious ways, she thought.

He didn't seem overly pleased to see her, but she could tell he wasn't keen on anybody's company right now. She reached out with the Force, found the tangled skein of his distress, stretched taut beneath his mind's surface. He was wrestling with a very different problem than his feelings about clones, but no matter—he needed quietude, and that she could provide.

Flowing with the Force, very lightly, she touched the tight, knotted strings of his dilemma, quieting their thrumming as a finger passed over the strings of a quetarra could subdue a chord.

He seemed surprised. He looked up, meeting her gaze with his own uncertain one.

Barriss smiled. "You are troubled, Jos," she murmured. "You are fighting your own internal war, on as many different fronts as the Republic is on Drongar. I can't solve your crises, but I can guide you to a more secure place, from where you can deal with them."

"Why?" he asked. "I mean—what's so special about me?"

Barriss smiled. "I could say I want to ensure your ability to perform well in the OT, and there is something of that in my purpose. But mostly it's because I'm a Jedi, and a healer as well. My purpose is to aid and comfort."

Jos was silent for a moment. Then he said, "What did you mean when you said it was too late to fear falling in love with Tolk?"

"Exactly what I said. It's obvious you love her and she reciprocates. I would see it even without the Force's aid. If you don't believe me, ask any of your friends."

Jos lifted his arms in exasperation. "So everyone sees it but me?"

"One is usually blind when one is in the eye of the storm."

"But she's ekster," he whispered. "My family would be devastated."

"Most likely true."

"I'd be giving up *everything*—my family, my friends, my practice . . . and for what?"

Barriss looked at him. "For love," she said.

Jos was silent for several long minutes, his eyes downcast. Then he heaved a great sigh and looked at Barriss.

"I can't," he said.

She nodded. She could sense his anguish, and that he spoke the truth. Perhaps it was the right decision. It was not her place to judge him, only to aid him.

"Choices of the heart are never easy," she said. She

looked at the sky, saw that the sun was setting in a blaze of reds and oranges, its light reflecting off the spores in the upper atmosphere.

"It will be dark soon," she said. "Best we return to the base."

Jos glanced at his wrist chrono and nodded. "Yeah, I promised Zan I'd be back in—"

A light brighter than a dozen suns seared Barriss's vision. An instant later, a giant hand lifted her, then smashed her full length into the mud.

The attack took Jos as much by surprise as it did the Jedi. At first he was not sure what had happened; only that there had been a brilliant flash of light, a deafening explosion, and when he regained his senses he found himself lying across Barriss's still-unconscious form, both of them half buried in warm mud. Not far away, in the grove of broad-leaved trees, one tree was now a shattered, smoking stump, its sap having been instantly superheated by the energy of a powerful laser blast that had turned the tree into an organic bomb. Jos's face tingled painfully, and he realized that his skin had been peppered by tiny splinters. It was a miracle he hadn't been blinded.

He looked up. His vision was blurry, and he was nearly deaf from the explosion, but he could see well enough to realize that a battle droid was standing on the other side of the bota field, its telescoping chest cannon still extended. It looked like it was lining up another shot.

Jos scrambled to his feet—or tried to; Drongar suddenly seemed to be rotating in several directions at once, and he fell again, this time landing alongside Barriss. His face wound up in the mud, only a few centimeters from hers.

He saw her open her eyes.

Another cannon blast scorched the ground a meter in front of them, ripping up rows of bota and raining fragments of the plant down around them.

Barriss rose to her feet—just how, Jos could not have said. She seemed to levitate—one moment she was sprawled on the ground, and the next she stood upright. Impressive as that was, however, it was nothing compared to her next action.

As Jos watched in astonishment, the Padawan *leapt* across the bota field, covering a distance of at least ten meters in a single bound. As she arced through the air toward the droid, Jos saw another flash of light. At first he thought the droid had fired again, but then he realized the glow came from Barriss's hand.

She had drawn her lightsaber.

Jos had seen images and holos of the Jedi weapon in use, but he had never before seen one in real life. Barriss's energy blade was an azure streak about a meter in length. It made a sound like a nest of angry wingstingers, and, even over the noisome stenches borne on the breeze from the nearby swamp, he could smell the acrid scent of ozone it produced.

He watched, openmouthed, as Barriss landed next to the battle droid. Before it could fire again, she struck a single blow with the energy weapon that sheared halfway through the droid's torso. Sparks erupted, and the droid collapsed.

Jos managed to get to his feet and stay there as the Padawan deactivated her lightsaber. Hooking it to her belt, she walked back to him, taking care to go around the bota field to avoid causing any more damage to the precious growths.

"That . . . ," he said, at a loss for words for one of the few times in his life. "That was . . . you're *amazing*."

She made a grimace of annoyance. "I'm an unwary amateur," she replied. "Had I been more mindful of the Force, that droid would never have gotten close enough to attack us.

"We'd better get back. I think that was a single scout that managed to penetrate our lines, but there might be more." She started back toward the base, and Jos hurried to keep pace with her.

"I can't believe it missed us," he said.

"It appeared to be battle-damaged; perhaps its targeting computer was malfunctioning. In any event, I doubt such luck will be ours more than once. Best we hurry. Also, we need to get you treated—you look like you've been shaving with a raven thorn."

Jos was in ready agreement with that. Suddenly facing Tolk in the OT didn't seem nearly as traumatic. This was an aspect of the war he had not been exposed to until now. It wasn't one he was eager to experience again.

And, of course, Zan was not impressed when he did get back.

"You're ten minutes late," he said.

"I nearly got killed by a battle droid," Jos said.

"No excuse. It didn't kill you, didn't even burn off a leg or anything."

Jos only half heard him. His mind was occupied with the memory of Barriss Offee battling the droid. She had been spectacular using that lightsaber. So far, most of the ekster women were a lot more exciting than the enster women he remembered back home . . .

34

Jos had enough on his mind that he was paying scant attention to the chip-cards. The coins, flasks, sabers, and staves upon them held no real meaning for him. Around the table, the other players looked at their hands, brooded, or made classic comments:

"Son-of-a-bantha, who dealt this mess?" This from Zan.

"That would be me," Den said. He glanced at Jos. "I tried to cheat in your favor, Doc—didn't you get a pure?"

"Very funny," Jos replied. "If this bomb was any bigger, they'd be calling this the Drongar asteroid field."

"Spoken like a being trying to up the bets," I-Five said.

"You going to bet, fold, or just whine?" Tolk asked Jos.

Her tone of voice was like a sonic disruptor fired straight into his chest. To his surprise, he'd found that nearly getting killed while out trying to clear his head yesterday had not bothered him nearly as much as Tolk's new coolness toward him.

But that's what you told her you wanted, wasn't it?

He looked at his hand. What with holding the Queen of Air and Darkness, the Evil One, *and* the Demise, he was so far below negative twenty-three that there was no way he could win, given the mathematical laws of this particular galaxy. When his turn came, he folded.

Bets went into the hand pot. After the next card, Zan folded also.

Den dealt the remaining players—Tolk, I-Five, Barriss, and himself—another card. The Jedi dropped out.

Zan leaned back and said, "So, Den, weren't you going to write a story about Phow Ji?"

The reporter paused a beat in his deal, then resumed. "Yeah."

"So when are we going to see it?"

"With any luck, never."

Jos thought this was odd, since Den seemed to have pretty high opinion of his abilities as a writer. He'd told his sabacc cronies a few days previously that he planned on eviscerating the Bunduki in pixels. Naturally, Den had cautioned them, this data wasn't to be considered broadband, as the Sullustan had no great desire to be rendered into shaak fodder by Ji. "What happened?" Jos asked.

Den didn't answer. Tolk called, the hands were turned over, and she won with an even twenty-three. Of course.

"Lucky at cards, unlucky in love," Den said.

Tolk glanced at Jos, then smiled at Den. "So why won't we be seeing the story, Den?"

"Oh, you'll see it, if you bother to look. They . . . butchered it. I laid it out as how our friend Ji was the scum of the galaxy and that feeding him feetfirst to a hungry rancor was too good for him."

"And . . . ?" Barriss said.

"And they . . . *twirled* it, so that now he doesn't sound . . . so bad." Den shuffled the cards. "Not bad at all, I'm afraid. Seems the audience is tired of grim news at the moment. According to my editor, they've been getting a lot of that lately—battles lost here, systems cut off there, and so on. Dooku's forces might be getting their metal behinds kicked in the long run—if you believe the Republic flacks, anyway—but it doesn't sound like that to the viewing public. They want heroes."

"Phow Ji is not in any way, shape, or form a hero," Zan said. "He's a murderous thug who kills people for fun."

"A fact I went to great pains to point out, believe me. But that doesn't matter. Ji can be trimmed and lubed enough to fit the slot. So it has been decreed by voices louder than mine, and so, apparently, shall it be."

There was a moment of shocked silence as the other players digested this.

"That's not a twirl, that's a Class-One troopship's gravity-gyro on full spin," Jos said.

"We gonna talk, or are we gonna play cards?" Den said, passing the deck to him. "Your deal, Doc."

"The way my luck is running, talk is a whole lot cheaper," Jos said. "I'm already down fifty creds."

Zan looked like he'd just been hit with severe vestibular disorder. "But—they can't make a coldhearted no-crèche like Ji into somebody for people to *admire*!" he sputtered. "The man keeps *trophies* of all the people he's murdered!"

"Enemies of the Republic, each and every one," I-Five said. "That's how they'll twirl it."

"This is unbelievable news, Den," Barriss said. "You must be horribly disappointed."

Den was quiet—he seemed to be editing his thoughts. "It is. I am," he said finally. "But I'm not all that surprised. I didn't just fall off the purnix lorry yesterday, after all. I've seen it happen to others. I've even had it done to me before—though never to this degree." He snorted. "Our warped Phow Ji will probably get a rich entproj contract out of it, if he doesn't dice the agent who offers it to him. 'The Hero of Drongar,' coming to your home three-dee soon."

"Sweet Sookie," Jos said.

"Heroes are transient," Den said, in a tone that sounded like he was trying to convince himself more than the other players at the sabacc table. "They come, they go, and they tend to die more often than everybody else in wartime. If one is real and another is a product of the media, it's all the same, in the long run. None of it really matters."

"I'm going to go out on a spiral arm here and guess you have no use for heroes," I-Five said.

Den shrugged. "They make good copy sometimes. Other than that, no."

"So there's nothing for which you would risk your life?"

"Good maker, no. I don't believe in all that spiritual stuff. I don't expect to be recycled as something higher up the food chain in another incarnation, or to see the Spectrum at the end of the galaxy, or discorporate and become one with the Force. For me, what you see is what you are, and when the lights go out, that's it. So why should I court the Eternal Sleep any sooner than I absolutely must? No risk, no loss. Heroes are, save for those who wind up being in the category completely by accident, either fools or selling something."

Jos looked at the droid. "What about you, I-Five? Given your construction, you could last five hundred, a thousand years or more. Would you put your durasteel neck and all those centuries on the line if there was a good chance somebody would ax it?"

I-Five said, "It would depend on why. I've mentioned before that I still have some memory damage I'm endeavoring to repair, and it seems from some of the recently recovered bits that I may have performed some 'heroic' actions in my past." He fanned his cards. "I must say I'm interested in learning the circumstances."

Den shook his head, then looked at Barriss. "You, I expect it from—you're a Jedi, that's what you do. The medical folks—well, I've seen some of them who'd charge a particle cannon at the drop of a glove, so they're as crazy as clones, too, in my 'cron." He glanced at Jos, Zan, and Tolk. "No offense," he added.

"None taken," Zan said.

Den shifted his gaze back to I-Five. "But I didn't expect to ever encounter a *droid* with delusions of valor. You, my metallic friend, are in need of some serious rewiring."

"And you," I-Five replied as he tossed a credit into the hand pot, "need a damper slapped on your cynicism chip."

Jos, Zan, and Tolk smiled. Zan took the deck of cards. "Maybe my luck will change," he said.

"It better not while you're dealing," Jos said.

Zan shuffled, then put the customary blank card at the bottom of the deck, marking where the shuffled cards stopped. He put the deck down for Barriss to cut. As she did so, he said, "I guess I'm what they'd call a devout agnostic. I don't know if there's something bigger than us or not, but I think that we should attempt to live our lives as if there is."

"A philosophy more beings should espouse," Barriss said.

Den rolled his eyes but said nothing.

There flashed into Jos's mind once again an image of CT-914's quiet grief for his comrade. He looked up from his cards and saw Barriss watching him, a look of sympathy on her face.

He glanced at I-Five. The droid was studying his cards, but he appeared to sense Jos's attention, because he looked up. Jos had gotten quite good at reading the subtle shifts of luminosity in I-Five's photoreceptors, but this time the droid's expression was enigmatic.

The moment stretched.

"Jos," Zan said. "It's your turn."

"What are you going to bet?" I-Five asked.

What indeed?

Jos dropped his hand and stood. "I'm out," he said. "I'll see you all later."

Zan blinked. "Where are you going?"

"To pay a sympathy call," Jos said as he left.

35

Jos walked across the compound, slipping an osmotic mask over his nose and mouth as he did so, because the concentration of spores in the air was unusually heavy. He was so preoccupied with his thoughts, however, that he barely noticed them, or the syrupy heat of midday.

He was thinking about space travel.

His training was in medicine, not applied and theoretical physics—he smiled slightly, remembering the irascible Dr. S'hrah, one of his teachers, who had zero tolerance for any discipline outside medicine—"You're a doctor, not a physicist!" would be his take on Jos's woolgathering—but he knew the basics and the history, as did anyone with anything more than a dirt clod for a brain. Travel between star systems was made possible by moving through hyperspace, an alternate dimension not all that different from realspace, in which superluminal velocities were easily reached. In ancient times, this had been thought impossible, since the legendary Drall scientist Tiran had proven conclusively, more than thirty-five thousand years ago, that time and space were inseparable, and that the speed of light was an absolute boundary that could not be crossed.

But Tiran's Theory of Universal Reference did not prohibit anything traveling *faster* than light—it only disallowed traveling *at* the speed of light. If the "light-speed barrier" could somehow be bypassed, one could theoretically shift easily from realspace to hyperspace and back.

Galactic colonization had initially been accomplished by generation ships, and this made it impossible to knit the separate worlds together in a viable galactic civilization. Finally, after centuries of experimentation and frustration, the best scientists of the Republic found a way to create and contain negative pressure fields strong enough to power a portable hyperdrive unit. At long last, affordable and ubiquitous superluminal travel had been achieved.

This accomplishment, of course, had quickly led to the Great Hyperspace War and various other forms of unpleasantness, but that wasn't where Jos's thoughts had taken him today. The problems of achieving FTL speed made a nice metaphor for breaking through to new concepts. If you could somehow make it past the initial barrier of perception, then the galaxy you found yourself in wasn't really all that different from the one you'd left behind. In his case, it was a galaxy in which artificial intelligences and cloned personalities had to be judged on an equal emotional footing with organics, but, once that concept was grasped, it proved to be not that hard to assimilate.

It did, however, require some adjustment—and some apologies.

Barracks CT-Tertium was the largest of the three garrisons at Ground Base Seven, which was located at the edge of the Rotfurze Wastes, a region of severe ecological blight two kilometers from the Rimsoo. Jos requisitioned a landspeeder and was there in less than ten minutes. He was far enough behind the lines to feel relatively unconcerned, although he could hear, on several occasions, the distant crackle of particle beams and the muffled *whump*! of C-22 frag mortars. Apparently the Separatists weren't all that worried about bota damage anymore.

At GB7 he was directed to a tiny 4.5-square-meter billet, barely large enough for the bunk-and-locker combination that constituted CT-914's home away from—actually, Jos realized, it was just his home. Unless one counted the vat from which the clone had been decanted in Tipoca City on the waterworld Kamino, CT-914 had no place else he could call his own.

The bed had been made to military precision, the blankets as smooth as the surface of a neutron star. The locker was ajar, and closer inspection proved it to be empty.

What was puzzling, however, was the spot over the head of the bed, where the trooper's designation should have been. Instead of reading CT-914, the frame was empty.

Jos spied a Dressellian corporal nearby and hailed him. The Dressellian, surly like most of his species, saluted somewhat resentfully upon recognizing a superior officer. Jos asked him where Nine-one-four was.

"In the recycling vats, most likely," was the shocking reply. "Along with most of his platoon. They were ambushed by a Separatist guerrilla attack two days ago."

The Dressellian waited a moment, then, seeing that the human captain was not likely to be asking any more questions immediately, saluted again and continued about his business.

Jos slowly left the garrison, stunned. In the last hour or so he had come to think of Nine-one-four as exemplifying all of his newfound knowledge of the clones' essential humanity, and to suddenly learn that he was dead was almost as big a shock as hearing of the death of an old friend or a loved one. He had felt compelled to seek the clone out and apologize to him, hoping that, somehow, such an expiation would simplify some of the challenges of an awareness that now included respect toward more than organic life alone. But instead he'd found that CT-914 had joined his vat-brother, CT-915, in death. And Jos knew that it would be a long time, if ever, before their deaths, and all the others perpetrated by this war, would seem to be anything but senseless and despicable.

He tried to still his racing thoughts for a moment, to have a few seconds of silent respect for the fallen warrior. But it seemed that, no matter how still he willed his mind to be, it kept filling up with images of Tolk.

On board the MedStar frigate, Admiral Tarnese Bleyd studied the flimsies before him, the results of his latest round of inquiries into any suspicious or surreptitious 'casts from the personnel of Rimsoo Seven. With a growl he swept them off his desk and onto the floor. Nothing— just the usual air and space chatter to be expected. Nothing to give him the slightest clue as to who might have been spying on him when Filba died, or why.

Bleyd growled again, an almost subsonic sound, deep in his throat. As long as whoever on the other end of that spycam remained at large, he, Bleyd, was in danger. The recording might even now be circulating over the HoloNet, or being viewed in the private chambers of some investigative committee back on Coruscant. The situation was intolerable.

Think, curse you! Use that hunter's brain, those predatory instincts. Who would be the most likely being to possess a surveillance cam, and who would have reason to shadow him, to attempt to record him in some kind of illegal activity?

Perhaps Phow Ji, that Bunduki martial artist he'd encountered? Bleyd considered, then shook his head. Such undercover activity would be much too subtle for such a thug. Perhaps he should reconsider the possibility of Black Sun—

His eyes narrowed in sudden thought. Was he coming at this from the wrong angle? He was assuming that he had been the target of whoever had done the espionage. But what if he was wrong? What if *Filba* had been the subject?

Bleyd activated the flatscreen desk display, quickly constructing a new search algorithm. In a moment he had the data he needed.

On several separate occasions there had been public complaints made by the Sullustan reporter, Den Dhur, concerning Filba. While Dhur was hardly the only one in the Rimsoo to have some kind of grievance against the Hutt, the fact that he was a reporter meant he most likely had access to surveillance equipment.

Yes. Yes, it made sense. Dhur must have been recording the Hutt's actions at the time of the latter's death—and had, by unhappy coincidence, gotten the incriminating interchange between Filba and Bleyd.

Unhappy indeed, for the reporter . . .

Bleyd stepped out from behind the desk, wearing a grim smile. He would order Den Dhur arrested and brought up from planetside immediately. With any luck, there was still time to rectify this mess before—

The door to his office opened.

Bleyd blinked in surprise. It was the robed figure of a Silent who entered, but Bleyd knew immediately who was hidden beneath the vestments.

Kaird, the Nediji. The Black Sun agent.

Bleyd stepped away from his desk. Almost automatically his hand slipped around to the back of his uniform, releasing the knife from its hidden belt sheath. It slipped comfortably into the folds of his hand. It was a ryyk blade, much smaller than the traditional weapons fashioned and used by the Wookiee warriors of Kashyyyk, but no less deadly. It had proven the difference between victory and defeat, between life and death, for him before, and he intended that it do no less now.

The bird-being folded back his hood, revealing his sardonic face and blazing violet eyes. He cocked his head in greeting.

"Admiral," he said. When he lowered his hands from the hood, the right one held a gleaming blade in it.

Bleyd did not reply to the greeting. He circled to his left, his knife held low by his right hip, the point extended downward from the little finger side of his fist, edge forward, in a reverse grip.

Three meters away, Kaird kept the circle complete, moving to his left, and the short and stubby blade he held jutted upward from the thumb side of his grip, the edge also facing his opponent.

Bleyd seemed outwardly calm, although he was thinking furiously. His office was fairly large, but it was still on board a starship, where every cubic centimeter of space was at a premium. With any luck, the enclosed area would negate the Nediji's speed. He couldn't dodge if he didn't have room, and once he was backed into a corner, Bleyd, who was larger and stronger, would have him. He would take some damage—no way around that—but damage could be repaired, wounds could be healed.

"Let me guess," the Black Sun agent said. "Mathal didn't 'accidentally' fly his ship into the wrong orbit."

"Mathal was greedy. He wanted to fill a freighter with bota, to make a killing, and Samvil take the stragglers. Doing that would have made me a fugitive from the authorities for life. He didn't care about that. He got what he deserved."

"You should have contacted us. Black Sun would have dealt with him. We take a longer view of our business, and we frown on rogues."

Bleyd shrugged. "As far as I was concerned, he *was* Black Sun. I could not allow him to ruin what I had set up here."

Kaird shifted his stance, turning so that his right side faced Bleyd. The Admiral noticed that the dark blue swatch of feathers around his opponent's neck had grown darker still, and had risen in a stiff ruff—no doubt an atavistic warning for predators. The Nediji was in full combat mode. He spun his knife, twirling it around his fingers. A showy move, the more so because it indicated he was not tight with fear.

"It's not too late," he said. "As you said, Mathal got what he had coming. We can overlook that. No need to ruin a business that's making everybody profit."

Bleyd shook his head. Just to show that he wasn't nervous, he also shifted his knife, turning it with a little move that switched from a mountain climber's pick to a sword fighter's hold. "Too much of the profit lines Black Sun's vaults. I can store the bota far away from here, move it myself, and make much more—if I cut out the middle beings."

The Nediji laughed. "Starting with me, eh?"

"Nothing personal."

Kaird laughed again. "Pardon me, but I take my death *very* personally." And with that he lunged, impossibly fast, and the short knife flicked out in a blur.

Bleyd saw it coming, but even so, he barely had time to get his own knife in position for the block. Durasteel clashed with durasteel, and Kaird hopped back, grinning, before Bleyd could counterattack.

"Just checking to see if you're awake, Admiral."

"Awake enough to cut you down, Nediji."

"And what if you manage that? There are many more where I came from. Do you think Black Sun will just shrug and forget to send another agent? Perhaps next time it will be a team of shockboots, real shoot-first-and-ask-no-questions types. Most unpleasant folk."

"Teams need a ship," Bleyd said. "Enemy ships tend to be shot down in wars. By the time the next agent or agents get here, I can be far, far away—far enough to make it financially unfeasible for the Republic to pursue me."

"You think having the authorities looking for you is a problem? You can't imagine how that pales compared to having *us* after you." Kaird flipped the knife from hand to hand. "And Black Sun *never* gives up the chase."

"I'll worry about that later. Right now, I'll deal with you."

"I don't think so. You're larger and much stronger, true, but I'm far faster. You are obviously adept with these"—he waved the knife—"but I still have the advantage."

It was Bleyd's turn to laugh. "You really think so? I'm a hunter and a warrior, bird-man, and I've killed half a dozen opponents with this very blade. You are fast, yes, but your bones are hollow and your feathers no protection against cold durasteel. No matter how fast you are, you can't get to me before I gut you."

"You're forgetting something," Kaird replied. "I'm an assassin."

Bleyd raised an eyebrow. "Which means . . . ?"

"It means that getting the job done is more important than how I do it."

Bleyd frowned. *What—?*

Kaird whipped his hand back suddenly, snapped it forward, and *threw the knife*—!

It came too fast to dodge. Bleyd instinctively swatted at the incoming weapon, and, with reflexes honed by centuries of natural selection, managed to deflect it— barely. It nicked him on the hand, but that was all. A mere scratch.

He grinned as the Nediji's knife fell to the floor, clattered, and bounced to his feet. He crouched swiftly and scooped it up, then stood, a knife in each hand.

"Now you have no weapon," he said. "You don't stand a chance, barehanded against two blades. Fool!" He brandished the knives mockingly.

The Black Sun agent backed up a couple of steps, until his back was against the transparisteel port. He rose slowly from his fighting crouch. What was he up to? Bleyd wondered. Did he have another knife hidden on him? Or a small blaster, maybe?

The Sakiyan paused, considering his next move. Then, to his surprise, the Nediji slowly shook his head.

"You could have taken me just then," he said. "If

you'd come in fast enough, you might have backed me into the corner before I could have maneuvered around you. But you hesitated. And now you've lost."

"Lost? Nothing has changed. I still have you cornered." Bleyd smiled, a feral gleam of teeth. "Frankly, I was hoping for more of a fight, Nediji. I expected better of a Black Sun killer. Now we finish this."

"I don't think so," Kaird said. His posture was quite casual now; he could have been carrying on a conversation on a Coruscant street corner. Despite himself, Bleyd felt a slight sting of uneasiness. "Something has changed," the bird-being continued. "Time has passed. And all of a sudden, you feel . . . *tired*, don't you, Admiral? As if you can hardly hold your weapons. As if all your strength has been used up."

Bleyd snarled. "Are you a Jedi, to try infantile mind tricks? Trust me, I'm immune to such claptrap."

"But you're not immune to dendriton toxin."

Bleyd blinked. Then, suddenly, the pulse of uneasiness bloomed into full-blown shock.

The Nediji's knife! The cut on his hand!

Bleyd gathered himself to charge, but his legs abruptly would no longer obey him. He tried to leap, and instead staggered to one side. Tried to take another step, and his left leg, now completely numb, gave way. He fell to one knee. He kept his grip on the knives, but he was so weak! And now a sudden fire raged within him, roasting his muscles, torching each individual nerve . . .

Kaird moved toward him, reached out, and took one of the knives from Bleyd's burning fingers. The other one fell from the Sakiyan's nerveless grasp.

"Dendriton toxin is a bad way to go," Kaird said. "Painful, slow—you're literally immolated from inside out. But you were a brave adversary, Admiral, and I admire bravery. So, even though my superiors wish you to suffer, I'll spare you the toxin's effects."

He stepped to the side, caught Bleyd's head in one hand, and tilted it back.

Bleyd felt the touch of the knife against his throat, but it wasn't painful, just cold. An almost pleasant momentary respite from the fiery agony.

His consciousness started to fade, then, the colors of his office leaching into grayness. He realized numbly that he wouldn't be able to cleanse his family's honor. That knowledge hurt even more than the molten venom in his veins.

He managed to shift his eyes, to look at the Nediji before he faded out completely. Kaird gave him a small and slow bow, a final salute that held no mockery.

"Nothing personal," he said.

And the darkness claimed Tarnese Bleyd, forever.

36

The medlifters came at dawn.

Barriss Offee was asleep in her quarters, in the middle of a Force dream. They had not been coming to her as often of late, these subconscious connections with the galactic life-energy field. When she had first felt the Force awaken within her, the dreams had been frequent and powerful, never to be remembered in their entirety upon awakening, but always leaving her with a sense of increased strength and control.

As always, she was momentarily confused upon awakening—then she recognized the sound of the approaching lifters. Hastily donning her jumpsuit, she started for the OT.

She caught a glimpse, through the spore clouds, of the lifters hanging low in the eastern sky, just above the bloated oblate sphere that was Drongar Prime. Other Rimsoo personnel were already running from their cubicles and quarters, some still pulling on clothing. She saw Zan Yant and Jos Vondar heading toward the landing area.

Then, suddenly, she stopped.

Something—*someone*—had called to her.

It had been a cry for help, nonverbal, but no less strong. She had heard it echo in her mind as if its author had been standing right behind her. A cry of rage and despair.

A death cry.

She knew where it had come from—the edge of the Kondrus Sea—and, though she didn't know who was dying, she knew why. For one unmistakable and mercifully brief moment, she could see, as clearly as with her own eyes, the killer's face as he loomed over his victim.

Phow Ji.

Without a moment's hesitation Barriss turned and ran away from the lifters, away from the Rimsoo, and into the lowlands that sloped toward the sea.

It did not even occur to her to wonder until she was deep in the fetid marshes why she had made the decision to abandon her duty—to turn her back on dozens of Republic soldiers wounded in battle and go seeking out one unknown casualty instead. There could only be one reason, and she was loath to admit it, because it flew in the face of everything Master Unduli had taught her about working for the greater good, not to mention the Jedi Code. She had let her emotions take over, had let herself be swayed by anger and, yes, a desire to punish.

But even knowing this, even fearing that she was running toward the dark side, she did not stop.

She emerged from the swamp vegetation, pushing through a last clinging cluster of snarlvines, and saw Ji—the only one still standing amid the carnage. Seven men, all wearing Separatist uniforms, lay dead about him. He had a shallow vibroblade wound on his right forearm, and a blistered left cheekbone where a laser beam had narrowly missed. Other than that, he was unmarked.

He was waiting for her, that sardonic smile she had

come to despise on his lips. "A drunken t'landa Til makes less noise than you do," he said. "Nevertheless, it's always a pleasure to see you, Padawan Offee. To what do I owe the honor of this visit? Have you come to congratulate me on my latest victory for the Republic?" He gestured mockingly at the bodies strewn about his feet.

Her rage threatened to overwhelm her. She felt the desire and the will to destroy him. In that moment, Barriss Offee knew exactly what Master Unduli had meant when she had spoken of the dark side's seductive power. She wanted nothing more than to turn him into a pile of ashes, and, worse yet, she knew that she could. The dark power lived and shouted within her. It wouldn't even require an effort—all she had to do was release it.

Phow Ji must have seen the truth of this in her face, because his eyes widened in slight surprise. "Do you seriously think you can stand against me? I am a master of teräs käsi, of Hapan, *echani,* tae-jitsu, and a dozen other deadly styles. I am—"

"You are a murderer," she interrupted him, her voice quiet but with an edge that stopped his tirade. "And I will see that you murder no more."

Ji smiled and shrugged slightly, recovering his aplomb. He shifted his feet, settling into a stance. "Come ahead, then—*Jedi.*"

After it was all over, Barriss spent many a sleepless night wondering what she would have done. Would she have given in, accepted his challenge, and used the Force to destroy him? Or risen above her baser impulses and used only enough power to render him helpless? In short, would she have succumbed to the dark side or not?

She never got the chance to find out.

Phow Ji suddenly staggered, his eyes snapping wide in astonishment. Barriss realized he'd been hit from behind by something. He turned, and she saw the vanes and stubby tail of a hypo dart protruding from between his shoulder blades. Another Separatist soldier, shooting from the cover of the nearby swamp, had nailed him. For all his vaunted strength, skill, and speed, there was no way Ji could have dodged something he hadn't seen coming.

Barriss expanded a bubble of awareness outward, with herself at the center, realizing even as she did so that, had she not been blinded with rage at Ji, she might have sensed the intended attack in time to warn the martial artist. But now it was too late. He had fallen to his knees, and, as she watched, he toppled heavily into the wet sand. He lay quite still, save for slight, rhythmic twitches of his fingers.

She could detect no further danger—evidently the shooter had not stayed to see the results of his ambush. Which meant she was safe for the moment as well, although that could change at any time. She kept her expanded awareness in operation while she knelt beside Ji, examining him.

His hands and fingers were cold, and the twitching had not abated. Paresthesia, most likely, she decided. She pinched back an eyelid, saw that the pupil was contracted. His breathing was rapid and shallow—it seemed obvious that Phow Ji had been hit with a potent neurotoxin of some sort—Paraleptin, perhaps, or Titroxinate. The Separatists had been known to use such biochems, and worse. If something was not done quickly, he would die.

There was no time to call for an evac, even if there was an available medlifter, which was problematic. But there was another way to treat him.

The Force.

Without even stopping to reflect on the irony of it, Barriss knelt beside Ji. She pulled the dart out, then rolled him over and put her hands on his chest. It occurred to her that it would be quite easy to just let the paralysis of his central nervous system do the job that, only a few minutes before, she had been all too willing to take on herself. But that temptation had passed. She was a Jedi healer. Here before her was a life in need of healing.

There was no need to make it any more complicated than that.

Barriss Offee closed her eyes and opened her heart and mind to the power of the Force.

The droid approached Den Dhur as the latter headed toward his quarters. It was one of the standard harvesting units, a little weather-worn and dented, but moving well enough.

"You are Den Dhur, sir?" the droid said.

"Who wants to know?"

If it was possible for a droid to look confused, then this one surely did. "I have a delivery for you, sir."

"And who caused this delivery to be sent to me?"

"Lieutenant Phow Ji."

Uh-oh. Den looked at the package, then at the droid. "It isn't going to blow up, is it?"

"Unlikely, sir. The item in question is a holoproj recording. There are no explosives contained in it."

Den nodded. "All right." The droid extruded a carry

drawer from its chest and removed the device, which, Den noticed with relief, did look like a standard holocron cube and not a bomb.

As he took it, Den said, "Ji gave this to you?"

"No, sir, he did not give it to me. He did, however, ask that I witness his activity and record it. This is the result, which I was to deliver to you."

Den was still trying to wrap his mind around the concept of a gift from Phow Ji. "He specified me by name?"

"Not by name, sir. His exact words were, 'Give it to that pop-eyed little womp rat who thinks he's the galaxy's gift to news media.'" The droid added, "This required some extrapolation on my part."

"Now I believe you. All right. Thank him for me."

"I am afraid that will be quite impossible, sir. Phow Ji is no longer among the living."

A herd of curlnoses couldn't have kept Den from hurrying into his cubicle to view the recording. He darkened the chamber, inserted the cube, and activated the projection unit. The three-dimensional image flowered in front of him.

The scene was of a small clearing in a jungle. As Den watched, a Separatist combat droid scout eased into the clearing, did a quick 360 scan, then started across.

Phow Ji stepped into view in the foreground, his back to the cam. He wore a pair of blasters in low-slung holsters on his hips. The droid didn't appear to see or hear him, but this changed when Ji yelled, "Hey, mechanical! Over here!"

As the droid turned toward him, Ji snatched the blasters from their holsters so fast that the action was a blur, and fired. The twin bolts caught the droid's visual sensor array, instantly blinding it.

Ji ran to his right, five or six fast steps, and dropped prone. The droid fired his laser cannon at the spot where Ji had been standing a moment before.

Ji rolled up to his knees and shot the droid again, and the bolts—there must have been at least six or seven hits—lanced into the chink under its control box. This was, Den knew, a weak spot on this model's armor, but so small that it was seldom a problem in battle.

It was a problem this time. Blue smoke erupted from the droid's casing, the thing listed to one side, then ground to a halt, critically damaged.

Ji leapt up and ran, again to his right.

A trio of Salissian mercenaries came out of the woods, blaster rifles working. Streaks of incandescent plasma scorched the air.

Ji dodged, dodged left, then right, then stutter-stepped as enemy bolts fell short or to the sides. He also shot as he ran, once, twice, thrice—and all three mercenaries were hit with fatal body strikes. They went down.

A heavily armored super battle droid emerged from the woods, followed by two more mercenaries, but Ji was on top of them almost before they realized it. He bodyslammed into one of the mercenaries, shot the other, and fired three times more at the droid, which erupted in fire and smoke as had the one before. Den watched in astonishment. Mother's milk, but this was *incredible* shooting, extremely accurate for sidearm fire, especially from a man running full out over uneven terrain and using both hands.

Ji holstered his blasters, straddled the remaining merc, who was still alive and trying to get up. He grabbed the man's head from behind and jerked it powerfully to one side. Den could clearly hear the Salissian's neck snap.

He'd thought his capacity to be astonished had reached its limit. But then his jaw dropped as two more mercs emerged from the woods, and Ji drew both blasters and *shot the guns out of their hands*!

Den had never seen anything like this, not even in entertainment holodramas.

The small 3-D image of Ji holstered his weapons again and ran to engage the surprised Salissians in hand-to-hand combat. The first man went down from a hammer fist to the temple; the second caught an elbow to the throat. Then Ji drew his weapons again, so fast that they seemed to just appear in his hands, and fired into the woods at unseen targets. He shot until the blasters depleted their charges, turning this way and that as he spied new targets. When the charge chambers were empty he tossed the useless weapons away, and charged into the forest out of sight.

A moment passed—then a mercenary pinwheeled into the clearing and hit a patch of rocky ground head-first. Again, the snap of cracking vertebrae was audible.

Another mercenary staggered into view and collapsed, clutching a blackened, smoking wound in his midriff.

Ji backed into the clearing from the woods, a blaster rifle now in hand. He was firing on full auto, hosing more hidden enemies.

More Salissians emerged from the forest, shooting rifles and blasters of various makes. A pellet from a slugthrower hit Ji a glancing blow high on the right leg, ripping open the cloth and the flesh. Blood oozed, soaking his pants. He spun toward the man who'd shot him and blasted him squarely in the face.

Another discharge took Ji low on the right side, vaporizing cloth and punching through his body. Not fatal, because the beam's intense heat instantly cauterized the wound, but serious nonetheless. Ji turned calmly and shot his attacker in the chest.

Then things got really interesting.

A large shadow obscured the light. Ji looked up, and the angle of the recording cam tilted as well, to frame a large drop ship hovering about fifty meters overhead. A dozen Separatist soldiers, using repulsor packs, settled down into the clearing, firing as they did so.

Ji shot eight of them, leaping, dodging, and rolling as plasma bursts peppered the ground all around him. It was a Jedi-like display of acrobatic skill, but finally the Separatists found the range. Phow Ji went down in a hail of sizzling blaster bolts.

He lay on the ground, obviously mortally wounded. The remaining soldiers approached him cautiously.

As they reached the dying man, he pulled a thermal grenade from his pocket and held it up. He smiled as he triggered it.

They tried to run, but there was no escape. The grenade blasted the clearing into a blaze of heat and light that, even with the cam's automatic dampers, whited out the 3-D image. When the glare cleared, all that was left of Phow Ji and his enemies was a smoking crater in the damp ground.

Den realized he was sweating, even in the relatively cool environment of his cubicle. He reached out an unsteady hand and switched the unit off.

Then he realized he wasn't alone.

He spun about with a gasp—then relaxed as he recognized the figure behind him. "Did—did you see the whole thing?" he asked.

"Yes," the Padawan replied. "Phow Ji made sure I received a recording as well."

"What—why did he—" Den couldn't finish the question. He'd been on a lot of planets and had seen a lot of violence, but he had never seen *anything* like this.

Barriss Offee was quiet for so long that Den thought she hadn't heard him. Then she sighed and said, "I saved his life. Earlier today. He'd been hit by a poison dart, and I brought him back through the power of the Force."

Den nodded slowly. "I'm guessing he was less than grateful."

"He was furious. I thought he was going to attack me right there. I don't know why he didn't. Instead, he just turned and walked away.

"I went back to the base to do what I could for the wounded. Soon after we got the last man stabilized, a droid handed me a copy of this recording."

Den pulled the cube from its slot and looked at it. It would be worth a small fortune, given Ji's newfound heroic reputation. Had the Bunduki known this—had he wanted Den to profit from it, given that it had been the reporter who had, albeit unintentionally, caused that reputation? Had Phow Ji, in his own twisted way, been trying to repay Den?

"It still doesn't explain why he did it. One man, purposely starting a firefight against a whole platoon? That's crazy."

"He was *m'nuush*," she said.

"I beg your pardon?"

"That's what the Wookiees of Kashyyyk call it. To Trandoshans it's *davjään inyameet*—the 'burning in the blood.' Humans call it 'going berserk.' It's a state of suicidal rage and fury, a point where one's life no longer matters, and the only important question becomes, *How many can I take with me?*"

"I've heard of it. So you think Ji committed a kind of ritual suicide?"

"I suppose that's one way to look at it. With a considerable amount of genocide mixed in."

Den sighed. He slipped the holocron back into its case and put it on a wall shelf.

"What will you do with it?" Barriss asked him.

"I'm not sure. I could make some serious creds off it, no doubt about that. But I'd also be helping to twirl Ji as a war hero."

"And you have no use for heroes."

"I never said that," Den replied. "Properly indoctrinated, they're great at drawing fire away from those of us who are smart enough to know we're cowards and cynics."

Barriss smiled as she turned to go. "Rest assured I'll keep this knowledge to myself, Den, but just so you know as well—your aura is not the aura of a cynic's, nor a coward's. It has definite glimmerings of hero, in fact."

So saying, she left the cramped chamber. Den stared after her.

"Oh, no," he murmured. "Say it isn't so."

37

Even aside from the almost daily thunderstorms and mortar shell explosions that seemed a little closer than usual, the OT was particularly noisy. Jos was in the middle of a nasty bowel resection—the trooper on the table had apparently eaten a large meal a few hours before he had been hit by a chain-gun round that had perforated the small intestine—when the public address system came on. An excited voice, going too fast, said, "Attention, all personnel. Republic Medical Surgical Unit Seven will be relocating, commencing at eighteen hundred hours! This is not a drill! Repeat, this is *not* a drill!"

Jos said, "Put a stat on that, please."

Tolk hurriedly glued the incision closed, almost dropping the patch in her haste.

"Relax, Tolk. You have an appointment you're late for?"

"You heard that announcement?"

"Yeah—so?"

"Look at the chrono—it is now seventeen forty-five. In fifteen minutes, you're going to be standing in the middle of an empty swamp in the rain with war machines trying to zap your inattentive butt if you don't close this up stat."

"You think?"

Before she could answer, there came a *boom*! that shook the OT. The operating table vibrated enough so the patient jittered toward one edge.

"Blast!" Jos said. "What was *that*?"

Vaetes stuck his head into the room and said, "We just took a direct hit on the shield from a particle weapon. Main generator's out; we're on backup power. We don't know where they came from, but there's a battle droid force more than eight hundred strong less than ten thousand meters from here, coming across the Jackhack Slough at a goodly speed. The ground's too wet for the troopers to set up a defensive line. That'll also slow the droids down some, but it's still best you close up any and all open patients and get them ready to move, people. This mobile unit is about to live up to its name."

As if to punctuate his words, another explosion rocked the building, rattling it hard enough to knock bedpans off the wall racks. The pans hit with harsh metallic clangs.

"Aren't those supposed to be in the cooler?" Jos asked. "The better to make our patients uncomfortable?"

Behind him, Jos heard Zan swear, something in low Pugali that he missed most of, but which sounded appropriately vile. "If my quetarra gets damaged I'm going to personally hunt Dooku down, excise his reproductive organs, and feed them to the swamp snails."

"Glue this one shut and start a stabilization packet," Jos said to Tolk. "Soon as you're done, get your stuff packed. Where's our staging station?"

"Southeast quadrant, by the backup shield generator."

"Got it." He raised his voice. "All right, people, you heard the colonel. Time to close up shop and move it!"

Jos backed out of the sterile field, stripped off his gloves, and went to check on his staff and their patients. There was a procedure for moving the unit—there was a procedure for doing everything in the military—but they had been here for what seemed like forever, and Jos had gotten so used to it that he had forgotten most of the course of action.

Another vibration thrummed from the energy shield. If those hits were any indication, it was seeming more and more like a good idea to pack up the splints and hightail it to safer ground—assuming any such thing existed on the planet . . .

He hurried down the corridor. They had practiced the drill several times, during those rare instances when there hadn't been any incoming patients, and everybody in the unit was supposed to know exactly what to do should the real thing ever come to pass. Jos looked at the faces of the orderlies and other functionaries as they passed him, and was reassured to see that most of the staff didn't seem unduly worried; they were all doing their assignments, more or less.

He left the building. The rains had stopped, but there was still a strong wind trying to push the sodden air about. Disassemblers and ASPs were fast at work, he noticed, breaking down prefab buildings and cubicles, while the CLL-8s loaded them and other matériel into cargo lifters that had sat idle since before Jos had been assigned here. The patients were being loaded as well, by specially designed FX-7s using repulsor gurneys. Medlifters and refurbished cargo lifters would ferry them out of harm's way. Patients were the first priority, of course, but it wouldn't do to let the support staff be killed or captured.

It all felt rushed, hurried, and so strange it didn't seem real. One moment, they were operating on patients, repairing troopers as usual—and the next, hurrying to escape a war heading toward them like a runaway mag-lev train.

Jos hurried to his own cubicle and started to pack his essential gear. You were supposed to have a grab-and-go bag ready at all times, but after several months in the same spot, Jos had begun using the clean laundry and supplies in his travel bag, and as a result the kit was mostly empty.

The droids would load everything else in the cubicle, and far more efficiently than he could ever hope to do. Even if everything played out perfectly, though, there still wasn't any way under the merciless sun that the Rimsoo was going to be ready to leave by 1800—not unless the droids were all magicians.

Zan had gotten there ahead of him and was stuffing his socks into his quetarra case around the instrument.

"You can't take that on the transport," Jos pointed out as he packed. "It'll have to go on the freight carrier."

"I know. Why do you think I'm padding it with my socks?"

"Theft insurance? Anyone who opens it and gets a whiff of your socks will never steal anything again. Besides, I thought that case was reinforced duraplast." Jos zipped his go-bag shut.

"It'd have to be made of neutronium before I'd trust it with those droids. Some of the ASPs used to be starship cargo handlers. They could 'accidentally' destroy a block of carbonite in a durasteel safe."

"Attention, all personnel," came the PA 'cast. "The transports will be—"

A bomb went off in Jos's ear—at least that's what it seemed like. There was a deep rumble that suddenly dopplered up and into the ultrasonic, and the overhead light fell onto his bunk, shattering the tough plastoid legs as the bunk collapsed onto the floor.

"What—?"

"The energy shield backup generator just overloaded. It's down," Zan said. "Next direct hit's going to fry anybody outside protective shelter like a mulch fritter."

"How do you know that?"

"I spent one summer working for my uncle, who installed EM shielding and domes for the Vuh'Jinêau Mining Company. I know what a shield overload sounds like. We want to be somewhere else, fast." He snapped the quetarra case shut and grabbed his go-bag. "Hurry, Jos. The arrestors might help against lightning and even partially deflect a laser blast, but a direct hit'll vaporize them. Us, too." He gave the case a last concerned look, then hurried for the door.

Jos was right behind him. "Don't the Separatists realize that all these explosions are ruining the bota crops?"

"Maybe you want to wait here and bring it up with them. Me, I'd rather send them a nasty letter." Zan plunged through the door to join the exodus, with Jos following.

Den Dhur had been through hurried evacuations a couple of times before, so this one didn't worry him overmuch. Not until the shield went down. Then he started to get a little nervous. True, he was a journalist, and in theory the other side wouldn't shoot him if they

scanned his ID tag, but there was more than one war
zone with a cooked reporter or two to show that the
system wasn't perfect. The advancing Separatist troops
probably weren't targeting the medical facilities particularly—at least they weren't supposed to be—but collateral hits were bound to happen with all the
path-clearing bombardment going on, and whether
noncom or soldier, a body dead for a few days in this
weather smelled just as bad either way.

Den hurried toward his assigned evacuation spot, using what available cover there was along the way. Already big clouds of greasy smoke boiled up from the
swamp as high-oxy fires raged. You wouldn't think a
swamp could burn, but you'd be wrong—dead
wrong—if you based your survival on that. He'd once
seen an entire continent aflame on—what was the name
of that planet? He'd suddenly gone blank. Well, now
was not the time to worry about old dangers, not when
the stink of burning vegetation and ash falling like hot
black snow told him that a droid army was slashing and
burning its way closer every minute. Now was the time
to leave the party; he could jet down the memory space
lanes later—if he had a later.

Everywhere, transport droids, ASPs, and loadlifters
performed their tasks, breaking down shelters, packing
crates, working fast and efficiently. Also working in
company with the disassemblers were several small
wrecker droids, which shoveled up debris or used their
built-in plasma torches to melt down scrap metal, plasteel cables, and other rubble considered not worth hauling away, but still too valuable to leave behind as raw
materials for the enemy. Classic scorched-dirt policy,
and practiced by both sides.

It wasn't going too badly, Den thought. This place should be loaded out in twenty or thirty minutes and on its way to a more secure location. By the time the droid army arrived, all they'd find was a dry patch in the swamp, with nothing remaining behind in the fading evening light. With any luck at all, anyway.

The big problem, of course, lay in giving up the bota fields. Even though it grew like—well, like weeds—all over Tanlassa, official policy was to prevent Separatist access to it in any way possible. Even as Den continued on his way, watching the base literally coming down around his ears, harvesters both mechanical and organic were gathering up as much of the precious plant as possible—what little was still viable after all the heavy artillery pounding. A transport was standing by to carry the harvesters and their cargo to safety, while several modified decon droids waited to douse with herbicide the bota that had to be left behind. If you couldn't have it, you didn't want your enemy to have it, either. A shame to destroy stuff that valuable, but casualties of war and all that.

Five hundred meters away, there came a bright, actinic flash, followed by a loud *boom*! and the sense of air rushing in that direction. Then a wave of heat, noticeable even in this hellish place, washed over him.

Den grimaced. Had that thermal bomb drifted a degree or two in this direction on launch, he and the rest of the Republic personnel here would be charred history. It was *definitely* time to leave.

He saw part of the surgical crew in the rapidly darkening camp as they scrambled to get to their pickup points. Jos, Zan, Tolk, and a couple of the techs hurried through the gathering darkness toward a surgical evac shuttle that hovered a few feet above the ground. I-Five was with them.

More smoke blew into what was left of the camp. The heat rose as the fires grew, creating pockets of unique weather. An occasional charged particle or blaster beam lanced through the gathering gloom, still distant but all too visible, eerie green or red shafts of ionized air that Den imagined he could hear sizzling through the burning swamp.

Noise, heat, explosions, the stink of fear in the air. Different each place he'd been, but exactly the same.

Run! Fast! Hide! You could taste it.

Personnel transports floated into view, repulsor turbines thrumming and burbling, and worker droids began herding people onto them. Good, good—Den hurried toward them.

Something blew up on the far side of the camp—it sounded like a generator flywheel coming apart, judging from the metallic whistles that followed. Den hunched down lower as he scuttled along. Wouldn't want to be in front of those hurtling chunks of metal—sometimes a high-rev flywheel could send shrapnel screaming for kilometers before it buried itself deep into whatever it hit—be that dirt and mud or flesh and bone.

There were a thousand ways to die in a war zone, but the results were all the same . . .

38

The evac point for Jos, Tolk, and several others was just ahead, and Jos saw there was a vessel waiting for them. He didn't recognize the type, but it looked big enough, fast enough, and empty enough to suit him just fine. He felt a sense of relief. They were going to make it!

Through the smoke and the gathering gloom he could just make out Zan, Tolk, I-Five, and one or two other med techs hurrying along with him. "You people doing all right?" he called. "Anyone need help?"

"Yes—all of you," the droid replied. I-Five was striding rapidly along, more sure-footed on the uneven ground than any of them. "For example," he said, looking at Jos and pointing ahead of him, "you're about to walk into a large patch of purple stingwort."

Jos drew up short. The droid was right—a swath of the venomous plant, one of the nastier examples of Drongar's indigenous flora, coated the ground directly ahead of him. I-Five's warning had saved him from days of excruciating pain, if not possible anaphylactic shock and death.

Before he could change course, the droid's right index finger, which was pointed at the stingwort, fired a needle beam of bright red coherent light at it. Without slowing his pace, I-Five carefully moved his finger back and forth, incinerating a one-meter-wide path through the dangerous growth as he passed through it.

"Thanks," Jos said as he moved quickly along the trail the droid had cleared for him. "I didn't know you packed a laser."

"I didn't either, until about thirty minutes ago," I-Five replied. "Another link in my grid became accessible. I also have some unique harmonic vocalization abilities, it seems."

"Really," Zan panted as he tried to keep pace—the Zabrak had never been big on physical fitness, and was paying the price for that now. "We'll have to try some duets together—assuming we make it through this move in one piece."

"Don't worry," Jos said. "This time tomorrow you'll be serenading us all with that thing you've been working on—you know, the one that sounds like someone strangling a Kowakian monkey-lizard?"

"If you're referring to my latest tone poem," Zan replied somewhat stiffly, "All I can say is—"

Whatever he was about to say was lost as another particle beam blast, perhaps a hundred meters away, showered them all with mud from the nearby bog. The organics cried out in disgust—I-Five just kept on walking as the effluvium slid from his metallic skin.

"Nice trick," Tolk said as she tried to wipe her face with her sleeve, which merely moved the thick sludge from one place to another. Jos resisted an urge to try to help her—after all, he wasn't any cleaner than she was.

"Isn't it? I'm rather pleased with it," I-Five said smugly. "My integumentary sensors analyze the mud's chemical composition and viscosity coefficient, then electrostatically repel it. Another little trick of which I am capable that I discovered only recently."

"I'll remember to ask for that when I have my next upgrade," Tolk said.

"Of course, some of the same effect can be accomplished by ultrasonic vibration. Please allow me."

"Wow!" Zan put both hands to his ears as he stumbled slightly. "Easy, will you? That hurts!"

After a moment's puzzlement, Jos realized that Zan, whose ears obviously accommodated notes his own could not hear, was reacting to an ultrasound that I-Five was producing. A moment later he realized why—the result was much the same as a sonic shower. A considerable amount of the muck and mire seemed to magically evaporate from their skin and clothes. They weren't clean, but at least they no longer looked like Fondorian mud puppies.

"I-Five, I take back every nasty thing I ever said about you," Jos told him. "Except for the times you beat me at sabacc."

They reached the evac vessel's boarding ramp and hustled into the vehicle. A few people were already on board, including Klo Merit and Barriss Offee. Jos blew out a soft and quiet sigh. *Safe.*

"Are all your memory gaps closed now?" Zan asked I-Five as the ship lifted on its repulsor beams and began its ponderous journey.

I-Five said, "Not quite. But the process seems to be heuristic—the more connection nodes my cyberinformatic programs implement, the faster the process goes."

"Good," Tolk said. "I'm looking forward to learning about your heroic moments."

"You and me both," the droid said.

Jos glanced through the viewport, but there was nothing to see save an occasional flicker of what might be either heat lightning or Separatist weaponry. Other than that, the Drongaran night was as black as an assassin's heart.

"How does the idea of being a hero make you feel?" he asked I-Five, and it was only after the question had left his lips that he realized that it had not felt odd in the least to ask a droid about its feelings. *Welcome to stochastic hyperspace, where all bets are wild . . .*

I-Five seemed to be giving the answer some thought. "It's intriguing," he said at last. "Somewhat exciting as well. As I explained to Padawan Offee, human behavior fascinates me, and a big part of that is your ability to *choose* the path that harms the least. Not all species have that option.

"Obviously my emotional and intellectual parameters were determined by human manufacturers. My fear is that I've been programmed—or reprogrammed—to sacrifice myself, if necessary, for the greater good. If a moment for such a heroic act comes, *I* would want to make the decision, not some predetermined algorithm. And I'd like to believe I'd choose the greater good."

A utilitarian droid, Jos thought. *Who'd have thought it?*

A burst of sickly greenish light from above leaked through the viewports. It didn't fade, and after a moment Jos realized that the Separatists had fired one or more hover-flares. A moment later an explosion, uncomfortably close, rattled the vessel's framework.

"I hope they're not getting our range," Zan said. He glanced through the still-open cargo bay entrance—and suddenly froze, his face registering stark horror in the putrid light.

"*No!*" he screamed, and leapt for the open ramp.

39

Den saw his transport idle to a halt at the pickup point just ahead. At least the big, rectangular vessels had some armor plating—once you were inside you would have a little more protection than being out in the open afforded. He aimed for the transport. In the pallid lights of the hover-flares he saw his favorite pubtender, Baloob the Ortolan, clamber up the boarding ramp into the craft. He grinned. *Good. A being who can mix drinks that well deserves to survive—*

Another ear-smiting explosion rocked the area, knocking Den from his feet. A good thing, too—before he could get up, several chunks of metal, one the size of a landspeeder, hurtled just above him like meteors, the shrieks of their passage splitting the air. Den grabbed his ears in pain.

A freighter barge went past on his other side, repulsors humming. Two of the smaller flywheel chunks hit it hard enough to embed themselves in its hull. The impacts momentarily canted the barge, and whoever had packed it had apparently missed a pressor field node or two, because several pieces of luggage fell off and went bouncing over the wet ground.

Somebody'll be looking for clean underwear tonight, Den thought. *Too bad—*

"*No!*" somebody screamed.

Den glanced at the surgical evac vehicle, fifty meters or so ahead. He saw I-Five restraining Zan, who looked like he was trying to jump from the vessel. Den followed Zan's frantic gaze and saw the reason: one of the fallen pieces from the cargo carrier was an instrument case—the one Zan carried his quetarra in.

Most of the base's personnel were loaded and moving away from the chaotic scene now, and Den was about ten meters away from joining them on his waiting transport.

"*Stop!*" Zan screamed again, nearly breaking free. If it wasn't for I-Five holding him, the Zabrak would have leapt from the carrier in a futile attempt to save his quetarra. Futile, because by the time he'd reached the instrument all the transports would be too far away and moving too fast for him to catch. He wasn't an athlete, the Zabrak. And what pilot would risk a ship filled with patients and doctors to rescue just one man, no matter how impressive his music?

As Den watched, I-Five and Jos Vondar hauled the stricken Zan back into the carrier, which continued to move off into the twilight, slowly picking up speed.

Den headed for his own transport at a trot. He looked at the quetarra case. It was only a dozen meters away— if he changed course now, he might possibly be able to grab it up and still reach his transport—

Something else blew up, much closer this time. He heard the unmistakable *thwip*! of shrapnel zipping past him, mere centimeters away. Not as big as the flywheel fragments, but big enough to punch a hole through him and let his life out very quickly.

Your ride is over there, *Den! Go, go, go!*

But Zan's anguished cry echoed in his mind—the cry of someone who had just lost a big part of himself.

Without further thought, Den turned and trotted toward the fallen instrument case.

His inner voice went straight to lightspeed: *Are you milking insane? Get on the transport, now!*

"In a minute," he said aloud. "Just got to grab one more thing—"

His inner voice was not placated. *Fool! Moron! Idiot! You would risk your life for a—a—musical instrument? This is beyond lunacy!*

"You heard him play," Den said. "A guy like that needs his art to survive."

His inner voice called him names that would make a Slime Sea sailor blink.

But by then, he was there. He grabbed the case without slowing down, even though it felt as if his arm was being pulled from its socket—how could such light and beautiful music come out of such a heavy instrument?—and veered back toward the transport.

He could see several beings gathered at the open cargo gate, among them Zuzz, the Ugnaught who had spilled his guts—or whatever Ugnaughts used for guts—about Filba. It felt like months ago; hard to believe it had only been a week. They were all waving frantically at him to hurry. And he was trying, but the blasted case seemed to be increasing its mass exponentially every minute. And it was too awkward to carry by the handle. He swung it up and over his head, hanging on to the case's neck with both hands and letting the body cover his back like a bizarre carapace.

Something big and heavy slapped the case from behind suddenly, knocking it into Den's back and sending him sprawling. The sound of the explosion took half a second to reach him after he was up and moving again, so it wasn't *that* close, he told himself.

Just close enough to almost kill him.

Den set his teeth, grabbed the case with both hands, and ran for all he was worth.

Eager hands reached down, grabbed him, pulled him on board. The transport swooped up and forward, leaving most of Den's viscera back on the ground, or at least that's how it felt. He glanced over his shoulder and saw that the ground where buildings had stood only moments before was now scorched and pitted dirt. As he watched, another mortar hit, producing a blast that nearly burst his eardrums and almost fried his optic nerves. He realized that both of his droptacs were gone—probably knocked out of his eyes when he was hit by that concussion wave. Ditto his sonic dampeners.

Everything was far too bright and noisy. But at least he was alive to notice.

He looked at the case and saw that the top was scorched and pitted with shrapnel. Not enough to penetrate to the instrument within, but, had that been his back, he probably would not have survived.

"See?" he said quietly. "It saved my life."

If you hadn't gone after the milking thing, you'd have been in the transport when the blast hit! Fool! Don't ever try to be a hero again!

Den looked at the case, startled. A hero? That was the last thing he'd wanted to be. He didn't grab the instrument out of any noble gesture, he'd just done it . . . well, because . . .

Because . . . ?

"Because to lose Zan's music would be a *real* tragedy

of war," he murmured. His words were low, and he doubted anyone heard him over the rumble of the thrusters. But his trusty Inner Voice evidently heard, because the condemnations inside his head stopped.

Den shook his head. Yar, he was a fool. But it still felt good. At the very least, Zan owed him a drink. Several, in fact. And here was a war story he could dine out on for a long time. *I ever tell you about the time my hide was saved by a quetarra . . . ?*

"Did you see *that*?" Tolk asked in disbelief.

"I did," Jos said, shaking his head. "I don't believe it, but I saw it. This from the guy who swore he'd never risk his life for anything or anybody? He must have bent a drive rod."

"Carbon-based life-forms," I-Five said. "Just when you think you've got them figured out . . ."

The three of them looked at Zan. "When this war's over," he said, "if Den wants it, he can have a position in any of my family's companies—high enough that he'll need an air tank to breathe—for as long as he likes. I'm forever in his debt."

"Zan," Leemoth said, "it's just a quetarra."

"No, it isn't. It's much more than that. I wrote my first conserlista using it. Learned the first of the Berltahg Sonatas on it. It's as much a part of me as my arm. I will never forget what Den Dhur did, not as long as I live."

Jos grinned. He'd never tell Zan, of course, but he would have missed the playing almost as much as his friend would have, even though he'd have to put up with more of that demented meewit screeching that Zan called Zabrak diaspora music—

And then something smashed into the carrier, harder than an extinction-level meteor. Jos felt the vessel drop and hit the ground. He instinctively reached for Tolk to protect her, but before he made contact, the world vanished in a red haze.

40

Jos swam up out of unconsciousness. His head hurt—*hurt* really wasn't the word, but he doubted any language could describe how it felt—and his vision was blurry. He was aware of the transport listing slightly to starboard, and of Tolk kneeling next to him where he lay on the floor. She was wiping his face with a damp pad.

"Hey," she said.

"Hey, yourself."

"How do you feel?"

"Like I was fanned over by a transport. What happened?"

"We got blasted by something. You hit your head on a bulkhead. We sustained some damage. We're slower, but still mobile. About ten klicks away from the new camp, out of range, apparently. You've been unconscious for almost an hour."

Jos tried to sit up, but a wave of stomach-churning nausea and vertigo overwhelmed him.

"You have a concussion," Tolk said. "Lie still."

"Yeah, I hear that. Everybody else okay?"

Tolk's mouth set in a firm line. She shook her head. Tears welled then, and she blinked them away.

"Who—?"

But he knew.

Despite the vertigo and nausea that tore at his brain and gut, despite the fiery pain in his skull, Jos rolled over and struggled to his hands and knees.

"Jos, you can't help him. He's gone."

Jos heard the words, but they didn't register. He crawled. Zan was only a couple of body-lengths away, lying on his back, seeming to recede and then advance in Jos's vision. It wasn't until he could touch his friend's face that he knew he'd reached him. Zan looked as if he were sleeping—there wasn't a mark on him.

"Zan," Jos croaked. "Don't do this, Zan. Don't you do this. This is not right, you hear me?"

He put out a hand to touch Zan's face again, and the effort spun the carrier around him. He collapsed, his fingers touching the Zabrak. Still warm, a dispassionate part of his mind noted clinically. Still warm.

But Zan wasn't there anymore.

"Zan! This isn't funny! You always go too far, you know that? Now get up!"

Jos abruptly vomited, emptying his stomach mostly of bile and water. He managed to turn away enough so as not to splatter his friend.

His head felt slightly clearer now. "Tolk," he managed.

She crouched down in front of him. "We tried everything, Jos. He took a piece of shrapnel in the brain stem. All his autonomic functions went out at once. He—" She swallowed, and bright tears overflowed her eyes again. "He just shut down—it was instantaneous. The last thought he must have had was that his quetarra had been saved. He was . . ." She swallowed again. "He was smiling."

"Let me help you, Jos," a soft voice said. Jos looked up, saw the Jedi standing beside him. Behind her, leaning in the canted vehicle, watching soberly, were I-Five, Klo Merit, and a few others. Barriss put out a hand toward him. "I can't bring him back. But I can help you deal with—"

"No," he said between clenched teeth. "No. I don't *want* to feel better. My friend is dead. Nothing can change that. Nothing is going to make that right, or better, or easier." He looked up at her. "Do you understand? I won't be anesthetized. I owe him that much."

Tolk's tears flowed freely now, and she reached out to touch Jos on the shoulder, but that wasn't going to help, either. *Blast* this war! Blast the governments and the corporations and the military!

This could not go on. Something had to be done. He had to make sure that *something* was done.

Zan. Ah, Zan! How could you leave?

Column stared through the viewport in the transport, watching the militantly verdant swamp pass beneath them. The air scrubbers were strained to capacity, and still the stink of pollen and stagnant water seeped into the fetid atmosphere. Zan Yant was dead, and Jos Vondar was injured. A shame. Yant had been an excellent artist, and a most likable fellow as well.

A shame. A real shame.

The message the spy had not gotten around to translating earlier had been, of course, a warning of impending attack. Column sighed. Would it have made any difference if the attack had been known of in advance? Maybe. Maybe not. It would have been nice to have been prepared mentally, even if there was nothing physically that could have been done.

There was, and probably never would be, an answer to that. Column, Lens, the spy—use whichever name you liked—they all lived in a subtle, shifting world, a world in which black was far too often white, a world where loyalty could change on an almost quotidian basis, where friendships were both luxuries and liabilities— risks too great to be considered, much less taken.

Column frowned. Still objective enough, hopefully, to realize when procedural mistakes were being made. Was this one of those times? Was paranoia encroaching, gaining a foothold in that heretofore magnificently objective brain? If so, it had to be resisted, fought against, and, ultimately, triumphed over.

Perhaps it was time to step up the plan. After all, it would do neither Dooku nor Black Sun any good to have their behind-the-scenes endeavors exposed.

Column nodded. It was a narrow strand of web to be walked, over a chasm deeper than time itself. But failure, now more than ever, was not an option.

Barriss could not recall ever feeling more helpless— more *useless*—since she was a child. She had saved Ji, had felt virtuous for that, only to have him wade back into the thick of battle as a berserker and be claimed by death anyway. True, it had been his choice, but still, the question would not leave her: could she have saved him? Would she have worked harder if he had been somebody she had liked, instead of somebody she detested? Personal involvement wasn't supposed to matter to a Jedi. A Jedi was supposed to be able to control her feelings and do the right thing for the right reasons.

Would she ever be able to function at that level?

She had not been able to deflect the attack that had killed Zan—she hadn't even felt it coming. And after the metal splinter had lodged in the base of his skull, she had still not been able to save him, though she had used every bit of the power supposedly under her control.

She could not even soothe Jos's grief over the death of his friend. Even if he would allow it, did she have the ability? A few hours ago, she would not have doubted it. But now . . .

Now, suddenly, everything was in doubt. The immensity of the war seemed far beyond the capabilities of the few remaining Jedi; certainly, even this small part of it was more than she could control.

Jos had managed to sit, leaning back against the wall of the transport as it limped along. Tolk, who loved him, knelt beside him and ministered to his physical injury, which was nothing compared to the damage to his psyche. Doctors dealt in such things, they were trained for it, but they were not immune to personal feelings. Zan Yant had been a good person, a dedicated surgeon, a wonderful musician, and now all that had been cut short. *And for what?* Barriss asked herself. Because two opposing factions wanted more power and control over the citizens of the galaxy. Was there ever an uglier activity than war? Organized slaughter of vast numbers for reasons that never seemed justified, or even sane?

She looked at the medics in the transport. Sometimes the price that had to be paid was dear, and she had sworn to pay it herself, if ever the need arose. But she was also a healer, one who could use the Force to repair those who were sick or hurt. Right now, however, she felt like a single grain of sand against the force of a massive, moon-driven tide. It was all so . . . *senseless*. So overwhelming. And there was nothing she could do to stop it. Nothing.

How could she ever become a Jedi Knight, feeling as she did?

I-Five said, "I understand the motivations of biologicals to a degree, but I cannot understand how they can shrug off the consequences of some of their actions."

"Welcome to the mystery," Barriss said.

"It does not appear as if I will be the one to solve it anytime soon. That last impact seemed to have scrambled my recovering circuitry somewhat. My heuristic memory process has ceased functioning."

Barriss reached out with the Force, but the droid's mind, as others like it, was untouchable. She could not help him, either.

Jedi Knighthood seemed no closer at that moment than far Coruscant, and the carefree days of her childhood.

Den made a lot of notes, speaking into his recorder, capturing images. Once they finally came to a halt, the droids began to set the Rimsoo back up, even though it was the middle of the night. Under the harsh glare of artificial light being swarmed by clouds of mindless insectoids, the noises and sights of the construction encroached on the warm and wet darkness.

The shock of Zan's death had washed over him like an ocean breaker, a hard, sudden, and overpowering surf. Den retreated to the shell of his work, the same tactic used by soldiers and doctors and reporters galaxywide: keep moving, and don't think about things better left alone for now.

People and droids did their work, and he did his job. He moved around, getting reactions, taking it all in and saving it.

He came across I-Five, who was directing orderly droids in the placement of patients inside a just-finished ward.

"Too bad about Zan," Den said.

"A great loss," the droid said. "If it is any consolation, his final sentient moment was a happy one. He saw you save his musical instrument. His expression of gratitude seemed both genuine and deeply felt."

Den shrugged. "Small comfort, friend droid."

"Perhaps. But is that not better than no comfort? My emotional circuitry is not on the same order of depth and complexity as yours, but the sadness I feel is mitigated by the knowledge that Zan Yant's demise was both quick and essentially painless—plus his mental state was, for lack of a better term, one of grace. You had just saved his most precious possession. It seemed a peak moment of joy for him. I should think that, given a choice, most sentient beings would choose to leave life in that state than in one of fear or suffering."

Den could not repress the sigh. "Yeah. I suppose. Not much of a choice, the kind of death. A being like Zan shouldn't have had to make it."

A pair of droids went by, carrying a section of building that Den recognized as belonging to the cantina. Good. Sooner that place was reassembled, the better.

"No being should have to make that choice," I-Five replied. "Yet this is the galaxy in which we exist, and until the powers-that-be come to the realization that war is inefficient and costly in terms of life and property, such choices will always be with us."

Den shook his head. "I still haven't gotten used to a droid as a philosopher. You are something quite special, I-Five."

"Get used to it. I don't expect I will be the last such droid ever created. I can say this: if droids ran things, war would not be an approved activity."

Den nodded. "Wouldn't that be nice."

"You would be out of a job as a war correspondent."

"I could find other work. Believe me, it would be worth it."

I-Five went back to his patient coordination, and Den drifted off. Walking across the compound, he passed several troopers who were obviously newly arrived—though they did all look the same, there was a sort of naïveté to the ones newly arriving that set them apart from the more experienced troops. They were chattering to each other, no doubt finding all this tremendously exciting. Had he ever been that innocent? If so, it had been flensed from him a long time and many worlds ago.

He'd miss Zan Yant—the man's music, his wit, his card playing. But I-Five was right: this was how things were. Not likely to change anytime soon.

In the meantime, he had work to do.

"Excuse me, friend tech, can you tell me how you felt about the recent attack on this Rimsoo . . . ?"

EPILOGUE

Eighty kilometers southeast of the old encampment, Rimsoo Seven was now set up. Outside, it looked much the same. The trees were in different places, the small hillocks had slightly different shades and shapes of fungi, and there was even another bota patch close by. They were still a Rimsoo on a forsaken planet, only now Zan was gone and the war was still out there, crouched to spring like a monster from some dark and dank cave.

Jos sat on his new bunk, in the same quarters he had shared with Zan, staring through the solid wall into infinity.

Everything was the same, but everything had changed.

Droids had the capability to be more than he had thought, and clones were not as simple as he had comfortably believed. The world had turned upside down, but somehow things were still dropping out of the sky onto his head.

He still couldn't get his mind around Zan's death. Just couldn't get a grip on it. Intellectually he knew that his friend was gone, gone to that place from which none return. But emotionally Jos still expected the door to open any minute, expected to see Zan enter, lugging his quetarra case, griping about the rain, or laughing at some bit of business in the OT, before unpacking the instrument and wandering off into some classical fugue.

That was never going to happen again.

People died almost every day in the OT, some of them under his hands as he frantically tried to save them, but this—this was not the same.

Zan had been his *friend*.

"Jos?"

He looked up.

Tolk stood in the doorway. She was in her surgical whites, and his heart leapt to see her—then fell and shattered. His tradition, the centuries-old customs of his clan, denied her to him—his family and history and social constructs all told him that he and Tolk could never be together. And he had believed, up until this moment, all this to be true, had accepted that it was anathema to even think of defying canon.

But Zan was dead. And that simple, searing fact now brought home to Jos, in a way that nothing ever had before, the truth of the old saying that he had heard bandied about all of his life, had even said himself on occasion, but had never really understood:

Life is too short.

Too short to waste on things that aren't important. Too short to waste on anything that doesn't, in some way, enrich you or your loved ones. Too short by far to let mindless rules and traditions tell you what you could do, where you could live—

And whom you could love.

Here stood Tolk, before him. Jos looked at her, felt tears start to gather. He stood and opened his arms. "Tolk—" he began.

That was all he needed to say. She ran to him. They

hugged, then kissed, tenderness flowering into passion as they discovered the ages-old tonic for the horrors of war. The truth that was always known but always hidden: that the past was frozen, the future unformed, and that, for everyone, eternity was in each heartbeat.

In war—as in peace—it was the only way to truly live.

The moment was short. The drone of incoming medlifters broke it. For a moment, Jos stared at her.

"Time to go to work," she said softly.

He nodded. "Yeah."

They started from the cube toward the OT.

STAR WARS REPUBLIC COMMANDO™

PLAY THE GAME!

Contact has been lost with a Republic assault ship. Turmoil has erupted in the lower jungles of the Wookiee planet Kashyyyk. Order has been abandoned on Geonosis. You've been chosen to lead a highly specialized squad of Republic Commandos into these conflicts and resolve them. Your only backup is each other. The missions are difficult. The odds are worse. Your training and resources will be tested severely. Hesitation will cost you your life. There is no room for error -- or fear. Your team is considered the most elite and powerful one in the Republic. Prove it.

GET THE GUIDE!

Prima's Official Game Guide includes all the vital information players need:
- Maps and walkthroughs for all 6 environments
- In depth coverage of the intricate squad command system
- Details of all weapons & enemies
- Multiplayer game strategies... and more!

READ THE BOOK!

Star Wars Republic Commando: Hard Contact.
Don't miss the gripping new *Star Wars* adventure novel from Del Rey Books, set in the dark, military world of the Clone Commandos. When a Commando pod loses a member on a dangerous mission, will the remaining three go on without him, or will they set out to find their missing brother, stranded deep in hostile territory?